MASTERY OF MANAGEMENT

AUREN URIS

PLAYBOY PRESS
PAPERBACKS

Other Books by Auren Uris

Keeping Young in Business

Turn Your Job into a Successful Career

The Executive Breakthrough: 21 Roads to the Top

The Executive Job Market

Mastery of People

The Management Makers

The Efficient Executive

Developing Your Executive Skills

How to Be a Successful Leader

(Techniques of Leadership, paperback title)

MASTERY OF MANAGEMENT

Copyright © 1968 by Dow Jones-Irwin, Inc. All rights reserved.

Published simultaneously in the United States and Canada by Playboy Press, Chicago, Illinois. Printed in the United States of America.

Books are available at quantity discounts for promotional and industrial use. For further information, write our sales promotion agency: Ventura Associates, 40 East 49th Street, New York, New York 10017.

ISBN: 0-872-16616-3

First softcover printing July 1971.
Third printing September 1979.

PREFACE

Here's a conversation between two top executives, overheard during a break in a recent management seminar:

"This morning's session made me realize that management is changing at a terrific rate. Most of the stuff we covered was unheard of five, certainly ten years ago—participative management, for example, and the task-force concept."

"Yes. It's a new ball game."

"No, it isn't! And that's what's so confusing."

"What do you mean?"

"If it were a *new* ball game, it would be a lot simpler. What confounds me is that it's partly an old ball game, partly new. If it were *entirely* a new ball game, we could just junk the old rules and start from scratch. But today, practicing management is like playing on a regulation diamond with sixteen players out in the field. And when you hit the ball, instead of running to first, second and third base, you head to third base, *then* to first, second and home."

"Your example is a little farfetched, but I get the point. . . ."

The nature and rate of change in the management field today is indeed so extreme that basic reappraisal and reorientation are necessary for both the students and the practitioners of management. And what's required is the integration of new insights and information into what remains useful of the old.

If one adopts a broad perspective for the moment, it becomes clear that management is changing because the world at large is changing. Tremendous developments have been bombarding our society. According to some authorities, we have undergone more change in the last ten years than in the previous hundred. Everywhere one looks, the drastic nature of developments becomes visible. In the sciences such as biology and physics, developments of DNA, new understanding of the make-up of matter, the applied science represented by our giant steps in space spell out a picture of change. In medicine, organ transplants, cryogenic techniques, the development of drugs and antibiotics, new understanding of longevity revolutionize prospects for the health and life-span of the individual.

And on the social scene, innovation and upset are rampant.

New attitudes toward work and leisure, the so-called sexual revolution and its effect on the behavior of young people, cracks in the foundations of organized religion, the concept that "God is dead" all add up to a world with new values, new attitudes and fresh ideas about how to spend one's life and develop one's career.

No wonder, then, that the world of management, with its roots in an exploding technology and human relationships on the work scene, is undergoing a revolution.

The problems suggested by the conversation between the two executives must be met by a reappraisal of management concepts, procedures and practices. Accordingly, *Mastery of Management* aims to supply a realistic and useful view of management in an era of change. It offers a context in which the origins, the present status and future course of development of key areas in the field are examined and clarified, to the end that managers and executives, present and future, can update their management understanding and practices. Again, new knowledge must be blended with traditional wisdom.

In attempting this ambitious work, the assistance of many individuals contributed to the final result. Most of the indebtedness to authorities in the field, as well as to experienced executives who shared their views and insights with the author, is acknowledged at appropriate points in the text. In addition, these acknowledgments are gratefully made:

Marjorie Noppel, for inspired editorial assistance in planning, developing and editing the final manuscripts.

Evelyn Sheehan and Halina Mazur for library services, the supplying of references and news items that added substance and validation at many points in the development of this work.

Doris Horvath, Angela Rapuano, Sheila Bernard, Rosalie Civello and Charlotte Braunhut for intelligent and painstaking secretarial services. Also, typing by Bettina Uris.

And, finally, to my family for their interest, encouragement and accommodation to the sometimes difficult schedules which the production of this book required.

AUREN URIS

CONTENTS

INTRODUCTION

"Can anyone write a book that will help the practicing manager—and the countless thousands who will fill the ranks tomorrow—catch up, get reoriented in the whirling, changing world of management?"

This is the challenging question—and urgent need—to which *Mastery of Management* addresses itself. Obviously, no one book, nor ten volumes for that matter, could do the complete job. Nevertheless, it is hoped that *Mastery of Management* does provide a foundation for the updating process that the inroads of the "management revolution" demands.

Behind the problem

"It's a lot tougher to be a good manager today."

That's the feeling both of practicing executives and of expert observers of the management scene. Why? Two factors explain this development.

Management problems are becoming more complex. With the disappearance of a traditional technology operated by authoritarian business leadership, both the hardware and the human problems of today's business establishment are developing ailments less easy to diagnose and requiring more sophisticated methods of treatment.

Management itself is becoming more complicated. The old ways are no longer the good ways. Such standbys as company loyalty, acceptance of authority, punishment-reward motivation are rapidly fading from the work scene, requiring new and more sophisticated management tools to keep both the people and the machines operating at satisfactory levels of performance.

A particular and personal victim of the management revolution is the obsolete executive. The obsolescence of managerial skills has been widely noted. In a world where experience may be a handicap instead of an asset, today's *better* manager may be the one in for the greatest shock from the advent of change.

Twenty years ago, a young man starting out in business could take comfort in the fact that his new world of work was, by and large, similar to that of his father's generation. But in the last decade, the forces of change have shattered old systems and means:

Automation, the computer and mathematical concepts of planning and decision making have altered the content of work.

The findings of the behavioral scientist have also demolished traditional concepts. The fact is, today's manager must cope with "new" people. On the one hand, managers must work with subordinates who are more highly educated and have more realistic aspirations than in the days past. At the same time, companies are hiring high school dropouts, educationally and economically disadvantaged individuals unused to the world of work. Problems of new attitudes and values must be met by new techniques.

Toward a mastery of management

What is needed for a mastery of this changing, complex field? Essentially, a new orientation, a fresh view of the work scene and its new directions. Accordingly, *Mastery of Management* attempts to do two things:

First, provide in broad perspective a backward and forward view of the art/science of management, so that the reader can get a meaningful orientation in the field —see the big picture of where management has been and where it is going.

Second, provide specific courses of action that will help the reader review and update his management skills, so that he will be prepared to manage in today's and tomorrow's business world. To this end, the first three chapters and the last one conclude with carefully selected lists of recent books for those who want to further explore the subject areas of the text. All the other chapters conclude with "Points for Executive Thought and Action," material designed to help executives develop personal insights and practical "how-to-do" aspects of the subjects covered in the respective chapters.

In short, this volume aims to equip the manager with the insights and techniques required to manage successfully in the rapidly changing contemporary work situation. To do so effectively, key areas and concepts of management have been organized under four major headings:

Part I   *Dynamics—The Big Picture*
Part II   *Environment*
Part III   *Tools*
Part IV   *The Future*

In these four areas, then, *Dynamics—The Big Picture, Environment, Tools, The Future*, are shown the parameters in which the executive of today and tomorrow will be working. It is hoped that the material assembled within the covers of this volume will provide a realistic and practical view of the executive's domain that will make it possible for him to continue to excel in his profession and, in so doing, help build a better world for tomorrow.

PART ONE/DYNAMICS–THE BIG PICTURE

The first three chapters define the transformation of the executive, comparing what he was in the first half of the century with what he is and does today.

The two major forces that have created change on the work scene are discussed in detail: the technology that has influenced the man behind the executive desk; next, the role of behavioral science as it influences executive techniques and procedures. These chapters add up to a broad overview of the management field, with emphasis on the major change factors.

ONE/TRANSFORMATION OF THE EXECUTIVE

"Today's manager is a new breed."

Almost unanimously, observers of the business scene note that today's executive is a different man, doing different work, in different ways from those of his predecessor 25 or 40 years ago. It is clear, too, that the changes in the executive's job have been real, substantial—and accelerating. Yet several key questions are often left unanswered:

Why is today's executive different?

How is he different?

What new or continuing changes in his job lie ahead?

Answers to these questions are important not only to the hundreds of thousands already in the management profession, but to the much greater number who will be tomorrow's practitioners.

Useful perspective is gained by looking backward to see what the executive was and how he operated in previous decades; then we can measure his progress, appraise his achievements and consider the direction of his future growth.

The executive circa 1870—a fictional record

Although we have no sociologically accurate study of the early executive prototype at work, artistic sources provide helpful data. One colorful piece of evidence is the description of a New England businessman in the 1870s provided by William Dean Howells in his novel *The Rise of Silas Lapham*.

Lapham is a successful paint manufacturer, and in the first chapter, a journalist, Bartley Hubbard, comes to interview him for a newspaper article. The meeting of the two men in Lapham's office provides a vivid glimpse of an executive of 100 years ago in his working environment. Here are excerpts from Howells's description:

When Bartley Hubbard went to interview Silas Lapham for the "Solid Men of Boston" series . . . Lapham received him in his private office by appointment.

"Walk right in!" he called out to the journalist, whom he caught sight of through the door of the counting room.

He did not rise from the desk at which he was writing, but he gave Bartley his left hand for welcome, and he rolled his large head in the direction of a vacant chair. "Sit down! I'll be with you in just half a minute." . . .

"There!" Lapham pounded with his great hairy fist on the envelope he had been addressing. "William!" he called out, and he handed the letter to a boy who came to get it. "I want that to go right away. Well, sir," he continued, wheeling round in his leather-cushioned swivel chair and facing Bartley, seated so near that their knees almost touched. "So you want my life, death and Christian sufferings, do you, young man?" . . . He put out his huge foot and pushed the ground-glass door shut between his little den and the bookkeepers in their larger den outside. . . .

Lapham suddenly lifted his bulk out of his swivel chair and led the way out into the wareroom beyond the office partitions, where rows and ranks of casks, barrels and kegs stretched dimly back to the rear of the building and diffused an honest, clean, wholesome smell of oil and paint. . . . "There!" said Lapham, kicking one of the largest casks with the toe of his boot. "That's about our biggest package. And here," he added, laying his hand affectionately at the head of a very small keg as if it were the head of a child, which it resembled in size, "this is the smallest. We used to put the paint on the market dry, but now we grind every ounce of it in oil—very best quality of linseed oil—and warrant it. We find it gives more satisfaction. Now, come back to the office and I'll show you our fancy brands." . . .

[Finally Bartley is ready to leave.] "Good afternoon, Colonel."

Lapham put on a straw hat, gathered up some papers lying on his desk, pulled down its rolling cover, turned the key in it and gave the papers to an extremely handsome young woman at one of the desks in the outer office. She was stylishly dressed, as Bartley saw, and her smooth, yellow hair was sculpturesquely waved over a low, white forehead. "Here," said Lapham with the same prompt gruff kindness that he had used in addressing the young man, "I want you should put these in shape and give me a typewriter copy tomorrow."

"What an uncommonly pretty girl!" said Bartley as they descended the rough stairway and found their way out to the street, past the dangling rope of a block and tackle wandering up into the cavernous darkness overhead.

Looking backward 100 years

From the American novelist's vivid paragraphs emerge a number of key observations about the management world of the 1870s:

Working environment. Silas Lapham's office is right next to an active operating part of his business, the warehouse. The office is there because of a necessary relationship. In the formative days of business, the head of the firm usually located close to the working heart of his business, since he was the direct supervisor of the work. A mine owner's quarters were built near the mine shafts. A foundry proprietor spent his working day in an office adjoining the foundry operation.

Staff subordinates. Although Howells doesn't mention them, a group of warehouse workers were probably on the premises, tending the incoming and outgoing stock.

He does describe the office staff—William, the office boy; a group of bookkeepers; and a typist, "an extremely handsome young woman."

In this early version of the executive suite, these people are direct extensions of the entrepreneur's own activities. They help to initiate or refine work that in smaller businesses the company head did himself—tending accounts, getting off correspondence, and so on. Conspicuously absent—and not to appear on the business scene as a significant group for several decades—are the middle managers, those executives who take over parts of the top executive's responsibilities and supervise others in getting them done. They include such functions as the treasurer for money matters, a head of accounting in charge of the firm's record keeping, a director of purchasing for supplies and materials procurement.

Equipment. Howells mentions several familiar pieces of office furniture and equipment. Lapham sits on a swivel chair—an early innovation that recognized the executive's action-filled role. He has a rolltop desk, a most inventive means of insuring protection and confidentiality of the executive's papers by the simple means of rolling down a wooden barrier and locking it in place.

We don't know what his secretary's typewriter looked like, but it must have been a most primitive model, for it wasn't until 1873—a few years later—that the gunmaking firm of E. Remington and Sons signed a contract to develop and produce a practical machine that could exceed the speed of the pen. In early 1874, the first improved machines reached the market.

Executive profile—a one-man sample. The most interesting contrast between the business scene of today and 100 years ago is provided by Silas Lapham himself. In the presence of the journalist, Lapham is relaxed, informal, at ease in a way that would do credit to today's most public-relations-conscious executive. And although Lapham's paint company is a highly profitable international operation—he sells in Europe, Asia, Australia—his is literally a one-man company. Lapham is a rough-

cut individual whose Civil War experience has given him
some feeling for command. But essentially he is a "promoted farmer," a man of the soil, supported in his executive role mostly by his native shrewdness and, interestingly, a wife who aids and abets his business efforts.

One hundred years after Silas Lapham

How does today's executive stack up against Silas?
For purposes of comparison, consider the hypothetical
person of Cyrus Lapham IV, vice-president (marketing) of Universal Paint:

Cy, driven down to the Tarrytown station by his wife
to catch the 8:10, arrives at teeming Grand Central station at 8:50. He walks the few hundred feet to 277 Park
Avenue, enters the gleaming lobby and takes an automatic elevator to his floor.

Walking through large glass doors into Universal's reception room, Cy is greeted by vivid blues, reds, greens
and yellows purring at him from walls and floors. There's
nothing dim or dusty about today's office decor. En route
to his inner sanctum, he passes through a line of sleek
desks belonging to the secretaries of the firm's executive
staff. Outside his own quarters, he is greeted by Miss
Smith, who is arranging the bouquet of fresh roses
which Universal's personnel department delivers daily to
maintain the élan of the secretarial corps.

Lapham sits down at his desk to go over the mail that
Miss Smith has already sorted. His executive desk is a
gleaming crescent on which stand two telephones, a dictating machine, an intercom and an adding machine.

Soon Miss Smith enters with a huge pile of sheets that
have been coughed out by the computer the previous
night, showing the production, sales and inventory of
Universal's domestic plants and one foreign branch.

"Conference at nine-thirty with P.J., Mr. Lapham,"
Miss Smith reminds, and the paint executive's working
day is off to a fast start.

Clearly, there are many differences between the two
generations. In everything from their clothing to what

they eat for breakfast, their modes of life are dissimilar. But what makes Cyrus Lapham IV a brand-new breed is something more basic—he is not the owner of a business but a professional manager. Moreover, he represents a large and constantly increasing group. A century ago, there was a relative handful of Silas Laphams—entrepreneur-businessmen. Today, there are tens of thousands of Lapham IVs.

Hal A. Salzman is chairman of the board of Odell, Inc., a conglomerate corporation operating wholly owned subsidiaries in toiletries, plastics, home furnishings and fashion products. He has had ample opportunity in his business career to assess the difference between the traditional and the contemporary executive. Here's how he describes the difference:

"The old-time manager worked mostly by the seat of his pants. He was a rugged individualist, a guy who knew every facet of his business. He knew production, sales, financing, and what's more, he insisted on working in all these areas. He wore many hats and would brook no intrusions into what he considered his personal and private domain. Today's executive is a vastly different type of ballcarrier. He's a member of a team; he's usually a specialist, a man who does one thing exceedingly well, depending on which function he came up through—marketing, finance, and so on—and he depends heavily on the support of his teammates to take care of their various specialties."

The vital statistics of change

Quite apart from appearance, Lapham IV and his colleagues have made several other crucial breaks with the past.

A classic study by Mabel Newcomer[1] pins down some of these changes. For example, today's manager is more highly educated than his counterparts of the past. Miss Newcomer offers these figures:

---

[1] Mabel Newcomer, *The Big Business Executive* (New York: Columbia University Press, 1955).

COLLEGE EDUCATION OF EXECUTIVES

	Some College Education with or without Degrees	With College Degrees	With Engineering Degrees
1900	39.3%	28.3%	6.8%
1925	51.5	40.2	13.2
1950	75.6%	62.1%	20.0%

In 1964, *Scientific American*[2] sponsored an updating of Dr. Newcomer's study, and this was one of the findings:

"As the percentage of big business executives with academic degrees of all kinds increased from 28.3% in 1900 to 74.3% in 1964, the percentage with degrees in science and engineering increased from 7% to 33%."

Another study, by the Research Institute of America[3], compares a group of business managers of 1957 with a similar group in 1967. The findings indicate that the latter group, on the average—

—is younger,

—is better educated,

—has been in management for a shorter period of time,

—has been with the company a shorter period of time.

The figures below spell out the specifics of the Research Institute study:

Age	1957	1967
Under 25	1.0%	8.7%
25–34	20.4	36.0
35–44	34.6	24.3
45–54	24.3	22.5
55 and over	11.0	5.5
No answer	8.7%	3.0%

Education	1957	1967
Elementary school	6.2%	0.0%
Started high school	16.3	3.9
Finished high school	27.4	28.5
Started college	18.6	21.3
Completed college	19.2	33.2
Advanced degree	4.0	10.6
No answer	6.3%	2.5%

Number of Years a Manager	1957	1967
Under 3 years	15.6%	36.5%
3 to 10 years	43.4	29.4
11 to 20 years	23.0	24.1
Over 20 years	8.4	8.0
No answer	9.6%	2.0%

Years with Present Company	1957	1967
Under 3 years	8.3%	26.4%
3 to 10 years	32.2	33.2
11 to 20 years	26.6	25.3
Over 20 years	24.0	11.9
No answer	8.9%	3.2%

While the Newcomer study investigated the big busi-

[2] "The Big Business Executive/1964," a research study (New York: *Scientific American*).

[3] Confidential Report for staff use only, Research Institute of America, January 1967.

ness executive—that is, top executives from large corporations—the Research Institute study matched two groups of 500 middle-level managers from a broad cross section of business and industry, including small and medium-size corporations. The indication, then, is that the change in characteristics of the manager is pervasive, applying to all echelons and all types of business.

Another interesting aspect of the Research Institute study is that the changes revealed, although quite sharp, took place over only a *ten-year* period. This highlights one other aspect of the change taking place in the management group—the tempo is accelerating, the advances made in the last ten years taking place at a more rapid rate than before.

Of course, behind the large overall figures are specific hard facts. *Nation's Business*[4] recently reported that college graduates with a master's degree in business administration—plus an undergraduate technical degree—have been at the top of the job recruiters' shopping lists. June graduates were offered $10,428 a year—$850 more than in 1966. These salary figures reflect the heightened demand that exists in today's business world for the educationally qualified young man. The College Placement Council, Bethlehem, Pennsylvania, the source of the figures, states that for the first time since it began surveys of starting salaries offered college graduates, Masters of Business Administration led the list.

The top executive has completely reoriented his attitude toward "the college kid" in business. Here's how Hal A. Salzman of Odell, Inc., states the case:

"In the bad old days, a college education was something a trainee had to get knocked out of him before the hard practicalities of the business world could make themselves felt. Today, college training, especially business training, is excellent preparation for business. Subjects are taught differently, rapport the students have with their professors is much better than it used to be, and the boys that come out of school today can go into business and, in the first year, can be quickly oriented to

---

[4] "Executive Trends," *Nation's Business*, September 1967.

business needs. Most college boys coming into business today, though they may still be wet behind the ears in some ways, from the viewpoint of organizational abilities and administration have much more orderly minds, have learned a method of approach, and have a much better predisposition toward computerized operations."

What the executive recruiters report

A group of executive-recruiting specialists, members of the Association of Executive Recruiting Consultants, were asked to describe some of the changes in employer specifications they had noted in the past 15 to 20 years. This was the consensus as to qualifications of executive-job candidates:

He must be computer-oriented. Even if he himself can't prepare a program, he must know what a computer can do, both in order to direct the work of the specialists and to utilize the almost limitless variety of management data it can produce.

It helps if he's a dual-threat man—a man who has had line experience but has the analytical abilities ordinarily associated with staff functions. For example, the controller's job used to be mainly an accounting function; now it's a control function which may not be accounting-based at all. The controller must be able to advise on the financial consequences of a new warehouse, a different pricing system or a new marketing program. The sales head is no longer a director of salesmen, he's a marketing man, and so on.

He should be a master technician. Particularly for the higher-echelon jobs, companies are looking for managers capable of the "McNamara approach." [5] Very much in demand is the troubleshooter and planner who can view company operations from a broad systems standpoint and come up with answers that have the backing of mathematical formulation.

---

[5] Robert S. McNamara, ex-president of Ford Motor Company and former secretary of defense, especially noted for innovating advanced business methods in running the Defense Department.

The accelerating rate of change

Not only have many changes occurred in a period of 100 years, but the rate of change itself has accelerated. It is significant that greater changes have occurred in the past 20 years than in the previous 80. And the rate of change itself is a major fact in the contemporary business world.

One evidence of this is the phenomenon of executive obsolescence. Job obsolescence is no stranger to the business scene. We'd have to search far today to find a buggy-whip winder or a hand turner, for example. However, the last decade has witnessed an unprecedented development—the *obsolete executive.*

Some figures supplied in an editorial in a business journal[6] fill out the picture of accelerating technology:

"Thirteen years ago, the first computer for commercial use went into operation. It processed data for an electric company. Today, there are some 35,000 computers in operation, and a technical journal has classified 1000 separate ways in which they're used. The number of computers will double not in another thirteen years, but in a mere three. The pace of change accelerates so rapidly that we not only see 'tomorrow' fairly clearly but speculate with some assurance about the day after tomorrow. What to do about it? We've only room to say, 'Learn. Learn what to learn. Then learn it. Then keep on learning.' "

Today, people are being nudged out of their executive positions, not by their age or a health failure, but because their executive skills, adequate when they started in their jobs, are no longer sufficient to tackle current work problems. They have failed to accept the fact that in today's world of business, education must be a continuing process.

The increasing rate of obsolescence in the executive ranks highlights the fact that the executive job is changing more and more rapidly. It is to the problem of anticipating and preventing executive obsolescence that the following chapters are addressed.

---

[6] *Administrative Management,* February 1967.

FOR FURTHER EXECUTIVE THOUGHT

Argyris, Chris. *Organization and Innovation* (1965). Richard D. Irwin, Inc., 1818 Ridge Rd., Homewood, Ill. 60430.

Bassett, Glenn A. *Management Styles in Transition* (1967). American Management Association, 135 W. 50th St., New York, N.Y. 10020.

Beaumont, Richard A., and Helfgott, R. B. *Management, Automation & People* (1964). Industrial Relations Counselors, Inc., 1270 Avenue of the Americas, New York, N.Y. 10020.

Howells, William Dean. *The Rise of Silas Lapham* (paperback edition, 1962). Collier Books, a division of Crowell-Collier Publishing Co., New York, N.Y. 10022.

Jennings, Eugene Emerson. *The Mobile Manager: A Study of the New Generation of Top Executives* (1967). University of Michigan, Bureau of Industrial Relations, Graduate School of Business Administration, Ann Arbor, Mich. 48106.

Mitchell, William. *Business Executive in a Changing World* (1966). American Management Association, 135 W. 50th St., New York, N.Y. 10020.

Randall, Clarence B. *Executive in Transition* (1967). McGraw-Hill Book Co., 330 W. 42nd St., New York, N.Y. 10036.

TWO/TECHNOLOGY AS A CHANGE AGENT

In 1967 there was considerable concern that the United States might lose its lead in the "technology gap" vis-à-vis Europe.

A *Wall Street Journal* editorial warned dourly that while European countries would benefit from tariff-free exchange of goods within the European Economic Community, the U.S. Government might well damage the competitive position of U.S. business by "manipulating the economy with price-wage 'guideposts' and other devices." While many would disagree with the *Wall Street Journal's* pessimism about "government manipulation," the editorial did serve to dramatize the incredible advances of business and industrial technology in the U.S. since the end of World War Two.

The *Journal* went on to note that underlying the great leap in technology were: a huge domestic market unhampered by tariffs or trade restraints; a free flow of capital, making possible profitable investment in innovative directions; and a high degree of business competition. As a result of this last factor, new products and processes are quickly put to the test of the marketplace, where the weak ones are rapidly eliminated. The nation's resources aren't wasted for long on anything that is inefficient or worthless.

To understand the impact of accelerating technology on business, one must examine two sets of factors involved in all technological developments. One can be described as "hardware" and the other as "software." The nature of each and its relationship to the other explain a good deal of how the job of tomorrow's executive will differ from the activities of his predecessors.

The hardware of the technological advance

Two words sum up the physical aspects of the technological leap since World War Two: *automation* and *computerization*. They are probably the most overworked and least precisely used words in the business dictionary; so it is important to define exactly what they mean.

Automation. Professor Herbert A. Simon of the Carnegie Institute of Technology provides this graphic description:[1]

"At the heart of the increases in productivity that mark the industrial revolution is a great burst of tool-building activity. . . . Man discovered fire for the second time—this time as a source of energy, many times more powerful than his own.

"With mechanical energy came mechanization—the devising of tools for applying that energy to the process of production. The human worker remained essentially part of the system of production but his main function became that of guiding known human forces rather than applying his own. In recent years, in speaking of 'automation,' we mean to note the fact that man's toolbuilding ingenuity has not limited itself to capturing and harnessing mechanical energy but is now extended, also, to the processes of guiding and controlling that energy."

From Dell S. Harder of the Ford Motor Company[2] comes this personal reminiscence:

"As some of you may know, I coined the word *automation* in the year 1935, although the term didn't come into extensive use until about 1947. At that time, its meaning was largely limited to the linking of man's tools with automatic transfer and handling equipment. Today, however, its meaning goes far beyond the definition it had even those few short years ago. Its meaning has expanded and changed with each new application."

---

[1] Speech at the University of Toronto, October 26, 1966.
[2] Bittel, Meldon and Rice, *Practical Automation* (New York: McGraw-Hill, 1957).

Other definitions of automation abound. For example, one authority holds that "automation is the completely automatic manufacture, assembly and preparation of products for shipment."

According to another widely held view, automation always includes the elements of electronic control and "feedback," that is, the ability of equipment to keep track of its own output. If the output or process develops measurable faults—such as too high a degree of heat or parts that are outside of tolerance—such equipment either alerts an operator or readjusts itself.

One practical but essential aspect of automation—as opposed to mechanization—is the automatic handling of work between production operations, so as to tie separate pieces of equipment into one continuous, fully automatic process.

For example, phonograph records used to be made on hydraulic presses run with an electrically timed cycle under the control of an individual operator. Today, records are produced by an electronically controlled injection process. A group of six machines with just three standby operators can outproduce the old-time department of 50 hydraulic presses and 50 operators.

In only two decades, the electronic computer has become one of the most revolutionary tools available to man. The advent of the computer has created new problems and new opportunities for the executive. Says one company president, "A computer is like an unbroken stallion: Running wild, it can do a lot of damage. Properly controlled, it can provide useful service."

The impact of the computer has already been tremendous. Some of the consequences already felt will be discussed shortly. But it must be remembered that the *technology of our technology* continues to advance. The development of the computer, from its practical beginnings in the 1950s, in a mere 15 years has already entered a fourth generation of machines (see chart, chapter 10). Undoubtedly, the generations will continue to develop and, with them, new capabilities will be available to managers.

The software of the technological advance

As a result of automation and the availability of the computer, new management methods have been developed that have revolutionized traditional practices in the software areas. The most important of the new techniques are briefly mentioned here and treated in greater detail in chapter 9.

PERT. The full name of this management tool is *Program Evaluation and Review Technique.* The U.S. Navy used the approach to expedite its gigantic *Polaris* missile program. The technique is also known as *Critical Path Method.* Regardless of label, the idea is basically simple and has broad application. It can be used to hasten the construction of a submarine missile, to overhaul a plant or to make bread. Essentially, it helps people to organize a series of interrelated operations so that time and costs can be optimized.

For complicated operations, it takes an engineer with a computer and a knowledge of parametric linear programming to apply CPM. But the basic principles may be applied even to the simple tasks. To some extent, PERT, or CPM, is like the housewife's approach to preparing a multicourse meal: She uses several burners and the oven simultaneously, starts things that take longer first, and ends up at dinnertime ready to serve.

Operations research. Richard S. Leghorn, president of Itek Corporation, has defined operations research as "a systematic application of the scientific approach to the investigation of current or expected operational problems which require decisions by managers."

Basically, operations research is a management approach to solving logistic and production problems. In the form we know it today, OR was developed during World War Two in Great Britain, when Britain's top brass assigned teams of scientists to solve some of its strategic and tactical problems. For example, the military was concerned with making the best use of its radar system, the best deployment of aircraft on bombing missions, and so on.

By 1950, American industry began to apply OR to

business decisions involving such questions as: How can our facilities be used in most economical fashion? What is the best price for our product under various market conditions? And so on. In general, operations research may be defined as the means by which a sequence of actions can be optimized by quantifying the elements involved in these operations.

The important role of specialization

With increased technology comes specialization—of work, of know-how, of organization. Specialization, in turn, has brought many changes in the management function. For example, consider the financial executive's job. Several decades back, in the typical company, he would be responsible for all activities related to the use of company funds. Today, as a result of increasing competition and a greater pressure for better performance, as well as the increased magnitude of the function itself, the job may be divided among a group of executives:

1. controller
2. treasurer
3. tax specialist
4. real-estate advisor
5. investment specialist
6. capital-budgeting specialist
7. acquisitions specialist

Specialization has also taken place in company operations. In the last decade, for example, materials handling has been recognized as a distinctly separate part of the overall manufacturing process and, at the same time, an integral part of the total system. The result of specialization is to deepen and refine the area of the specialty. Knowledge about the specialty becomes more sophisticated. Tools and techniques tend to become more highly refined and potent. Operation times and lead times tend to shorten and, most important of all, the specialist is expected to produce superior results.

John Kenneth Galbraith, in his important book *The New Industrial State*,[3] asserts that, increasingly, the

[3] (Boston: Houghton Mifflin, 1967).

"technocrats," or specialists, are the ones who are running the corporation. Top management—the president, officers and vice-presidents—can no longer be personally adept in the areas of expertise necessary to make day-to-day decisions. The specialists, individually or in groups, will be given problems to solve. Their conclusions and recommendations will be weighed by top management, whose major job will be to ratify decisions by the specialists.

The technological advance: many fronts

When technological change is considered, attention often focuses on automation and computers. However, technological changes of a different and broader dimension are also occurring, and they are having a subtle but decided effect on the world of business and the working life of the executive.

The conquest of space, starting with *Sputnik* in 1957, and the resulting need for exploratory craft that can withstand extreme pressures of temperature, speed, and so on, resulted in new standards in many production areas. Frontiers of production knowledge are being pushed further and further back. By-products of the advance number in the hundreds. Subminiature computer parts, developed to get small, efficient computers on board space rockets, turn up in small office computers that occupy only as much space as a desk. New materials, developed to make space rockets withstand the conditions of space and reentry, appear in coffeepots and cookware in the housewife's kitchen.

Space science is only one of the many areas in which technological advance is creating a general business feedback. Oceanographic study and development promise a world tomorrow of underocean resources and activity. Armies of executives will have to be trained to become familiar with the conditions of underwater operations.

In the field of medicine, basic research is creating still another revolution affecting not only the world of business but our entire civilization. Birth control, organ replacement, antibiotics and drugs with astonishing properties for healing and minimizing old diseases and ailments set a breathtaking pace of change. Consider just one problem posed by the medical revolution: When the life-span is increased to 100 or even 125, what will happen to our traditional ideas about retirement age, executive succession, the need for new blood to update an executive staff, and so on?

Impact of technological change on the executive

Later chapters will discuss in detail the impact of some of the changes. Here, however, it will suffice to describe briefly some of the consequences for the executive of our accelerating technology.

The young executive on the work scene. Traditionally, the veteran, the "man of experience," was of supreme importance in the business world. It was the experienced executive, with "know-how" built up over the years, who could help his company anticipate or circumvent problems. Now experience, the very quality that formerly was a virtue, threatens to become a handicap. The more today differs from yesterday, the less pertinent is the experience an individual has accumulated. Accordingly, it isn't the veteran but the master of the newest techniques who's likely to become the mainstay of effective management.

This doesn't mean that college graduates will move in and take over. What is suggested, however, is that the understanding of the veteran and the technical, specialized approach of the newly trained youngster must be united for the most effective solution of problems.

Higher education. Education is clearly a growing need for the employee of tomorrow at almost all levels. The manager and the rank-and-file employee will have undergone thorough training before they are permitted to handle the responsibilities and mechanisms of tomorrow's company. Investment in machines, products and markets will be much too great to permit mistakes due to ignorance or lack of preparation.

The administrative executive will be expected to know finance and engineering and to have an understanding of mathematics. Advanced degrees, once an academic asset, are now becoming a business requirement.

Information handling. The so-called information explosion is already upon us as a result of computerization and high-speed communication. The traditional problem was how to get information. The problem the manager faces today is how to absorb and use available information.

At a recent conference held by the National Industrial Conference Board[4] on the problem posed by the great proliferation of information, the panelists were asked to consider how industry might make the most of scientific and technological knowledge being acquired by such agencies as the Atomic Energy Commission and the National Aeronautics and Space Administration. There was agreement on two points:

> Conventional methods of disseminating technological information are clearly inadequate in an age when five million articles are published annually.

> A new discipline, that of the "technoeconomic analyst" is being encouraged, to bring together the creators and potential users of new knowledge.

An exchange between two of the panelists, Martin R. Gainsbrugh, senior vice-president and chief economist of NICB, and Dr. Arthur M. Bueche, vice-president for research and development, General Electric Company, provide two related but somewhat different views of the problem:

Gainsbrugh: Businessmen hear a lot about this problem of coping with an accelerated rate of change. Does anyone here have any reservations about the reality of it? Is there evidence that it is getting worse? Just the other day, the statement was made that in the past decade there has been as much addition to human knowledge as there had been until then since man first walked this earth.

Bueche: It's a good topic for conversation. But when I

---

[4] Reginald H. Holland, "Technology Transfer," the *Conference Board Record*, September 1967.

talk to businessmen, I get quite a different emphasis. The question is not how to organize the increasing volume of scientific knowledge but how to organize the technical resources of a business to use that knowledge. Let me expound on that: The big change lies not in the increase in knowledge but in the fact that it has got beyond the ken of the few. This has meant that new organizational structures have had to be brought into being, the first step toward the harnessing of science for technological purposes. So, today, our real concern is not the growth of knowledge as such but how industrial organizations can be fitted into the picture.

Reaction time. Accelerating technology has another effect: It reduces the time between start and finish of many business processes.

This emphasis on speed inevitably quickens the pace of executive activity. Every moment of an executive's day, from answering the mail to making decisions, both large and small, has lost time latitude. Customers won't wait, competitors won't wait. The sandwich at deskside is already replacing the leisurely two-martini, two-hour repast that used to be one of the prerogatives of executive life.

A simple example illustrates the speedup phenomenon: A customer of the Owens-Illinois Glass Company ordered some containers. Shortly afterward, he changed his mind and called to cancel it. He found he couldn't—the shipment was already at his plant. This example could be multiplied in a hundred different ways. Electronic communication, plus jet airplanes, plus interlocking systems between production and sales, vendors and customers, customers and suppliers—all add up to a new business tempo.

Unification of function. To a large extent, everything from manufacturing to sales record keeping hangs on the same string. The production process that used to consist of a number of different operations is now much more of a unified whole.

It's this fact that has increased the use of the so-called

systems approach, in which the entire company operation may be viewed as a single operating system with inputs and outputs and in which the relationship between elements must be highly logical.

Restatement in brief

To recap: The emerging preeminence of the younger, more highly educated manager poses both a threat and a promise. The threat is to the mature executive whose training and experience lie in a past that to some extent is losing its relevance to a rapidly developing and changing present and future. The promise is for the young people of today and tomorrow, who will no longer have to wait for an opportunity to take over the managerial reins, and for the companies that will respond to the flexibility and drive that youthful management can bring to organizational life and its problems.

Of course, the mature manager holds trump cards in his confrontation with the new generation. While his *technical* experience may be outdated, his *emotional* experience, that is, his maturity, will still be an important asset in providing balance and judgment in developing and setting company policy and in assisting the young Turks in their interpersonal relationships, likely to be rough and edgy due to inexperience.

The problems posed by the rapid proliferation of information and the need for faster reflexes will have to be faced up to and countered by managers able to *(a) analyze* their working problems; *(b) solve* them in practical, realistic fashion; and *(c) organize* their energies effectively to cope with job routines and problems with reasonable timeliness.

Finally, the unification of functions that results from the new technology suggests that in a simple, direct sense, the executive tomorrow will increasingly become a generalist who will view his job, however specialized, as a part of a total system and will understand how his part of the operation meshes with the operation of the organization as a whole.

FOR FURTHER EXECUTIVE THOUGHT

Burck, Gilbert, and editors of *Fortune. The Computer Age and Its Potential for Management* (1965). Harper & Row, Publishers, 49 E. 33rd St., New York, N.Y. 10016.

Diebold, John. *Beyond Automation: Managerial Problems of an Exploding Technology* (1964). McGraw-Hill Book Co., 300 W. 42nd St., New York, N.Y. 10036.

Ginzberg, Eli. *Technology and Social Change* (1964). Columbia University Press, 440 W. 110th St., New York, N.Y. 10025.

Kanter, Jerome. *The Computer and the Executive* (1967). Prentice-Hall, Inc., Englewood Cliffs, N.J. 07632.

Laird, Donald A., and Laird, Eleanor C. *How to Get Along with Automation* (1964). McGraw-Hill Book Co., 330 West 42nd St., New York, N.Y. 10036.

Lothrop, Warren C. *Management Uses of Research and Development* (1964). Harper & Row, Publishers, 49 E. 33rd St., New York, N.Y. 10016.

Myers, Charles A. (ed.). *The Impact of Computers on Management* (1967). M.I.T. Press, 50 Ames St., Rm. 741, Cambridge, Mass. 02142.

Rico, Leonard. *The Defense Against Paperwork* (1967). The University of Michigan, Ann Arbor, Mich. 48106.

Schon, Donald A. *Technology and Change* (1967). Dell Publishing Co., Inc., 750 Third Ave., New York, N.Y. 10017.

THREE/THE BEHAVIORAL SCIENCES MAKE THEIR MARK

The beginning student of business learns almost immediately that "management has to do with the efficient control of men, machines, materials and money." But he may not discover for years what every experienced executive knows—"men" present the greatest challenge —and the most complex problems. As one manager observed, "Eighty percent of the problems that come across my desk have nothing to do with the 'hardness of material' but the hardheadedness of the staff."

The fact is, managing human beings is very different from managing money or machines. As one executive sighed, "If only people in business were more businesslike." People bring to the work scene emotions and attitudes ranging from apathy to aggressiveness. How they are handled determines their personal efficiency, their individual contributions and, ultimately, the profits of the entire company.

However, along with the "people problem" goes the promise of tremendous rewards when their full potential is tapped and channeled into the goals of the enterprise. When an individual or work group is skillfully managed, the resulting contribution can rack up more than average benefits for a company. (The executive of one company which is well known for its success in motivating its people admitted at a recent business seminar, "We've been making so much money, it's indecent.")

In recent years, in an effort to get more out of manpower resource, companies have turned to the behavioral scientist—psychologist, sociologist, anthropologist—just as they turn to the engineer and the maintenance expert to maximize the efficiency of their equipment.

As *Fortune* puts it: "Increasingly, business has turned to the academic world for help, particularly to the behavioral scientists—the psychologists, sociologists and anthropologists whose studies have now become the showpieces of the better business schools. A number of major corporations, such as General Electric, Texas Instruments and Standard Oil (N.J.), have brought social scientists onto their staffs. Some companies collaborate closely with university-based scholars and are contributing importantly to advanced theoretical work, just as industry's physicists, chemists and engineers have become significant contributors of new knowledge in their respective realms. Hundreds of companies, large and small, have tried one or another formulation of basic behavioral theory, such as the many schemes for sharing cost savings with employees and actively soliciting their ideas for improved efficiency." [1]

The scientist and the worker

From the outset, the behavioral scientist and the businessman have had one interest in common: identifying the factors that improve or inhibit production in the work group. The story of this quest is a fascinating one, and it provides an interesting picture of the relative success the scientist has had in contributing to business progress.

The first mark made by science on the business scene came around 1908 with the work of Frederick Taylor, called the father of scientific management. Taylor's training was in industrial engineering, but he became deeply interested in the problem of human efficiency. Not surprisingly, he approached it by measuring work and tools. He concerned himself with such problems as the most effective size, shape and handle length of shovels for moving coal manually and the average time required to produce a certain quantity of work.

Taylor's success in increasing efficiency through time

[1] Robert C. Albrook, "Participative Management: Time for a Second Look," *Fortune*, May 1967.

and motion standards made the somewhat startled industrial community realize that scientific methods had a place in the world of work. Since Taylor's time, not only has the alliance between businessman and behavioral scientist become stronger, but a whole crop of middlemen has sprung up. These include behavioral engineers, industrial trainers, management-development planners, and others who, acting as a bridge, have attempted to translate the insights and concepts of the scientists into practical tools and techniques for business.

From Taylor's time until the early 1930s, most of the work done by the scientist was in the area of time and motion study. The time-study man, the industrial engineer, gave birth to the concept of mechanical efficiency. But, gradually, a reaction set in against the mechanical coldness of time study and its "dehumanization" of the worker. During the depression of the 1930s, the "efficiency expert" was a hated figure, and it wasn't long before companies, for the sake of labor peace, eventually moved away from the time-study approach.

Even after the strict standards of the efficiency expert were watered down by time allowances—everything from fatigue to rest-room visits was factored in—management felt that Taylor's approach had run them into a dead end. Something major was still missing from the human work equation.

What this "something" was didn't suggest itself to management for several decades after Taylor. And then it seemed to appear in the work of an industrial sociologist, G. Elton Mayo.

Influence of the Hawthorne experiments

In the 1920s, the Western Electric Company was giving its people practically everything workers at that time had ever asked for. They had the best pension plans, sickness and accident benefits, recreation programs. Nonetheless, output wasn't going well—at least not well enough. The company decided to call on some research people from the Harvard Graduate School of Business to study the effects of lighting on production. Before the so-called Hawthorne experiments were completed, a large group of scientists worked on the problem and they turned up some startling facts. For example:

The researchers selected two groups of operators. Group 1 continued to work under the old level of light. Group 2 was given more light. With more light, output increased. This result had been expected. But the output of Group 1 went up, also.

Next they gave Group 2 less light to work by. Output went up still more. And so did that of Group 1. The researchers even put two workers in a room without any light at all, working by sense of touch. Despite this handicap, the workers kept up the increased output.

Trying to explain the unexpected developments, the researchers experimented further. They studied a group of six assembly workers.

They changed the group from time to piecework. The output went up.

The girls were given two five-minute rest periods. Output went up.

Two ten-minute rest periods were given. Output still went up.

Then the morning rest period was lengthened to 15 minutes and the girls were served a hot snack. Output was up again.

The girls were let off half an hour earlier. Output soared.

They were let off a full hour earlier and yet output remained at the same level.

The girls were put back to working that extra hour. Output was up.

It remained at that high level when weekly hours were cut from 48 to 40.

Finally, as a last test, the scientists restored the original conditions. The girls went back to timework. No rest periods, no hot snack and 48 hours a week.

Output hit an all-time high.

The unknown factor

The scientists *thought* they had restored the original

conditions. Yet these girls felt differently about themselves and about their work. The mere fact of being selected from among their colleagues to participate in an experiment made the girls feel important. They had become a "team" whose help the company needed. There was a purpose behind what they were doing, a purpose bigger than just turning out so many pieces of work.

The researchers developed another line of inquiry. Twenty-one thousand Western Electric workers were interviewed and asked how they felt about their jobs and the company and what complaints they had, if any.

At first the interviewers used prepared questions relating to the job in the company. But the workers tended to stray from the subject and talk about other things. After trying unsuccessfully to keep them on the track, the interviewers finally discarded their prepared questions and let each individual talk about whatever preoccupied him. The researchers made another discovery: Discussing his troubles made many a worker feel better about things in general, about his working conditions and about his boss in particular. Also, he responded favorably to being listened to. He was pleased to be considered as an individual, a person who had something to say.

Morale—the "x" factor?

If there was one word that summed up the implications of the Hawthorne experiments to management in the Thirties and Forties, that word was *morale*. To management, the goal now seemed both clear and obtainable. If worker morale were kept high, productivity would be high. One simply had to develop ways and means of "satisfying" the worker, making him feel good about his work, his boss and the company, and all would be well on the production front.

Psychologists at the University of Michigan's Survey Research Center, including Daniel Katz, Nathan Maccoby and Nancy C. Morse, were the front-runners in a new line of research involving morale.[2] In the early Forties, they proclaimed that there was a direct relationship between morale and productivity. Managers were told that if by proper supervisory practices they could make their people happy in their work, productivity would rise.

The only trouble with this finding was that it didn't hold up. Subsequent investigations demonstrated what many practicing managers knew by experience, namely, that the relationship between morale and productivity was neither direct nor simple. As a matter of fact, later research found that in some instances, high morale *depressed* productivity.

The morale-productivity relationship

Current thinking on the relationship between morale and productivity is almost a reversal of ideas current 20 and 30 years ago. As subsequent studies proved, there are different types of morale. One kind is marked by a high level of group concentration in completing assigned tasks—finishing the Jones order, for example. But consider this example:

Last night the boys went bowling, and the shipping department won a smashing victory over the addressograph department. Not surprisingly, morale is high this morning in shipping. Everyone feels great. But how about the work?

Well, as a matter of fact, the work is standing still. A few of the boys are a little tired after the big game. Some are bringing the others up to date on how they "carried" the team. The supervisor clearly has an output problem.

Researchers at the Survey Research Center of the University of Michigan discovered the same thing in a controlled experiment. They investigated the behavior of three very different groups: clerical workers in a large insurance company, railroad section gangs, and workers

---

[2] See Nancy C. Morse, "Satisfactions in the White-Collar Job," Survey Research Center, University of Michigan, Ann Arbor, 1953.

in a tractor-assembly plant. The results were the same with all three groups of employees, and there is every reason to believe that the same finding would apply in any department:

The fact that employees are happy doesn't mean they feel an urge to work harder or better. Surveys of employee attitudes show, in fact, that people can enjoy high morale and still fail to produce.

Yet, just because high morale doesn't guarantee high production, it doesn't follow that management can ignore the personal needs, the human satisfaction of employees. Employee morale plays a role in motivating people, for example. It can provide a springboard, a starting point. But good morale doesn't mean, by itself, that people will take the jump.

Participation, the next target

As the results of research in morale proceeded to disillusion and disappoint more and more managers, a new concept was sought. It was found in studies of "participation," largely in the field of group dynamics. Psychologists and sociologists had long been aware that people behaved differently in groups than they did as individuals. For example, studies conducted during World War Two showed that housewives who participated in group discussion on the dietary value of citrus fruits tended to use citrus fruits to a greater degree than matched groups that were simply lectured at, on the same subject, by dietitians.

The implication for management was clear: If employees were given the chance to participate in decision making, they would accept the final decision and be more wholehearted in working toward its implementation. Change, a continuing preoccupation of business, might then become more acceptable at the lower echelons.

Yet, here again, the easy answer does not always apply. For example: Professor Arnold S. Tannenbaum of the University of Michigan describes an experiment in which a company divided its clerical staff into two groups, one to be managed participatively, the other in the usual way, with management making all decisions. In the participative group, the clerks discussed and decided things like rules for office conduct, size of work groups, length of coffee breaks, and so on. The other group was not allowed to participate in decisions.

The results? Although productivity in each group went up and the clerks in the participative group enjoyed their work more, productivity in the *nonparticipative* group rose most.

Professor Tannenbaum accounted for the results by suggesting that productivity went up in the participative group because of increased job satisfaction and in the other group because of the manager's increased control. Tannenbaum further suggested that output might have gone up more in the participative group if the supervisor had realized that the purpose of participation was not to make personnel happy but to improve their functioning inside the organizational context.

Tannenbaum's final statement hits at the heart of a problem: the tendency of business to jump to conclusions about research findings and then to be disillusioned when they don't work out in a practical situation. This experiment, said Tannenbaum, suggests that participation and control are not mutually exclusive. There may be a time and a place for each.

Next target—motivation

At times when skilled labor is scarce or management needs top performance, motivation becomes of crucial importance. And the emphasis today is no longer on "coaxing or persuading people to do what's wanted," but on *creating conditions that elicit their best efforts*.

Traditionally, management has taken two approaches to motivation:

The "do-it-or-else" approach. In the "bad old days," let's say up to the end of World War One, the manager gave little thought to motivation. A man either did as he was told or got pink-slipped off the premises.

The "reward" approach. The company relied on the

carrot rather than the stick. In retrospect, the idea seems naïve: "Treat employees well and they will work harder out of loyalty and gratitude." This paternalistic view faded as cynicism and the harder realities of the work situation emerged after World War Two.

In recent years, behavioral scientists have learned more about the attitudes of people at work, and their findings have led to what may be called the *"internal incentive" approach*. The new and current phase embraces the thinking of psychologists and sociologists like A. H. Maslow and Frederick Herzberg:

Maslow's "basic needs" concept. Before Dr. A. H. Maslow's theory of human motivation was developed, puzzling facts were noted. For example: Money was supposed to be the great incentive. Yet, strangely, when people were asked what was most important to them in their jobs, money often took third or fourth place. Factors like "challenging work," "chance for advancement" and even, in some cases, "a good boss" ranked higher.

Dr. Maslow suggested a theory that explains the seeming contradiction. He suggested that there is a *hierarchy of needs* that exists for the human being. We give precedence to the first of these needs—*until it is satisfied*. When the first need is satisfied, the second becomes dominant, and so on, through the sequence. Here's Maslow's list:

Physiological needs—hunger, shelter, sex.

Safety needs—these represent our needs for protection against danger and threat either from the environment or from people.

Social needs—after the physiological and safety needs are fairly well satisfied, the needs for love, affection and "belongingness" tend to emerge.

Esteem needs—these have to do with the wish that most of us have for self-respect and the good opinion of others.

Self-fulfillment—last on the list but perhaps of most significance for future managers is the need for "self-actualization." This concerns the individual's feeling about the value and satisfaction of his work.

Failure to understand this need often lies behind the manager's complaint, "We've given our people everything—good pay, pleasant working conditions, all the physical comforts possible on the job—and yet they're dissatisfied." Dr. Maslow's concept explains the reason. It's precisely because employees have had the four basic needs sufficiently satisfied that the fifth—the need for self-fulfillment—emerges. It will cause discontent unless and until the manager finds ways of satisfying it.

Herzberg's motivator/hygiene-factor concept. Further insight into the nature of human motivation was provided by Dr. Frederick Herzberg, chairman of the psychology department of Western Reserve University. Dr. Herzberg's ideas help explain contradictions such as this one:

"I don't understand it," says manager Bill White bitterly. "One of my best men just quit. He'd been asking for air conditioning at his work station. I twisted myself into a pretzel to get a requisition through. I got him what he wanted—and a few months later he leaves for a job that actually pays him less than he was making here!"

White's sad tale may not be duplicated often, but similar cases are frequent. What makes a man satisfied or dissatisfied in his job seems unpredictable. Dr. Herzberg clarifies the situation considerably.

Herzberg developed the idea that two sets of conditions affect a man at work. He calls one set *motivators,* the other, *hygiene factors.* The first group is positive, has the power to *satisfy* an employee. The second group is negative, can *dissatisfy* or demotivate. These he calls *hygiene factors.* Of the former, the five most important, according to Herzberg, are achievement, recognition, the work itself, responsibility and advancement. Of the latter, the five most important are company policy and administration, supervision, salary, interpersonal relations and working conditions.

The distinction between them, says Herzberg, is that the first set of factors (the motivators) "describe man's relationship to what he *does:* his job content, achievement on a task, recognition for task achievement, the nature of the task, responsibility for a task and professional advancement or growth in task capability."

The dissatisfiers (or what Herzberg calls hygiene factors), describe an employee's "relationship to the context or environment in which he does his job." They "serve primarily to *prevent job dissatisfaction,* while having little effect on *positive* job attitudes."

This is a most important distinction. Dr. Herzberg's study shows that "the factors involved in producing job satisfaction are *separate* and *distinct* from the factors that lead to job dissatisfaction." The lack of satisfiers does not lead to dissatisfaction; the presence of hygiene factors does not lead to satisfaction but to *no dissatisfaction.*

In other words, the presence of good company policies and administration, good supervision, good salaries, good interpersonal relations and good working conditions will not motivate people over the long haul. What does motivate people is the challenge and pleasure they get out of the work itself, the sense of achievement they get from doing the work, recognition for a job well done, a feeling of responsibility and the desire for advancement.

The climate of work

Today it's generally agreed that neither carrot nor stick, incentive nor punishment, will win desirable results as motivational techniques in the long run. Superseding these "pushing" type of motivators is the concept of a "climate" on the work scene that will help the individual employee develop his own internal reasons for wanting to excel—for wanting to produce at high levels, to contribute ideas above and beyond his immediate tasks. In this general area, Douglas McGregor's Theory X–Theory Y approach is an outstanding example of the psychologists' approach to greater effectiveness on the work scene.

Theory X—Theory Y

In 1957, an important new idea was introduced to the world of management by Professor Douglas McGregor of the Massachusetts Institute of Technology. In a talk at the university, McGregor expounded his Theory X and Theory Y concepts of management. Three years later, he expanded his ideas in a book, *The Human Side of Enterprise*.

McGregor's now-classic work suggests that two different approaches, or philosophies of management, are possible in business. Each is based on a set of assumptions about people. One can see the differences in approach—and at the same time test one's own assumptions about people—by looking at McGregor's descriptions:

Theory X Assumptions about People	Theory Y Assumptions about People
1. Human beings are inherently lazy and will shun work if they can.	1. For most people the expenditure of physical and mental effort in work is as natural as for play or rest.
2. People must be directed, controlled and motivated by fear of punishment or deprivation to impel them to work as the company requires.	2. Man will exercise self-control in the service of objectives which he accepts.
3. The average human being prefers to be directed, wishes to avoid responsibility, has relatively little ambition, and wants security above all.	3. Under proper conditions, the average human being learns not only to accept responsibility but also to seek it.
	4. The capacity for exercising imagination, ingenuity, and creativity exists generally among people.

Which set of assumptions is true? Neither one in a clear-cut, objective way. But, in general, managers tend to evaluate people either by the Theory X or Theory Y assumptions. And whichever position a manager takes, there are direct consequences in the way he handles his people. For example, consider the implications of McGregor's first assumption:

"Tom Smith is inherently lazy and will shun work if he can" (Theory X). If Tom Smith's boss believes he has an allergy to work, Tom Smith will be managed by a considerable amount of direct and close supervision. Rigid work schedules must be set for him. His progress and level of performance must be checked continually. These methods belong to the Theory X arsenal of management techniques.

Compare this with the second assumption:

"Tom Smith is energetic, enjoys his work and prides himself in doing it well" (Theory Y). If Tom Smith's boss sees Tom as this type of person, he will spend considerably less time on direct supervision. Tom will be given the objectives of assignments and left to work out the ways of achieving them. He will also be trusted to turn out a satisfactory amount and quality of work without overly frequent checking. These methods represent the Theory Y approach.

McGregor's ideas caused a furor in management circles. Many people, including management practitioners and consultants, contested McGregor's view that Theory Y is best for managing people.

One of the more articulate opponents of Theory Y is the well-known management consultant Dr. Robert N. McMurry. In a recent issue of *Business Management,* Dr. McMurry points out a psychological basis for the superiority of Theory X:

"There appears to be little awareness that . . . the so-called victims [employees managed by Theory X] might relish their bondage. Why? For the simple reason that the rigid structure in which they find themselves is not fettering but reassuring. It is even conceivable that rank-and-file employees deliberately seek regimented jobs because these positions are more comfortable and less demanding than jobs requiring initiative, creativity and decision making."

In general, critics of Theory Y describe it as being impractical, unrealistic, out of place in today's world of business. Moreover, the anti-McGregors argue, Theory X, whatever its shortcomings, works. Actually, objective observers now believe that these opposed views are more the result of misunderstanding and failure to agree on basic terms than of the irreconcilability of the two approaches.

Psychologists and management experts are still discussing the pros and cons of McGregor's Theory X–Theory Y concepts. Yet Theory Y has not achieved the impact expected by some. True, many managers now give a responsible employee considerable latitude in his work, but more often than not, they've never heard of McGregor. What has failed to develop is any degree of broad and general application of Theory Y that might lend eventual support to either side of the argument.

In other words, practicality and personal preference rather than theory—either X or Y—rules. Managers and executives develop their personal leadership styles that often are a mixture of both X and Y assumptions about people. We have not yet developed a concept of climate building that is sufficiently surefire as to result in general acceptance and use.

The behavioral "engineers"

In addition to the behavioral scientists, there's a body of thought and practice in the field of management that comes from a group once removed from the behavioral scientists—the behavioral "engineers." Whereas most of the scientists are academicians, the engineers are closer to the work scene, and their ideas and contributions tend to be slanted toward practical application. This chapter would not be complete without a mention of one of the concepts that have come from this source.

Work simplification. Work simplification is a technique developed by Allan H. Mogensen and widely practiced by industry in the 1930s and 1940s.

In the 1960s, Mogensen added another dimension to his original concept. While still used by many companies in its original form, more recently it has been adapted to motivate employees and improve employee relations.

As used at the department level, work simplification tends to fall into two areas:

I. *Line industrial engineering.* Here W/S is considered essentially as a simplified industrial-engineering approach to cost cutting. Traditional tools such as flow charts and principles of motion economy are used. However, the basic tool is Mogensen's approach for methods improvement, taught at the frontline level to supervisors and, by them, to employees. The first steps:

1. *Select a job to improve.*
2. *Get the facts and make a chart.*

3. *Challenge every detail.* [Here the W/S practitioner is told to ask of the operation being examined, *What* is its purpose; *why* is it necessary; *where* should it be done; *when* should it be done; *who* should do it; *how* should it be done?]
4. *Develop a better method.*
5. *Install the improvement.*

II. *W/S as a motivational technique.* For many of the companies newly attracted to W/S, the benefits lie in the areas of morale and motivation. The same basic approaches—the five-step method, flow charts, and so on—are used. But there's less weight given to direct applications and immediate returns. Applied in this manner, W/S has helped—

1. overcome resistance to change. Employees exposed to W/S training become change-minded. They not only accept the need for change but are willing to contribute to improvement.
2. acceptance of company goals. Along with W/S training goes an indoctrination on the need for efficiency in such vital areas as productivity, waste reduction, safety, and so on. For example: In a midwestern electronics firm, operating personnel have been given a six-part program of training in W/S. Throughout the program, the company's need to compete with rival organizations on prices and quality claims were demonstrated. Employees ended the course with a new understanding of the need for improvement. "Believe me," says a top executive, "employee acceptance of our viewpoint was ninety-five percent of the battle."

Assessing the impact of behavioral science on the work scene

Starting with Frederick Taylor and his "scientific management" ideas, the behavioral sciences have had an impact both direct and indirect on the art and science of management. The direct contributions include the development of approaches which led to tools to solve specific management problems in the manpower area.

Taylor, for example, provided the concepts which eventually led to time and motion studies to increase the efficiency of frontline operations.

Subsequent contributions by behavioral scientists gave us the means of testing aptitudes, attitudes and personality, with their greater and lesser implications for job effectiveness.

The human-relations school started by Elton Mayo's "Hawthorne studies" proved that improved performance might be obtained by giving attention to the morale and involvement of employees in their work.

The insights into employee motivation provided by A. H. Maslow and Frederick Herzberg gave management a better understanding of how to motivate and, equally important, how not to motivate employees.

The important indirect consequences

Even more important is the contribution the behavioral sciences have made to the *climate and context* of the modern work scene.

The modern manager operates in a "semiscientific" climate decidedly unlike the primitive command-and-obey mechanisms typical of business before 1900. Today, an executive might not understand the sudden tears of a secretary, but he usually realizes they are understandable. Even though he chafes at a low level of productivity from an engineering-design group but wouldn't dream of applying Theory Y as a stimulant, he probably knows that some organizations use such approaches and swear by them.

In short, the behavioral scientist has demonstrated fairly convincingly that he can be of help in diagnosing and prescribing for some of the maladies that trouble the human being at work. And the manager, made aware by the insights of the psychologists and sociologists, can now analyze his human-relations problems and label them as being problems in communication, motivation, and so on. The fact that he may or may not apply some of the remedies suggested by the scientists is secondary.

FOR FURTHER EXECUTIVE THOUGHT

Blake, Robert R., and Mouton, Jane S. *The Managerial Grid: Key Orientations for Achieving Production Through People* (1964). Gulf Publishing Co., Book Division, Box 2608, Houston, Texas 77001.

Haire, Mason, et al. *Managerial Thinking* (1966). John Wiley & Sons, Inc., 605 Third Ave., New York, N.Y. 10016.

Herzberg, Frederick. *Work and the Nature of Man* (1966). World Publishing Co., 2231 W. 110th St., Cleveland, Ohio 44102.

Jennings, Eugene Emerson. *Executive Success: Stresses, Problems and Adjustment* (1967). Appleton-Century-Crofts, 440 Park Ave. S., New York, N.Y. 10016.

Landsberger, Henry. *Hawthorne Revisited* (1958). Cornell University Press, 124 Roberts Pl., Ithaca, N.Y. 14850.

Likert, Rensis. *The Human Organization, Its Management and Value* (1967). McGraw-Hill Book Co., 330 W. 42nd St., New York, N.Y. 10036.

McGregor, Douglas. *The Professional Manager* (eds. Caroline McGregor and Warren Bennis) (1967); *The Human Side of Enterprise* (1960). McGraw-Hill Book Co., 330 W. 42nd St., New York, N.Y. 10036.

Maslow, Abraham H. *Motivation and Personality* (1964). Harper & Row, Publishers, 49 E. 33rd St., New York, N.Y. 10016.

Sampson, Robert C. *Managing the Managers: A Realistic Approach to Applying the Behavioral Sciences* (1965). McGraw-Hill Book Co., 330 W. 42nd St., New York, N.Y. 10036.

Scott, William G. *Organization Theory: A Behavioral Analysis for Management* (1966). Richard D. Irwin, Inc., 1818 Ridge Rd., Homewood, Ill. 60430.

PART TWO/ENVIRONMENT

The next five chapters take a searching look at the executive milieu.

Changed hours of work and leisure, longer vacations, greater job mobility, the manager's new status, all play a part in shaping today's working climate.

The very framework in which the manager operates, namely, company organization, has been undergoing a metamorphosis. The hierarchical structure, which seemed as everlasting as the Egyptian pyramids, is now changing. Business organizations have been developing flexible structures, with consequent influence on the executive's responsibilities and his relationships up and down the line.

The executive's physical surroundings, his office, have been undergoing a transformation. New styles in executive suites both assist and shape his activity. One interesting note: The executive desk, once the indispensable fixture of the executive workplace, may be on the way out.

Members of the human constellation that surrounds the executive—his subordinates, his staff, service people —these, too, are shifting in relationships, importance and function. Today's executive works with different kinds and quantities of people from those familiar to his predecessors. The manager must alter his approach to these new people in everything from the way he issues instructions to the manner in which he attempts to maintain their level of performance.

A new climate of labor-management relations will affect what he can do and does with his subordinates. Some of the changes he confronts have been legislated for him. For example, the changing role and status of women is just one of the many new elements that make the future less and less like the past.

FOUR/THE CHANGING CLIMATE OF WORK

Almost every type of job that has outlasted the passage of time has changed radically in its context.

The blacksmith's craft, for example, has survived into the automobile age, but today's smith plies his trade out of a station wagon, not under spreading chestnut trees. And instead of waiting for customers to come to him, he makes the rounds of farms and stables, shoeing horses on their home territory.

In the comparatively short span of 75 years, the working environment of the executive has altered radically, both in the general sense of his role in society and in the specific one of his conditions of work. He has changed from a hardworking, imaginative but predatory entrepreneur to a still hardworking but social-minded and respected citizen.

This chapter spells out some of the shifts in the context in which the executive works—his operating "climate" in the broadest sense—covering such key elements as his professional standing, his work span and his community status. The chapter concludes with some recommendations that can help the practicing executive improve or make the most of his personal working situation. The executive office, obviously a major aspect of his working environment, is given special attention in chapter 6.

The professional executive versus the entrepreneur

The earliest executives in business were entrepreneurs. An individual became a "boss," top administrator or order giver because he started the enterprise, put up the

capital and assumed the risks that gave it birth and substance. As the business grew and flourished, he needed
additional managers. Typically, he brought in members
of the family or friends.

The "family business" persisted into the late decades
of the 20th Century, exercised by a tight core of kin
with prerogatives of ownership and management. By
the 1950s, however, the number of privately owned corporations had declined radically.

What accounted for the drop? If today you asked an
entrepreneuring family group why these companies have
been going public in droves or have merged with larger
firms, they'd inevitably cite personal reasons: death of a
founder, illness, onset of retirement age or business operation becoming too difficult.

But management consultants, often called in to doctor
failing family enterprises, see the picture very differently.
According to Joseph B. Vandegrift, head of his own consulting firm: *"Almost invariably, these closely held companies reach a point beyond which they cannot grow.
The founder doesn't want to let go of the reins. That
fact alone cuts off growth possibilities because competing firms, usually run by professional managers, become
too tough to stand up to. Over half my business is devoted to family businesses that are in trouble because
obsolescent management can't compete in a modern business climate."*

The replacement of the entrepreneur by the professional manager, with his scientific and systematic approaches, has created one of the most profound changes
in the business climate. The appearance on the business
scene of the professional manager changed attitudes,
values and behavior. "Management" no longer means
guidance by the methods of primitive paternalistic and
authoritarian leadership. The "personality powerhouse"
stereotype has been largely replaced by the sophisticated
and highly educated executive who quotes Plato as easily
as the afternoon stock-market prices.

Professionalization of the manager is so important a
factor in the changing world of business that it will be

treated at greater length in chapter 13. At this juncture, the essential point is that professionalism brings increased structuring and a more systematic and ordered climate to the business enterprise.

Working hours

Paradoxically, while today's manager may put in pretty much the same number of hours per week as his predecessors (50 or 60 a week), his subordinates are working considerably fewer. For example:

In the 1920s and 1930s, offices in large cities whose operations were essentially clerical, like banks or insurance companies or headquarters of factory operations, were open five and a half days a week. Then came the end of World War Two, and the half-day work on Saturday started to disappear. By the 1950s, the five-day week was widespread in office and factory alike, except where the economics of production—high investment in equipment or continuous-processing operations—or the needs of producers pushed by cost-price differentials made the longer week necessary.

Many executives have duties that can be performed independently, however, and a practice developed—referred to as "briefcase-itis"—of taking work home. Studies of executive work schedules show that a 50- or 55-hour week, inclusive of work done "after hours," is quite common. Sixty or even 70 hours per week is not uncommon among executives at the highest echelons. (Generally, they are individuals whose interests, commitment and compensation are such as to justify the business cliché that "they live their work.")

The workweek for rank-and-file employees, meanwhile, shows a downward trend, which will undoubtedly continue as a result of automation, computerization and increased productivity. In 1929, the average number of hours worked per week was 44.2; in 1966, this had dropped by ten percent, to 41.4.[1] This figure includes

---

[1] "Economic Report of the President," Department of Labor, Bureau of Labor Statistics, 1967, p. 244 n.

overtime hours, hours reflecting the booming economy in 1966. The difference in the standard workweek is even greater—a 40-hour week was prevalent in 1929. Today, a 37½- or 35-hour week is common for many firms, and the number in this category is growing.

Vacations and leisure

The basic way of regarding time has changed considerably. One might say that the manager of 50 or 100 years ago didn't have any leisure. There were simply periods when he wasn't at work.

Today our views are very different. Leisure time has come to be regarded as a positive factor in itself rather than as a nonwork period. One indication is the trend toward a liberalized vacation policy for blue- and white-collar workers.

In the period 1960 to 1966, the percentage of companies that gave their employees three weeks' vacation after ten years of service rose from 38 to 66 percent for office workers and from 27 to 52 percent for plant workers. Moreover, 56 percent of the companies now give four weeks' paid vacation to office workers after 25 years of service, and 44 percent of the companies grant the same to plant workers.

As for new employees, 76 percent of a cross-sectional group of companies surveyed give office workers two weeks' vacation after only one year of service, though only 20 percent provide the same allowance to plant workers. (The practice of treating office workers more liberally than blue-collar workers has not changed, although many unions are now trying to narrow the gap.)

A desire by companies to protect the health and well-being of their key men also favors leisure. It is now widely accepted that leisure is essential to executive health and vitality. It is hoped that in the fast-paced business world, the executive will become more efficient if he's had a chance for physical and psychic refreshment off the job.

A growing number of companies also encourage the use of leisure by their executives to broaden their views and horizons. "Sabbaticals," once only for the academic world, are now appearing on the work scene.

A contemporary attitude that is most revealing of the changed view that organizations have of executive leisure is the attitude the executive himself may adopt. In the "bad old days," say, ten or twenty years ago, the executive bucking for a raise might "let slip" to his superior the fact that "I haven't taken a vacation this year, T.J. Just couldn't get away."

Such a confession was supposed to make old T.J. aware of the serious-minded and dedicated attitude of his subordinate. Nowadays, the reaction would more likely be, "This guy must be doing a poor job of organizing his work," or, "He's going to arrange to take his time off. We don't want him having a heart attack or breaking down on the job because of overwork."

The executive as traveler

At one time, salesmen were the "travelers" of the business world. Today, the top brass is just as likely to be on the wing. While there are, of course, many executives who are deskbound and whose responsibilities are such that they need never set foot outside company premises, the typical executive is due to log even more mileage in the future for two reasons:

Rapid transportation facilities. The rented automobile, the jet airplane and the helicopter make practical a trip that in previous years would have required a costly investment of time. More and more companies are buying their own airplanes, and often the pilot is the president or another executive. Company-owned aircraft are no longer simply status symbols—they are often credited with considerable increases in business. Says one company head, *"If a customer five hundred miles away calls up with a problem, our chief engineer can be in his shop within two hours. If an important prospect wants to iron out some points before signing a big order, I can see him before he calls in a competitor. Our company plane is worth its weight in gold."*

Expanded executive horizons. The manager's job responsibilities tend to be less insular. Today, operations of the multiplant company may be spread all over the map as a result of mergers and acquisitions. This often means that executives in charge of centralized functions, such as finance, purchasing, personnel services, etc., must make the rounds of the adjunct premises one or more times a year to fulfill their responsibilities.

Another factor is the trend to top-level or team selling. Where big orders are involved, it's common for a group of key men to visit the customer—perhaps a couple of engineers, a value analysis specialist and a salesman. If the customer is important, the president himself may jump into a plane and make the final sales pitch. Thirty or 40 years ago, he might have sent a letter or an aide.

The executive as a status figure

Today the executive who has achieved any degree of eminence is likely to be regarded by his community with as much respect as an elected public official.

This favorable public image is a relatively recent phenomenon. Only a few decades ago, the "businessman" was an unsavory character in society's pantheon of stereotypes. As early as Boccaccio, references to men of business implied that they were sharp, dishonest traders, whose main endeavor was to buy cheap and sell dear.

Closer to our own times, the entrepreneurship of the 19th Century was seen as one of exploitation and ruthless self-aggrandizement at the expense of the public at large. In this period, the businessman as robber baron was the common image, and often justifiably so. In later years, apologists for these exploiters pointed out that it was due to their efforts that the West was opened up, that our natural resources were converted into national wealth. While this is probably true, the implication that the public good was their objective, rather than an incidental by-product, is highly doubtful.

The executive's newfound respectability derives from several factors, of course. Chief among them must be counted the development of the American economy to the point where an American president of the 1920s,

Calvin Coolidge, with considerable insight, pronounced that "the business of America is business." And 30-odd years later came the echo of the same thought in the famous statement, "What's good for General Motors is good for the country," made by Charles Wilson, president of that company.

In a culture dominated by business, it is natural that outstanding performers of the business world gain special status in the society at large. This phenomenon is seen in the world of daily news developments:

Let a newsworthy event occur in the heavens—a comet appears or a total eclipse is due—and the astronomer becomes (if but briefly) king. In periods of drought, the water-conservation engineer is the hero of the hour.

In our present society, the businessman is considered both seer and doer. He is viewed as both the architect and the builder of our capitalist society, which has made the U.S. a world leader in technology, productivity, standard of living. His helplessness during the depression of the 1930s is still held against him by those with long and unpleasant memories. But he is certainly given credit for the prosperity of the post–World War Two years and the high standard of living generally enjoyed in the last two decades.

As the focus narrows down to individual executives and their respective communities, other factors emerge that account for his high rating as a citizen.

He is seen as a supreme "practicalist," a man who can be counted on to help a community solve its problems. Accordingly, he's much sought after to serve on everything from sewer commissions to art-museum boards. In smaller communities, he may even be elected to the part-time position of mayor, member of a board of trustees or other supervisory or administrative post.

The executive's professional ability, his talent for organization and his skills in "managing" are seen as a special expertise. The press, radio and TV have helped to foster the impression that today's business executive is a special breed, with unique skills to offer. This fact has been underlined for the public by the frequency with which businessmen have acceded to high offices: Robert McNamara as secretary of defense, George Romney as governor of Michigan, Charles Percy as senator from Illinois, and so on.

Executive mobility

Today's executive no longer lives out his life in the industry or company in which he started to work. Like the doctor, he may pick up his tools and instruments and move from New York to Los Angeles or from Bangor to Miami, and he often does. Moreover, since his executive skills are almost fully transferable, he may choose to work for a company in an entirely different industry and be sought after because his past experience in a given market situation or on particular technical problems is an asset to another employer.

As management methods become more systematized, as executive techniques become more sharply defined, managerial skill loses its individualism and its parochialism. A marketing executive who knows chain-store operations can function as well for a drug company selling to chains as for a food company. Financial management of a chemical-processing company may be handled by an executive whose previous experience has been largely confined to consumer goods. EDP operations are similar whether the input concerns textiles or textbooks.

Executive compensation

The president of the United States earns $100,000 per year; he also receives an expense allowance, a pension of $25,000 a year and, of course, many privileges. How do the earnings of the business executive rate?

According to a recent report, the business executive can count himself fortunate. Compared to his opposite number in government, a major university or a large labor union, he is the highest-paid employee in society. Here are some typical examples of top executive pay:

President, INTERNATIONAL HARVESTER
$218,426

Executive Vice-president, INTERNATIONAL HARVESTER
$121,098

Chairman and President, CURTIS-WRIGHT CORP.
$100,400 (plus
$ 75,000 additional compensation)

Vice-president, CURTIS-WRIGHT CORP.
$ 54,800 (plus
$ 14,200 additional compensation)

Chairman, GENERAL MOTORS
$200,000 (plus
$468,750 additional compensation)

Chairman, ALLIED CHEMICAL CORP.
$150,000 (plus
$ 90,000 additional compensation)

Chairman, AMERICAN TELEPHONE & TELEGRAPH CO.
$304,600

Chairman, INTERNATIONAL TELEPHONE & TELEGRAPH
   CORP.
$242,799 (plus
$225,000 additional compensation)

Chairman, RADIO CORP. OF AMERICA
$290,000

Chairman, INTERNATIONAL BUSINESS MACHINES CORP.
$100,000 (plus
$255,159 additional compensation)

> Additional compensation to executives includes in-
> centive plans, thrift plans, employee savings plans,
> retirement plans, stock-purchase plans, dividend
> units, contingent credits and, of course, bonuses.

Of course, the figures above represent salaries at the
very top. Salaries at the starting rungs of the management ladder are much lower. (Nine thousand dollars is
the figure used by executive recruiters as the starting
point for the executive category.) But by any standard of
remuneration, the management group fares well.

The competition for executives—especially those to head up large corporations—has pushed salaries up to such high levels that the problem has been not how *much* to pay but *how* to pay, so that individuals retain the benefit of their compensation rather than yield large chunks to Uncle Sam.

Accordingly, the executive's take-home pay is usually augmented by pension plans, profit-sharing arrangements, paid life insurance, deferred-compensation plans and stock-option plans. In addition, he can expect elaborate fringe benefits that may include anything from permanent use of a company limousine and chauffeur to a summer home on a lake, an airplane or membership in an expensive club.

Money as a motivator

The public tends to assume that money is the major incentive for the hardworking executive. While this is undoubtedly true for many, it is by no means so for all. Past a certain level of compensation, intangible factors such as pleasure in power, satisfaction in doing a tough job well, and so forth, play a crucial role. Clarence B. Randall, former head of Inland Steel Co. and an articulate spokesman for business and businessmen, describes the executive life-style and career incentive as follows:

"The image created by the society columns of the man of great wealth vacationing on his private yacht or leasing a villa on the Riviera for the season does not reflect either the way of life or the motivation of a working executive in a large American corporation today. Typically, such an officer is a man of simple personal tastes whose standard of living is unpretentious. He wants the best salary he can get, of course, but so does the garage mechanic who services his car. The published figure that sounds big to the public does not seem large to him after he has paid his income tax, built a home and sent his children to college. To the very end of his career, he has to watch his budget.

"It is obvious to him, if not to others, that he will never be rich, and he accepts that fact with equanimity.

*When his life is finished, he will leave behind no vast
fortune, will have endowed no hospitals and established
no foundations to benefit mankind for generations to
come. In industry today, it is rarely possible for a man to
accumulate such amounts of capital solely from his salary. He can, of course, make a ten-strike in the stock
market by buying the right security at the right time and
selling it at the propitious moment, but so can the lawyer, the doctor, the professor or the garage mechanic.
Such good luck, if it came, would be completely disasso-
ciated from his employment."* [2]

Nevertheless, in the climate in which the executive
works, a high level of compensation is important for two
reasons:

First, our society, rightly or wrongly, regards the dollar price tag as the outward and visible sign of a man's
inward and invisible worth. High salary commands respect in and outside of the business community.

Second, a high pay level gives the executive the satisfaction of knowing that his company recognizes his value.
Cold, hard cash still speaks louder than mere words of
commendation.

Together, these two factors strengthen the executive's
self-image as a person of importance, both on and off
the job. This is not to say that every executive becomes a
fortress of security by virtue of his pay. It does suggest,
however, that in a materialistic culture such as ours, the
average executive must feel himself a member of a special and desirable professional elite. His social worth
today is well established.

Executive fringe benefits and security

As Clarence Randall also points out, the executive of
today has one advantage that was not enjoyed by his
predecessor—financial security in retirement. Though
money may not be the main motivator, he knows that his
pension and/or profit-sharing plan will be adequate to

---

[2] Clarence B. Randall, *The Executive in Transition* (New York: McGraw-
Hill, 1967), pp. 24–25.

keep him financially independent and enable him to live comfortably when he retires.

One result of this security is that the executive behaves far more cautiously than his predecessors. In Randall's words:[3] "As he approaches middle age, he knows that it would be imprudent for him to jump ship and sign on with another corporation, no matter how attractive the salary, for no new employer could match the security that will accrue to him if he stays on." (Despite the fact noted earlier that he has greater mobility, he may thus choose to "stay put.")

Of course, where a man is so good that many companies seek him out, arrangements are often made to match the pension benefits of the company he's leaving.

The executive's unprivate life

Most of the changes in the executive work climate thus far discussed are logical and understandable. Since Western civilization has become increasingly business-dominated, it's natural to expect that business leaders would star in the pantheon of public leaders. With technology at the point where an executive can accomplish four or five times as much in 40 hours as his predecessor did in 60, it follows that his working time tends to diminish.

But some of the changes in the executive's work situation are not all that logical. The role of the executive's wife is a prime example. In Andrew Carnegie's time, her role was strictly limited to wife, mother and homemaker. Today, a prospective employer may interview her as well as her husband. Increasingly, she is considered a key in the development of his career—a business partner as it were, and not necessarily a silent one.

Today's executive works in a world in which the conduct of his wife is considered very much a matter of business interest. In big-company politics, a wife can often make or break a man's career, and an executive is rarely elevated to a top spot until his mate has cleared the inspection of top brass.

---

[3] *Ibid.*, p. 57.

The need to keep up appearances obviously censors and limits his freedom of movement. It may even influence his choice of a mate or tie him to an unsatisfactory marriage to keep up appearances. It may also make the executive feel he must conform in behavior and confine himself to those social contacts, institutions and organizations that will give him good marks (or at least not give him demerits) up in the president's office.

Not surprisingly, today's business executive faces the real risk of a conflict between his working and personal life. A *Wall Street Journal* headline makes the point:

GROWING JOB DEMANDS SHATTER MARRIAGES OF
MORE EXECUTIVES

According to the writer, *"The corporation is taking the place of the 'other woman' in the so-called eternal triangle—and the staggering impact on executive marriages suggests that big business is the most demanding mistress of all."*

Must their lives be an open book?

Business executives, like government officials, are finding it increasingly impossible to keep their private lives private in another sense.

A recent Special House Subcommittee on the Invasion of Privacy has been checking into possible misuses of the computer for what was criticized by one witness as "push-button snooping." The possibility that computerized dossiers on individuals can be made available to top managers for the asking is, to say the least, disquieting, and it's a possibility that will certainly one day have to be dealt with.

Even now, when executives are hired, they often must sign a release in which they grant to their prospective employer the right to conduct a personal investigation. As one top executive explains, "The possible adverse impact on the company's image of undesirable activities by individuals makes it impossible for us to remain uninterested or even to act as though we were."

Executives who pass through the hands of executive-recruiting firms have to endure searching scrutiny of many kinds. Probably the most extreme, if not typical, is the so-called stress interview—a series of unexpected, anxiety-producing questions designed to reveal how well the candidate can cope with the tensions of high-echelon life. *Life* magazine quotes one of the leading practitioners, Kurt Einstein, of Einstein Associates, as follows:

"We don't care what a man's views are. We just want to know how his mind works. We want to know whether in an anxiety-producing situation he can instantaneously make a meaningful, reasoned judgment and defend it. Flattery, sarcasm, disbelief, even accusations are used as psychological levers. We may lead him down a verbal lane of logic and then booby-trap him into contradicting himself. You sense a weakness—excessive sensitivity about something or an unwillingness to discuss a subject—and then you pursue it."

The article goes on to show how seemingly harmless small talk may be loaded with traps.

" 'Now, Bob . . . ah, do you mind if I call you Bob?' 'No, go right ahead.' The interviewer's face becomes harsh. He leans forward, looking into the candidate's eyes, and says, 'Why? What do you mean? Why can I call you Bob?' 'Well, I don't know. I guess it sort of makes things go along a little faster.' 'Oh? We've got all afternoon. How many seconds do you think it might save every minute? Isn't it really that you are trying to make me like you?' 'Well, I suppose so.' 'Do you think you are being successful?' " [4]

The interrogation techniques of the stress interview are not unlike those used on Nazi war criminals, where the aim was to so fluster the subject that he wouldn't be able to continue lying about his identity and war record.

(According to *Life*, Einstein feels that the stress interview is particularly successful, too, in exposing the "counterfeit" executive. This is the man who has maneuvered himself up to the higher echelons without any real productive ability.)

Many executive recruiters are appalled by such an ap-

[4] Chris Welles, "Test by Stress," *Life*, August 18, 1967, p. 72.

proach and wouldn't touch it with the proverbial ten-
foot pole. But, according to *Life*, the Einstein approach
has a growing number of adherents (apparently it
works), and many of his clients are using him to screen
men who are being considered for key positions.

We can be sure of one thing only: that the changing
climate of work, the pressures and circumstances under
which the executive operates, will continue to change.
One essential fact will determine whether the manager
becomes the darling of our society or its scapegoat. If
business, guided by political wisdom, succeeds in leading
us to an Eden of material and psychic well-being, the
manager will be hailed as chief angel. But if the ailments
of affluence and advanced technology, compounded by
political unwisdom, drag us down into the abyss, the
managers will be the money changers who will be driven
from the temple. And once again the climate in which
the manager works will change, and his status and self-
image will consequently change in accordance with the
new climate.

POINTS FOR EXECUTIVE THOUGHT AND ACTION

From your personal point of view as a practicing executive, the subject of work climate has a personal and
direct bearing on you and your work. The following
checklist can help assess an executive working situation,
which can pinpoint unsatisfactory areas and suggest
courses of action that can lead to an improved work
climate and the rewards and satisfactions that result
from it.

Working hours

In your case, do you think the number of hours
worked per week is "reasonable" in view of—
1. your responsibilities?   ☐
2. requirements of your off-the-job living?   ☐
3. the ideal from the point of view of efficiency?   ☐
*(Note: The executive who works more than 50 hours
per week may do so because of poor job organization or
failure to delegate. Studies show that working efficiency*

tends to fall off after working hours reach the 50–55-hour-per-week level.)

Vacations and leisure

1. Do you take all the time off granted within the limits of company policy? (Remember, the effective manager seldom says, "I can't afford to take my vacation because I'm needed on the job.") ☐
2. Do you try to allocate your vacation time in the most effective manner? (For some individuals, this may mean taking a month's vacation at a clip. Others may find it more satisfactory to take a two-week winter vacation and a two-week summer vacation.) ☐

Weekends, holidays can provide an important rest-and-relaxation period between the demands of the job:

1. Do you utilize weekends as a period for recharging physical and emotional batteries? ☐
2. Since executives must often neglect their families during the workweek, can vacation periods and weekends be used as occasions for family activities? ☐
3. Can you profitably combine business travel with personal or family vacations? ☐

Your personal status

While being an executive can give one community status, the process can be reversed. That is, community status can add to company and professional status. Accordingly:

1. Are there organizations in your community that can benefit from your executive skills? ☐
2. Would your participation in local politics benefit you personally and give your company better representation in local affairs? ☐
3. As a person of authority in your community, can you start new projects that would benefit the community and at the same time reflect favorably on your company? ☐

Building the executive image

You may or may not be susceptible to the crusader impulse. But whether you are or not, it's likely that the more favorably the executive is regarded on the national as well as the local level, the better off business will be and the better off the executive will be. Accordingly:

1. Do you join business or management organizations to help advance their status and good work? ☐

2. Do you lend your support to lower-echelon management groups—foremen's groups, for example —to help them grow in effectiveness and stature? ☐

3. Do you offer yourself as a speaker in church and civic groups to help keep the public at large informed of some of the advanced ideas and concerns of business executives? (One executive has become very much in demand as an authority on sensitivity training, another on the subject of job hunting and opportunities for young people in business. Think of the areas of business in which you have a particular interest and see if you can use your expertness in the field as a means for building understanding and goodwill both for yourself, personally, and for the executive profession in general.) ☐

FIVE/COMPANY ORGANIZATION
AS A DEVELOPING CONTEXT

According to the *New Yorker* magazine, a construction worker helping erect Frank Lloyd Wright's Guggenheim Museum was overheard to say, *"The way I figure it, this is the screwiest project I ever got tied up in. The whole joint goes round and round and round, and where it come out, nobody knows."*

Many an employee has felt the same way about the structure of his company's organization. Often he can't put his finger on the reason why. Unconsciously oppressed by the sheer size of a big company, for example, he may quit. The explanations given may range from "I've decided the commuting takes too long" to "Even though the people I work with are friendly enough, I feel lost." The real reason remains hidden in the psyche.

Size, of course, is not the only aspect of company organization that affects the manager. Illogical structure —a manager reporting at the wrong executive level— can cause anxiety and frustration. In one instance, an executive's nervous disorder was traced to the fact that he reported to a superior who, from the point of function, should actually have been his subordinate!

An article by three British psychologists[1] points out "that an understanding of the individual's 'life space' at work is dependent on an understanding of the social systems of which he is a part." In the world of business, the company represents a substantial unit of the executive's social system and its structure "organizes" all employees

---

[1] "Extending the Occupational Environment; the Measurement of Organizations," *Occupational Psychology*, Kerr Kinson, Roy Payne and Derek Pugh of the University of Aston, Birmingham; January 1967.

of the company into a subsystem. The precise interrelationships within the subsystem can be diagramed by company-organization charts.

While architects and sociologists have successfully conducted studies to define the effect on individuals of various types of architectural design, similar studies for company organization are still few and far between. However, we know that traditional views of organization theory are changing and that new organizational forms are developing to meet new business and technological needs. In the process, we are learning much more about how particular organizational patterns affect executives and their performance. In this chapter, we will look at some of the more important aspects of organization structure, past, present and future, and their impact on executives.

Organization structure—the executive's stage

The company is the executive's theater of operations. It provides the stage on which he acts out his role, exhibits his skills and personality, realizes his failures and successes. But it's the company's *organization structure* in particular that sets the limits of the stage, both symbolically and practically. Some of the factors are:

Company size. The magnitude of a company's operations, the size of its personnel roster, the number of plants it owns, all influence the manager's self-image and his feelings about company affiliation. A manager working for General Motors, with its worldwide name, has a different sense of himself than a manager working for "The Ajax Tool Co.," a 25-man machine shop.

Function. The activities a company engages in determine its character, too, as well as the number and types of departments which it has. Indeed, this factor may be more critical than size in determining the simplicity or complexity of the structure. A company with fewer employees making a variety of different products that require considerable departmental diversification and a large number of internal service departments will be more complex in its organization than a large-roster firm concerned with only a few products or services.

The foundations of structure—old style

Until recent years, corporate structure was governed by a rigid set of principles and considered to be largely unchangeable. The traditional organization consisted of line managers, who headed operating departments such as production, and staff managers, who provided services such as engineering, research, etc. Who reported to whom was set forth on the organization chart—a masterpiece of order with its neatly positioned boxes and lines.

The traditional organization structure was hierarchic. Everyone had a boss who, according to an inherent authority system, had almost absolute power over subordinates. The boss's assessment of a subordinate's performance could make him or break him. It could get him a raise or get him fired. It could give him a bright future in the company or put him in a dead-end situation.

The traditional structure also generated a kind of social conformity. Businessmen spoke of a GE type of executive, an IBM type or a Ford type. Even much smaller corporations hired or fired, promoted or stalled employees because they were or were not "company types."

What created the image of the "company man"? It was the personalities and behavior of the man or men at the top. The very structure of the corporation, like an elaborate dam, facilitated the filtering through all echelons of the "messages" from on high. Employees knew, almost without expressed directive, what was and wasn't appropriate behavior: the type of car they should drive, the part of town they should live in, the pace at which work should be done. The hierarchical structure also had psychic consequences for the manager:

Dependency. If a man's entire professional career and livelihood depend on a strong authority whose whims he cannot fathom, he's obviously not going to stick his neck out. The powers that be in the upper echelons must be pleased, coddled and mollified. This meant major concentration not on *doing* good but on *looking* good.

Constriction. For many managers, the traditional company structure imposed limitations on thought as well as behavior. There was no incentive to develop new ideas if the men "upstairs" refused to listen or preferred to sit tight.

The nine-to-five syndrome. There was little reason to tackle a job with zest or imagination. Originality, even though paid lip service by many companies, was likely to be shot down on sight and the real thinker labeled as nonconformist. If higher marks went to the executive who kept his nose clean, why bother to exercise imagination? Result: many good managers working at half their capacity on routine tasks and bored, bored, bored.

Flies in the ointment

That there were many flies in tradition's ointment tended to be disregarded or rationalized.

The fact that the line and staff organizations often were competitive and hostile was either accepted with a shrug or secretly encouraged as an expression of the aggressiveness and vitality of the American manager.

The fact that formal organization charts often failed to square with the reality of responsibilities and actual lines of command was usually regarded with a "yes, but—" attitude. It's an interesting paradox that the businessman, usually a stickler for precision and hard reality, was able to live with this ambiguity. The fact is, many corporate managements felt quite satisfied; they had the illusion that they were getting the best of two possible worlds. They were reassured by the fact that the nonformal organization by which the company actually ran was, in a sense, a triumph of practicality over theory. And having a formal organization chart gave the comfortable feeling that, basically, order and system reigned.

The fact that actual operating practice often contradicted organization theory was not regarded as inconsistent. There was always some explanation. For example, the concept of span of control was often expressed in specific terms, e.g., an executive should not have more than six subordinates reporting to him. In practice, the magic number was often exceeded without any notable loss in efficiency. The departure from theory was often explained by a modification:

"An executive should not have more than six subordinates reporting to him *unless the subordinates are doing similar work*." This explained why a sales manager might have as many as 15 or 20 field salesmen under him.

Emotional consequences of company structure

The ambiguities and rigidities of traditional company organization give rise to a variety of effects for the executive, both personal and professional:

The "up" stance. The "corporate ladder" is not merely a figure of speech but a kind of career road map in the minds of many executives. Great importance is attached to the relative position of one's rung, or echelon. Promotion—and its rewards—means moving up on the chart. Demotion—and its humiliation—means a descent to a lower rung. Emotionally, this entire cast of thought stresses a win-lose psychology that magnifies professional competition and its attendant stresses and strains.

Organizational schizophrenia. Differences between actuality and theory—that is, the reality of who reports to whom and who has authority over whom—can create friction and frustration. Says one executive, "I'm quitting my job to save my sanity. I'm supposed to have a creative, forward-planning responsibility, but I keep being put down by my immediate superior, who is afraid my ideas may look so good as to make him look bad. So I pull in my horns and just drift, but then my boss's boss presses me to be more imaginative and unorthodox in my approaches. I could make an explanation that would get me off the hook, but it would get my boss on, and I'm not one for knifing people in the back. . . ."

When the company is stultifying. "I'm frightened," says an executive responsible for a public-relations function. "The company's self-image is so far from reality, it's laughable, but I can't seem to get the old-timers to realize that the company that they see died ten years ago. They think that as long as the chart of organization is the same, the world is the same. Measured by the chart, the company is operating in a complete state of anarchy. No one is doing the job the chart dictates, and I'm afraid some day someone is going to say, 'The emperor isn't wearing any clothes,' and the whole place will fall apart."

The old order changeth

Following World War Two, the mysteries and contradictions of company structure started to surface. The impetus came, in part, from new techniques and technologies initiated during the war period to speed production of war goods. Under pressure to get out the shipments, the book was often thrown out the window. During the peacetime conversion period, many traditional theories and practices were called into question and found wanting. The average chief executive became much more sophisticated about the theory and practice of company organization and organizational planning. He started to recognize that structure is a *result* of operating need, not the product of abstract planning. He took a fresh look at the old either-or stand on centralization and decentralization and concluded that centralization is, of itself, no better than decentralization, and vice versa. Wisdom often dictated centralization of certain operations, decentralization of others.

Similarly, he began to approach span-of-control problems on the basis of desired results instead of following a pat rule or theory. It was realized that many factors affect span of control. The manager's personal efficiency was clearly one. An executive with a special talent for administration might be able to supervise twice as many subordinates as a less capable man.

The computer and company structure

An even more potent factor than increased sophistication of managers was to affect thinking about corporate organization. Companies involved in radical technological changes often found themselves making equally major changes in their organization structure. The most important example is the effect of computerization. As the charts on the next page show, when a computer goes into operation, it is often followed by severe disruption in the middle-management ranks. As functions are merged and responsibilities consolidated, the organization chart flattens drastically; instead of five distinct levels or hierarchies, for example, there may be only three. Many intermediate levels and functions become unnecessary. As they are eliminated, the flow, both of clerical and production work, tends to run in a continuous line from the starting point (when the order comes in the front door) to the finishing point (when the completed product and invoice leave the shipping platform).

Organization of Hypothetical Manufacturing Company

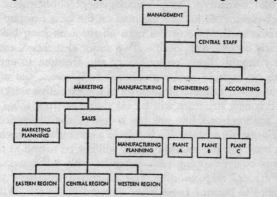

Possible Organization of Computerized Manufacturing Company

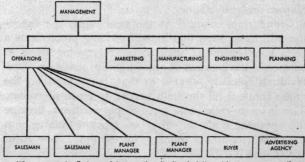

When a computer first goes into operation, it often is followed by a severe, sometimes violent, upheaval in middle-management ranks. Responsibilities are consolidated and functions are merged as this diagram from a classic work shows. (Source: *The Use of Computers in Business Organizations* by Arthur D. Little's Frederic G. Withington, published by Addison-Wesley.)

Reprinted by special permission from *Dun's Review*, November 1966, p. 42.

Consequences of the simplified organization

A major result of this new development has been the erosion of the classical hierarchical company structure, a consequence of great import for the present and future of operating executives.

If the lower chart is examined, it becomes clear that no layers upon layers loom over lower-echelon managers. Moreover, with fewer links to the chain, there is not only greater efficiency but also greater exposure. Management by result becomes not only logical but a virtual necessity. The old management obfuscations of buck-passing, of knifing the man on the next rung up or kicking in the face of the man on the next rung below clearly become less possible. Two major elements of company organization—responsibility and freedom to act—take on entirely new dimensions. As a result, the *attitudinal and behavioral* qualities of the executive working in this new structure will be far different from those of his predecessor. Here are just a few of the differences:

Target perception. He will have a clearer idea of what his basic job responsibility is. It will not be fuzzed at the edges by overlapping responsibilities with colleagues.

Personal responsibility. The executive will have the chance to become more inner-directed in his job. Without the presence of the arbitrary superior, he will work toward job objectives with a greater sense that they are his own professional ones.

Group responsibility. At the same time, the executive will more often find himself tackling problems as a team member rather than alone. A growing trend in business is the creation of special groups made up of individuals specially selected so that, taken together, the group contains all the skills needed to reach objectives. This is the so-called task force or project team. Because this approach is also bringing new types of training onto the scene (sensitivity training, for example), a word of explanation is in order.

The project team

A project team or group is usually set up to meet a

specific company objective or problem. In some cases it is brought into being solely to reach that target and is dissolved when the objective has been attained. In others,

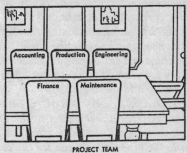

PROJECT TEAM

it may be a semipermanent group, convened at intervals to make decisions of a recurring nature, such as where to invest the company's retained earnings. In any case, the project team varies in makeup, depending on the nature of its objectives. A typical team formed to decide what kind of new numerical control equipment should be acquired might be constructed as shown above.

The manager in charge of such a project team will approach his job very differently from a department head or functional manager, because he's performing on an entirely different "stage," within a very different organization structure. By virtue of the team form of organization, he will have, for example—

—varied problems (he may be called on to solve a wide range of problems, from developing, producing and marketing a product to improving the safety or overall performance of a company or finding a location for a new company facility);

—more direct responsibility;

—greater performance measurability;

—greater group identification;

—greater role identification and involvement

Effect of computerization on the manager

The computer gives management the *opportunity* to modify the organization structure, observes Victor Z.

Brink, professor at the Graduate School of Business, Columbia University.[2] Dr. Brink sees these advantages in particular:

"1. Management has more opportunity to centralize or decentralize corporate functions.

"2. It has the option of combining functions or parts of functions in new and imaginative ways. For example, the cost accountant and the engineer have worked in each other's territory for years. The computer offers new techniques for these men to use together.

"3. Properly designed, a computerized data-processing system gives a manager direct access to the central data bank. He can interrogate the system on the status of a particular order or program. He can see the consequences of alternative decisions and choose the best alternative. No one stands between the manager and his information source.

"4. At the bottom of the organization chart, things will happen faster, also. New men will be able to participate in the decision-making process sooner. For example, in earlier days, the college graduate going into public accounting would work at basic, detailed auditing for from four to five years. Now the emphasis is on systems and analysis, and new men move up faster."

Other advantages of working in the organization of the future

Within the short space of one chapter, it is impossible to spell out all the changes that are taking place in the manager's job as a result of company restructuring. But there's no question that the newer forms of organization taking shape will give management much greater opportunity to run the company as it should be run. Executives at all levels will have greater freedom and responsibility —and be more directly accountable for results. The executive job will be far more demanding and far more rewarding. The handicaps of traditional functional organizations will disappear. For example, the executives

---

[2] "How the Computer Is Changing Management Organization," *Business Management*, July 1967, pp. 26–30.

in the new organization structure will not be as frequently hampered by the following obstacles, taken from a list provided by C. J. Middleton: [3]

No one in a functional organization besides the company or division manager is entirely responsible for project costs and profits. Functional department executives are concerned only with doing specialized work within budget.

Functional departments often are jealous of their prerogatives and fight to promote and preserve their specialties rather than work toward a unified project objective.

The total perspective of a project is lost among functional departments. They can be guilty of "tunnel vision"—that is, a concern for only their own portions of the task without regard for the impact of their actions on the company and on the project.

More and faster decision making is required on a new project, and it is slowed by passing interdepartmental problems to the top through all levels of functional departments. This process often delays important project decisions or prevents them from being made.

Function departments performing repetitive tasks often lack the flexibility and responsiveness to cope with new and rapidly changing project requirements.

Management's thinking along fresh paths has been stimulated and reinforced by the findings of industrial sociologists, organization experts, and others whose research into the actual workings of companies increasingly challenges and even conflicts with classical management theory. Professor Joan Woodward, lecturer in industrial sociology at Britain's Imperial College of Science and Technology, for example, makes the following distinction between the new views and earlier theories:

"The . . . so-called classical theories of management subscribed to Mary Parker Follett's view that 'no matter what the purposes to which human endeavour is directed, the principles of that direction are nevertheless the same.'

---

[3] C. J. Middleton, "How to Set Up a Project Organization," *Harvard Business Review*, March/April 1967.

My view is that the form of organization must depend upon the nature of the task to which the organization is directed." [4]

In short, Professor Woodward says there is no one "correct" organizational system, but *a number of correct methods, depending on the technology of the enterprise.* In her studies of British manufacturing firms, she found, for example, there was no direct correlation between a particular form of organization structure and business success for all firms; yet within groups of companies *engaged in similar work,* the correlation was very close.

The future of company structure

There's always a lag between what research discovers and what business applies. It can be predicted that in the years ahead, more and more companies will learn what the best organization structure is for their particular objectives and technology and make the necessary changes.

Clearly, too, the tremendous unification and centralization possible through automation and computerization will tend to *simplify* organizations of the future.

One sign that companies are becoming aware of the relationship between technological changes and organizational structure is the appearance of a new staff department during the past 25 years—the "department of organization planning." William F. Glueck, writing in *Personnel,* notes that at least 100 of America's top 500 corporations now have such departments and that in the opinion of knowledgeable observers, organization planning and development will be one of the five most important management activities in the future. According to Dr. Glueck, these departments invariably have these four objectives:

Help the firm achieve efficient use of resources, especially its human resources.

Help the company adapt to internal and external changes in order to achieve its current, not past goals.

---

[4] "Rewriting Management Classics," *International Management,* August 1967, pp. 26–27.

Prevent excessive or poorly planned organization change.

Help in management conflict within the firm so that a minimal amount of organizational resources is expended on internal-contest behavior.

Clearly relegated to a dying past are company structures consisting of departments with large personnel rosters. The existence of the latter made it necessary for the manager to have an authoritative leadership capability—he had to deal with large numbers of people. The executive of the future will deal with fewer people and more things. But he will deal with the people more naturally and the things more logically. The old distinction as to whether an executive is a "thing person" or a "people person" will take on a different implication. And, it is to be hoped, *his* superiors will have *greater* understanding of the following statement, made by the president of a small but highly successful company:

"Organization climate: the least tangible area of management, yet the most important—a gold mine for those able to control it. Proper climate, including morale, incentive and leadership, does not add a mere ten or fifteen percent to profit. It can easily double or quadruple it! Yet, oddly enough, it is the least expensive of all ingredients."

POINTS FOR EXECUTIVE THOUGHT AND ACTION

The practicing executive is not always in a position to take action in matters relating to company organization. Of course, it's his relative position in the hierarchy that determines what he may or may not do. If you're head of the company, or a sizable part thereof, you may be able to initiate the studies that will assess and propose improvements.

However, executives at any echelon can consider company or organizational structure with respect to their own immediate situation and to that of their subordinates. Questions of the kind posed below can lead to worthwhile appraisals.

Your situation

1. Is your actual organizational position—as defined by the person to whom you report and your subordinates—the same as the company-organization chart indicates? ☐

   Don't assume that the "real" structure, as exemplified by job responsibilities, job content and to whom you report, as well as who reports to you, *need* correspond to any formal chart. However, interesting information may be gotten by such a comparison, if a formal chart exists.

2. Are you satisfied with your present "report to" obligation? ☐

   This question is not intended to raise questions to which there are no practical answers. An executive may dislike his superior and may have to continue to report to him. The intention here is to start a process that might yield, for instance, the realization that the executive to whom you are reporting is no longer responsible for, or even concerned with, your function, since his job might have changed.

3. Are you satisfied with your present authority or prerogatives? ☐

   What is intended by this question is stimulation to thinking about job-organizational changes of *content* that have not been recognized by logical realignments in structure. For example, such a consideration might lead a sales executive to ask his superior, V.P. for sales, to have field reports from salesmen sent first to him rather than to a service department, since he is expected to keep up week-to-week contacts with field salesmen and respond as quickly as possible to their requests or complaints.

4. Could a discussion with your superior on the subject of organization structure possibly ease some of the strains or dissatisfactions that grow from illogical and obsolete forms? ☐

Your staff or department

1. Spend a few minutes sketching out a thumbnail organization chart of your division. Nothing fancy, just a rough pencil outline will do. Then consider:

   a. Everybody reporting to logical immediate superiors? ☐

   b. Do all subordinates know to whom they are supposed to report? ☐

   c. Do they actually report to the individual they're supposed to? (Many executives themselves are culprits here; they invite bypassing by permitting contacts from subordinates who should be reporting to the executive's assistants.) ☐

2. How about taking a stab at designing—or redesigning—a chart that represents actual departmental organization? (This could lead to constructive realignment of responsibilities, changes in job content, and so on.) ☐

3. If your area of responsibility meshes closely with that of another executive, could joint analysis of structure help—

   a. eliminate double bossing for some employees? ☐
   b. get rid of areas of overlapping authority? ☐
   c. fill some gaps where no one is responsible for a given activity that falls between the organizational stools? ☐

   Other? _____

4. Can you ease some of the organizational pressures of subordinates by—

   a. redefining their responsibilities? ☐
   b. discussing changes that they might want to suggest? ☐

   Other? _____

SIX/THE OFFICE AS ACTION-
ASSISTING ENVIRONMENT

The baseball player has his diamond, the scientist his laboratory, the executive has his office. The office is the executive's arena, his working habitat, the environment designed to assist him in his job. An analysis of the executive office not only reveals a great deal about the executive job, but also holds out the hope that an improvement of office design, making it more suitable to the individual executive, will thereby assist him in his work.

In the past, the typical entrepreneur's office adjoined the scene of production. When Bartley Hubbard, journalist, entered the private office of tycoon Silas Lapham, he knew he was in a paint factory. As William Dean Howells describes Lapham's place of work, it was small, close by the warehouse, redolent of the company's product and not too tidy. Cramped and unattractive though it was, however, it suited the needs of the time.

Today, the executive suite is separate from the factory —even thousands of miles away—and luxurious by Lapham's standards. Yet it is *also* functional and, therefore, an influence on the executive's job. Four stages of development in office design have made such change possible.

Executive suites—four stages in evolution

The *factory office* was characteristic of an era when production was the heart of an enterprise. The owner was more often than not to be found on the floor of the shop, shirt sleeves rolled up, discussing problems with his workers or repairing a balky machine. (In some small manufacturing businesses today, this is still a familiar scene.) Control over activities was exercised by observing operations firsthand. The boss who wanted to know how an order was progressing checked the work piled up on the floor between machines. His office was often small, because valuable space couldn't be taken from production, and much of his day was spent where the action

was—in the warehouse, factory, loading platform, etc.

The next three types of offices were developed in chronological sequence, but anachronisms, of course, exist. All *four* types of offices are extant today—and probably will be tomorrow. But time favors the more advanced office styles.

The white-collar office. As business grew, simple functions were split up into specialized tasks. Two developments ensued which marked a turning point in American business:

New managers were created to supervise the specialized activities of clerical workers, and paper work—records, reports, memos—became an increasingly important function in itself. No longer could the entrepreneuer and a few trusted employees carry the details of the business in their heads! This marked the start of what is known today as the paper-work explosion.

And, as paper work became a "production" in itself, office machines were developed to get it done faster. Result: The many activities involved in clerical work could no longer be crowded into a small space adjacent to the factory. The office was moved away from the dirt and noise of production. The managers' offices moved with it. With the physical separation of management from direct supervision of production, the status-oriented executive office made its appearance.

A visitor to the office of a manufacturing company in the early 1900s would have walked through rows of wooden desks lined up like cabbages in a field. At the head of a row sat the office supervisor, where he could see what was going on. His superior, however, would be marked as the member of a higher caste—for he would have a private office. And there'd be no mistaking where this manager belonged in the organization. If he were but one step removed from frontline management, privacy might be achieved by a ground-glass partition and a door. At the other extreme, if he were at the vice-presidential level, he'd have a large corner room with a special area outside for his secretary.

The "living room" office. Today, many executive offices are like living rooms with desks in them. Of course, the decor varies with the size of the company and the importance of the man. An executive vice-president of an international corporation may have a crystal chandelier, Chippendale chairs, oriental rugs and custom-made leather couches, while his counterpart in a smaller firm makes do with plain wall-to-wall carpeting, a sofa and coffee table from the local department store and prints instead of original oil paintings on the wall. But in both cases, the offices are planned *not* to look like working areas; the very absence of paper work, files, etc., signals to all who enter that here works an important man.

A Park Avenue advertising agency, for example, rewards those who make it to the vice-presidency with their choice of office furnishings. (The executive floor looks like a display of model rooms in a department store.) Next to a French Provincial drawing room lavishly furnished in white and gold might be found a room in the most austere Japanese style, almost bereft of furniture. Beyond that might be an Early American living room replete with maple bookcases, hooked rugs and pewter.

The executive workroom. With the advent of the computer, a new wave in office design is breaking. The resulting changes in the nature of the management job are leading to new concepts about working areas. The office that is emerging might be termed the *executive workroom*.

Characteristics that distinguish the office of the new executive from that of his more conservative colleagues are these:

It is achievement-oriented, not status-oriented. Size of the office has been dictated by the occupant's actual needs, not his position on the organization chart. Thus, the regional sales manager of a major furniture company has a ten-by-ten-foot nook in his firm's headquarters' showroom. His job takes him out of the office 75 percent of the working day, and he needs only a few tools, with some privacy, to accomplish his indoor work. In another

case, the designer-partner of a nationally known office-layout organization, Saphier, Lerner, Schindler, Inc., has a two-part office. The working area, small in size, contains a draftsman's desk and cabinets for blueprints, specifications and supplies. The conference area, larger, is equipped with a round table, chairs and fixtures for visual displays. When the executive, who travels frequently, is "in residence," the entire suite is his private office. When he's away, an overhead garage-type door is rolled down, sealing off the workroom so that the staff has an additional conference room.

It is tailored to the working style of the executive. "An office should provide a working climate to support and stimulate the capacities of its occupant to their maximum performance," asserts one specialist. The new executive recognizes this and tells the designer what he wants. It may be a table instead of a desk; it may be a telephone headset, so that he can take phone calls and still be free to move around; or it may be a "bulletin board" wall, so covered that information can be displayed pinup-style. In any case, executives are increasingly discovering that traditional office design is needlessly confining and that their own performance is furthered by furniture and fixtures tailored to their way of working.

It is communications-oriented. If the modern manager is miles away from the people on the shop floor, he must stay in close touch with those who direct the activities for which he is responsible. The style of his office will reflect the nature and amount of communication. Many face-to-face meetings? He'd have furniture in "conversation groups." Frequent larger meetings? A desk convertible into a conference table. Important phone conversations with company plant managers and customers? An electronic service center, with phones, recording equipment, coded dialing system, etc., built into a special unit.

The completely equipped office of the future (see sketches at the end of this chapter for one outstanding designer's ideas) is still "far out" for most firms. But slowly and surely, many of the ideas are being adopted piecemeal. Here are some of the specific features that characterize executive offices of today, the changes that have occurred and the changes that are likely to be accelerated as automation and other technological trends continue to make their mark.

Environmental engineering—or the new science of comfort

"The job we face in development of the modern office," says Jay Doblin, industrial engineer, "is to provide an environment which does not intrude. It is carefully controlled as far as temperature, ventilation and light go." In short, the ideal office frees the "human organism" to concentrate on the business at hand.

It is in the environmental aspects that the executive office has undergone the most fundamental changes in the past 50 years. To name the major ones:

Air conditioning. Thirty years ago very few executives had this luxury. Today it would be difficult to hire a secretary if one's offices weren't air-conditioned. The control of office climate is as completely accepted today as is heating in the winter. In fact, it's almost forgotten that, originally, most companies had to justify the installation of air-conditioning units on the basis of increased productivity. And this was not a myth: Tests made by many, including the country's biggest landlord, the government's General Services Administration, prove that employees working in air-conditioned space turn out more than those in similar space that is not air-conditioned. The GSA study found that output increased nine percent. Errors and absenteeism also tended to be less.

Lighting. Dramatic changes have also occurred in office lighting over the past 30 years. Most outstanding is the rise in intensity of illumination. Unbelievable as it sounds, in 1900 the recommended lighting level for offices was about two footcandles, and in 1920 it was about ten footcandles. By 1945 it was 50, and today the *minimum* level is 100. (Recommended lighting levels are established by the Illuminating Engineering Society.) One reason for the trend toward higher levels of light, say some authorities, is the nature of our living habits that is making nearsightedness increasingly common. Lenses worn by nearsighted people require more light because they diffuse vision.

One of the ironies of contemporary office lighting, however, is the fact that the newer glass-walled office buildings by no means obviate the need for artificial illumination. These structures are so huge that a high proportion of the work space on a floor simply doesn't benefit from the window area—that being reserved for private offices.

Light-generated heat. The newest development in environmental engineering is the use of the lighting system to generate heat as well. Room air is drawn through the lighting fixture so that it picks up the heat generated by the light source. This heat is then transferred to a water circuit, where it is circulated to heat the building. On very cold days or when the lights are off, more heat is needed than can be taken from the lighting fixtures. This is supplied by inserting electric heaters in the duct or waterline feeding each zone. Baseboard heaters along outside walls may also be used, regulated by zone thermostats that allow each zone to be independently controlled.

Noise control. The loudest sound in the average top-executive office today is likely to be the hum of the air conditioner. Street noises are eliminated by the closed windows. Internal sounds are deadened by acoustical tile on the ceilings, thick carpeting underfoot and draperies at the windows. One of the more interesting developments in soundproofing is soundproof glass. The writer visited a design firm in which most of the offices were placed in the inner core of the floor space and constructed entirely of soundproof glass. When the door of such an office was closed, none of the surrounding office noises were audible. (It was like watching television with the sound turned off.)

Interestingly, success in deadening sound within rooms has brought another problem to many firms. The contrast between inside quiet and outside office noises is often an unpleasant distraction. Inside walls and partitions are not always effective in preventing the entrance of sounds from other outer offices.

Color. Once executive offices tended to be painted pale green or beige, on the theory that it was least distracting to work. Then the color explosion started and all rules were shattered. Quiet, low-key pastels or white are still favored by most companies for executive offices, but bright blues, yellows or even reds are often used to break up the monotony of reception rooms and large clerical areas. The all-plaster wall and ceiling is a thing of the past. In modern buildings, wooden parquet flooring may be used to add interest to ceiling areas, walls may be covered in grass cloth, inlaid with tile, brick—there's no limit except the ingenuity of the decorator. The guiding principle is, what impression does the company want to convey? Old, solid, traditional? Walnut paneling may be the answer. Growing, in the modern spirit? Then expect to find huge photo murals of the firm's products, op-art paintings, clear, bright colors.

Hallmarks of status

It's been said in favor of business status symbols, as signs of the pecking order, they save a lot of time. In a large company, the new employee or the outsider will shortly learn who has the power and in what degree by such small but clear signals as size and location of an office, the type of desk and the "extra" furnishings such as tables, couches and chairs. As a business prospers, it inevitably upgrades office decor in general, both to create a pleasant working environment for employees and to impress prospective customers. At the same time, furnishings and space are seldom determined by sheer aesthetic or practical considerations. Who gets what depends on whether he is one of the important figures or a merely necessary one. Here, briefly, are the indicia of success as signaled by office allocation and design:

Size of office. This factor has always been a major sign of prestige. People are always prone to relate the size of offices with importance. It's no accident that over the years an informal rule of thumb for space requirements has developed that is used even today. Clerical worker, 50 square feet; chief clerk, 75; supervisor, 100; first-level executive, 200; intermediate executive, 300; top executive, 400.

The more progressive office designers take issue with this tradition. They believe it makes little sense to assign a tremendous office to an executive and cram secretaries and others into the middle of the floor, away from the light, barricaded by filing cabinets. Some specialists hold that the trend is toward more open space, fewer private offices, but, if so, it is gaining ground slowly. A big private office is still the common desire.

An anecdote is told of two government agencies that had to meet together on an important decision. One group consisted of scientists, the other of general–administrative officers. Out of deference to the most important man in the group, the head scientist, the first meeting was held in his office. By choice, however, he had taken a small office with a dilapidated desk, assigning the more spacious offices to his working subordinates. The members of the other group were so embarrassed to be discussing a momentous decision in surroundings that weren't in keeping, they suggested the next session be held in the office of an official of *their* agency.

Office of the president

The president of the United States traditionally works in a large oval office. Lyndon Johnson had it decorated with white walls, thick red carpeting, white sofas flanking the fireplace and a giant-size desk. His successors will redecorate to their own needs and tastes.

Of course, for the president of the United States, the oval office symbolizes the center of power of the free world. It has its ceremonial as well as its status value.

But as Stuart H. Loory[1] reports, for much of his workday, Lyndon Johnson (as did other presidents) uses a small den whose entire width at one end is occupied by a leather-topped writing table. The small area is a favorite workroom. Secretaries come and go with papers for the president, and it's here that incoming and outgoing calls are centered.

Loory reports that in the small office, LBJ feels free to pull the heavy green velvet drapes shut, settle into the green swivel desk chair, put his feet up on an ottoman and discuss informally with associates or visitors the problems of the world.

Regardless of individual preference, and while the more advanced planners tend to downgrade office size, the fact is that space is still indicative of power, and most new offices today continue to be laid out this way.

Location. The choice prestige locations are still high up (in metropolitan skyscrapers) and on the corners of the building. The man who has an office with a view has reached some sort of high status plateau.

Again, office planners have some ideas for changing this. One design firm advocates putting all private offices on the interior of the floor, with aisles around the windows so that all can enjoy the view.

Furnishings. Perhaps the most subtle status symbol

---

[1] "Special Report to the *New York Post,*" May 9, 1967.

is the "no desk" office.

Presumably, when an executive arrives at the point where he spends all of his time conferring with people, he's reached the pinnacle of success. Actually, for many men the desk has become obsolete, and with good reason. They've discovered that it's far more comfortable to talk to employees, colleagues and customers with no barrier between. If writing or reading is an important part of their work, they can do it more comfortably at a table. Papers can be stored in cabinets or credenzas. As one executive noted:

"I used to work behind a huge slab of a walnut desk, trapped in the kneehole. It was an effort just to get up and move around. Now that I've had this new office, I feel absolutely liberated.

"One thing I notice, too—people are much more relaxed and at ease with me without the barrier of that huge desk."

Of course, for a few executives, a large desk is an important accessory, rather like Linus's blanket in the *Peanuts* comic strip. As Michael S. Saphier, office designer and a deskless man himself, notes:

"Someone asked what kind of a man you have to be to work without a desk. The answer is, you need a strong sense of security and attractive legs."

Another important and increasingly prevalent sign of executive status is the art collection. Any top man worth his salt has one or more original works of art in his sanctum, be it a Miro lithograph, a Chagall oil—or his daughter's first finger painting. The merging of business and culture, once worlds apart, is a characteristic of the day. An executive who wouldn't be dragged to an art gallery or a ballet 30 years ago now willingly subscribes funds and even gives of his time to raise money, to advise on the budget or to help on planning. It's "good for business to support community effort, and culture is big in the community."

The sauna as symbol

Most top executives are content with the conventional

office luxuries: teak paneling, sofas, built-in bars, etc. Some men demand more. The object of their predilections might be categorized as the "health and recreation" extras. Starting with the modest black leather reclining chair (price tag $600) or vibrating couch, these specialties run on to such elaborate fittings as the executive sauna. While a Finnish steam bath might have been hard to justify to Silas Lapham's board of directors, in today's fast-paced business world many consider it a small price to pay to keep their high-priced president well and happy. When he's making decisions that can cost the corporation millions of dollars, a few thousands are not a quibbling point.

New directions in office design

Every office designer and many executives agree that the changing nature of the manager's job is fostering new concepts of office design. Exactly how they will be reflected in furniture and layout, and when they will take hold, is a matter of speculation. But here are the most likely changes on the horizon:

More open space, greater flexibility. The trend is away from enclosed private offices, except for top executives, and toward layouts that can be rearranged as the nature of the work changes. This doesn't mean lack of privacy. Workers who need quiet and isolation for concentration are given prefabricated office units that can be set up and dismantled easily. Such cubicles are like a roomette with metal and/or glass walls. The occupant has a writing surface, shelf space, cabinet and drawer space, room for chairs and files. While soundproof, these office-ettes provide a feeling of openness and enable easy communication with others on the floor.

In Europe, the idea of locating offices in the open has been carried to an interesting extreme. The idea is radical and it hasn't yet found widespread adoption either there or in the United States. Nevertheless, the concept merits a brief description because it is similar to the ideas expressed by some of America's top designers. The concept is known as "office landscape" (*Büroland-*

schaft, in Germany, where it was started). In such a layout, an office floor, or part of it, would consist of one large open room with no conventional walls, corridors or private offices. A bird's-eye view of the space would show clumps or clusters of work stations—desks, chairs, tables, etc., shielded from other work stations by an artful arrangement of filing cabinets, green plants and low screens. The desks of employees working together would be grouped, but arranged at odd angles, so that the total effect would be of a rather pleasant random design.

What's significant is the rationale behind *Bürolandschaft.* First of all, it's designed specifically for *nonroutine* work. Its proponents see more and more of the office job as becoming nonroutine. As the computer takes over lower-level decision making, office people will do far less paper work themselves; hence, there'll be no need to arrange desks in rows simply to facilitate the flow of paper.

In the new era of office automation, work will involve verbal communication to a much greater extent than before. Moreover, people will be working as teams on projects that cut across departmental lines, since much work will be of a problem-solving nature. Here's how one expert describes the kind of work for which the open space is designed:

"Because of the computer, staff work and teams shift constantly. Management assigns a project and (1) a team of specialists is assembled to work on the project, (2) the work is completed, (3) the specialists are assigned to new teams with new goals."

The open but clustered layouts are ideal for this kind of operation because the layouts can be shifted as the work shifts.

"Proxemics"—a new field of study

Design of the new offices is already being influenced by findings of the social scientists on the relation of space to communications. One new branch of study called "proxemics" examines how communication between two or more people changes with shifts in the distance between them and with changes in position. Where people's work depends on their communicating freely with each other, such studies may offer ideas for laying out offices that can result in a higher level of performance than conventional layouts.

The action office—tailored to the man

Embodying the newest ideas in office design and furnishing is the so-called action-office concept of Herman Miller, Inc., furniture designer and manufacturer.

In 1960, a consultant to the aircraft and lumber industries, Robert Propst, presented a memo to Herman Miller, Inc., stating his idea that a new approach to office furnishing could significantly increase productivity. First, Propst observed that traditional office furniture provides only one main work posture, forcing individuals to sit for most of the day. Because there's a direct relation between "whole body motion and mental fluency and alertness," added Propst, the net result is a drop-off in work capacities toward the end of the day.

Second, office conversations in the sit-down office tend to waste time because they're of the relaxed and diversionary kind. This memo proved to be the trigger for a four-year project into all possible areas bearing on the relation between a man and his immediate work environment. Propst himself discovered such pieces of information as—

- —the fact that people like to support their heads and hands,
- —they're irritated when they can't surround themselves with things they like,
- —body position can control exposure to visitors (working with your back toward an approaching visitor diminishes your chance of being interrupted),
- —talk over a disordered desk is distracting,
- —too much privacy lowers productivity,
- —exceptional performers develop extra work stations and surround themselves with extra visual and physical stimuli,
- —piled papers become obsolete and frustrating.

These and other findings about the needs of office

users were translated by Propst and George Nelson, Inc., industrial designer, into a line of furniture that supposedly stimulates work performance directly.

Here is a brief description of the main components of the action office:

Desks come in a variety of heights, sizes and types, to allow the office worker plenty of free movement. For example, there's a stand-up desk as well as a sit-down desk. One common characteristic is lack of drawer space for "dead storage." All desks have broad surfaces to permit the worker to spread out his papers on top. One of Propst's main tenets is that the visible display of data triggers action. What the worker sees, he acts on. Yet papers can be instantly shut off from sight by pulling down top covers, tambours or fold-down panels—the same principle as Silas Lapham's rolltop.

(This is in contrast to the prevalent idea that the cleared desk denotes the effective executive. No one has even done research, to the author's knowledge, to determine how many "clean-desk men" stash unread papers and reports away in drawers and cabinets simply to maintain this myth.)

A *communications center* is provided that looks like a modern acoustically insulated telephone table with back and sides. It is insulated for privacy and it has a phone panel and an open-tray drawer for electronic equipment. In the typical executive office a few years hence, this center will hold not just a phone but all the executive's electronic tools—tape recorder, microfilm reader, closed-circuit TV and speaker phone.

Discussion is facilitated by executive desks and tables with a flip-up panel in the middle that can be used to display information to colleagues in informal conferences. *Tables* are an important part of the furniture line. A large conference table has a file bin inserted in the middle of the working surface, with a flip-up cover. A team of people could work around such a table and have instant access to the working papers used on their project, which they filed there until it was completed.

All of the action-office furniture has a light, clean,

simple look—quite the antithesis of the heavy teak and walnut desks, upholstered couches and massive tables favored by many captains of industry. Such an office is clearly a working room, not a living room. A crystal chandelier would be as ludicrous with this furniture as an old-fashioned coal stove in a modern kitchen. The thinking behind the new direction in office design is aptly summed up by two excerpts from a descriptive brochure prepared by Herman Miller. While it applies to a particular furniture line, it could apply in general.

What an office shouldn't be:

"Today's office is a wasteland. It saps vitality, blocks talent, frustrates accomplishment. It is the daily scene of unfulfilled intentions and filed efforts. It is the equivalent of doing business on clay tablets in an age of the computer and instant communication."

What the office should be:

"A place to live better with your work—to do your work better. The office is a place for dealing in symbols. It rarely traffics directly with the actual objects its company may make, the actual money it negotiates with or the markets it serves. The acts and arts of working in an office involve the absorption, use and control of information. They include reading, thinking, writing and communicating—by face-to-face conversation, telephone and the use of other communicating or information-storing devices."

Finally, as one tomorrow-minded designer sees it, "The office should be a mind-oriented living space." The particular implementation of this concept will change and develop as new needs and facilities develop.

POINTS FOR EXECUTIVE THOUGHT AND ACTION

An executive's office should reflect both his taste and working needs. The pages you have read provide a useful background for practical considerations: Is your present office suitable for present needs? Are there changes you can and should make to improve your office situation for tomorrow? The following provides some of the practical information needed for reviewing and improving the utilization of office space and equipment:

The executive desk

The executive desk is a many-splendored object and has added to the executive's impressiveness over the decades. It affords—

—a conversation piece—when its design is unusual,

—a place to hide administrative vices,

—distance from outsiders and subordinates,

—something to chase a secretary around—at least back in the days when the spirit of Pan prevailed.

However, more and more executives are questioning the desk as a necessary office appurtenance. In place of the desk, there have appeared various substitutes that you may want to consider:

The small work table. The surface may be round, square, oblong or have an organic shape. The executive sits at it—sometimes in a lounge chair—and does the paper work still left for him to tend, frequently swiveling away from it when he is done so that while he is on the phone or talking with visitors, he will not have the sense that he is behind—or at—a desk.

The stand-up "desk." It is usually a small piece of furniture, located against a wall, recognizable as a desk only dimly. A number of managers like the "action feel" of standing up, leaning over a surface and scanning a report or signing a document.

The pullout shelf. This relative of the old hideaway bed has the advantage of occupying minimum space. For example, one executive has converted a shelf in his bookcase so that it swings out, carrying on its surface a phone, typewriter, a few reference books—leaving just enough room for an 8½-by-11 sheet of paper.

"I've never been happier," says one executive. "Back in the old days when I had a desk, I found that people wanted to leave papers—and problems—on it. Without a desk, they have no place to put them—and you know what? Some of my subordinates have actually become more independent."

Obviously, the decision to join—or not join—the anti-desk rebellion will depend on a number of factors: the type of work done, company policies and individual personality and work style. A number of managers have compromised with the trend by throwing out heavy, old-fashioned wooden desks, with their multiple drawers, and substituting the conference-style desk with minimum storage space.

Chairs

"Executives who sit pretty last longer," observes one office-furniture designer.

Another says, "The average executive is sedentary, overweight, out of shape and frequently complains of pain in the lower back. As far as his seating facilities are concerned, he'd usually be better off switching chairs with his secretary."

Dr. John Welsh, medical director of Union Carbide Corp., points out that man was designed "to function as an animal on all fours." Sitting is an unnatural position and so the spine, back muscles and ligaments were not constructed for that sort of thing. Over long periods, they may grow weak and need to be helped along in the form of low-back support. Good sitting is imperative. Here are some seating considerations that affect managerial comfort and fatigue:

Seat: Should be cushioned moderately and covered with woven or other rough-grained fabric to prevent sticking and/or shining the seat of the trousers. The manager who's stuck with a solid wooden or plastic seat can resort to a pad made of woven material. The height and depth of the seat should permit you to place both feet firmly on the floor when you are seated solidly against the back.

Back: Some chairs with extra-high backs afford head and shoulder support. While, in general, full support by the chair back is desirable for spinal relief, hot weather may bring discomfort to the perspiring manager. Where there is a problem, a "breathing" fabric, rather than leather or leatherlike material, can help.

Mobility: "Frankly," says one executive, "chairs on

wheels or casters are terrible. They damage my carpet. I've used a sheet of plastic on the floor behind my desk, but then I feel like I'm on roller skates." For most men, however, mobility in a chair is important and is achieved not only by wheels or casters but by swivel-and-tilt movement, too. If you're bothered by a back problem, try to select a chair with adjustable mechanisms.

Lounge chair? "Sheer relief!" is the verdict of an executive who has used a lounge chair for five years. This executive doesn't have a back problem and his activities grade him as the opposite of sedentary. Yet he feels the relaxation he gets by using the large, commodious type of chair is beneficial and helps maintain his personal drive and energy.

President John F. Kennedy dramatized the problem of low-back pain for many sufferers. His answer to the executive-chair question caused a surge in popularity for rocking chairs throughout the world. The fact is, the rocking chair may be an excellent solution for some executives.

For the executive who likes the sensation of motion but would rather not "do it himself," there's a motor-driven vibrating chair available that is said to stimulate circulation and to act as a piece of exercising equipment.

Office layout

For the executive who is concerned not only with his own working area but also with office arrangements for subordinates, a number of general principles can help assess present conditions or plan for improvement. The checklist below is based on generally accepted optimums and, of course, may be modified for particular situations or needs:

Are related departments or functions arranged in close proximity to one another to have the work flow conform to a straight-line principle? ☐

Are main aisles approximately five to eight feet wide, secondary aisles three to five feet wide? ☐

Is four feet of chair and work space allowed between rows of desks facing in one direction? ☐

Where chairs face each other back to back, is there an approximate allowance of four feet between chairs? ☐

Are vertical files arranged so that where their fronts face on aisles, a free space of 28 to 36 inches is provided for the opening of the file drawers? ☐

Ceiling-high partitions are desirable for privacy, but in large general-office areas, should you consider lower partitions to allow closer supervision as well as better light, heat and ventilation control? ☐

If space and usage requirements in a general office are changed, should you use metal movable partitions or panel dividers instead of solid walls for maximum flexibility? ☐

To insure effective nonglare lighting, do you avoid having anyone facing directly into the light (preferred lighting: main light comes over the individual's left shoulder)? ☐

For individuals doing detail work or work requiring considerable eye use, do you take particular pains with the direction, quality and quantity of light reaching their desktops? ☐

If desks are set in a row, do you have them facing in the same direction? (The generally desirable situation, except where two people work together.) ☐

Do you seek to improve both ease of supervision and communications by grouping personnel as near as possible to their immediate supervisor? ☐

In the interest of efficiency, do you place people who do the most moving about in the course of their work nearest the facilities they use or close to main aisles and exits if they travel to other office areas or other departments? ☐

Can you keep sufficient floor space flexible so that you have standby work area for office expansion under peak work-load conditions? ☐

If you are planning major changes and are in doubt about aspects of layout, are there experts—sometimes provided free of charge by utility companies —you can consult to optimize your planning? ☐

This page and the next provide a glimpse into the future of office construction and design. The sketches come from the work studios of Saphier, Lerner, Schindler, Inc., a leading space-planning and design firm. SLS has coined the word *environetics* to signify "the science of design of the things people use and the places in which they use them." As SLS sees it, *environetics* considers not only the requirements of the client's physical work space, but also extends to the systematic investigations of efficiency, comfort, visual effect and provision for expansion—and includes the projection of the client's corporate personality. In view of these principles, their offices of the future take on added interest.

Executive office emphasizing control function. "Control seat-console" moves laterally and also vertically—chair moves through doorway into elevator shaft which engages chair. Assistants (specialists) stand by.

Office of the Future No. 1. Saphier, Lerner, Schindler, Inc. Environetics. A Division of Litton Industries.

Secretarial-clerical work station. Equipment monitoring includes control and information-retrieval functions.

Office of the Future No. 2. Saphier, Lerner, Schindler, Inc. Environetics. A Division of Litton Industries.

Executive office combined with conference area featuring management information and display equipment. Emphasizes planning function.

Office of the Future No. 3. Saphier, Lerner, Schindler, Inc. Environetics. A Division of Litton Industries.

SEVEN/THE HUMAN CONSTELLATION

Executive Ben Bane entered the lobby of his office building, his mind still preoccupied by his perusal of the morning newspaper. What a bubbling mess, he thought —campus revolution, hippies, racial disturbances. It would be a relief to crawl into the snug capsule of his business life.

As he waited for the elevator, a young girl walked into the lobby and her appearance literally startled him. Her long, unkempt hair hung halfway down her back. She wore a Mexican-style blouse and a black leatherlike skirt that cleared her knees by a good three inches and hung suspended from her shoulders by gilt chain.

Bane turned for confirmation of his feelings to a fellow businessman, a nodding acquaintance from another floor. He smiled a half-smile and rolled his eyes, making a slight motion toward the outlandish female. The other smiled in agreement.

What screwiness was afoot, thought Bane. He got off at his floor, relieved at the comforting familiarity of the corridor and his office. He was involved in the morning mail when Miss Gretchen from Personnel came to the door. "Good morning, Mr. Bane. I'd like you to meet our new librarian, Natalie Moon." Bane got to his feet and tried to look pleasant as he shook hands with the girl in the black miniskirt.

The changing constellation

We know the machines of tomorrow will be different. What of the people who will operate and manage them? As executive Ben Bane discovered, the new wave of employees will be showing up on the work scene looking unlike what we've been used to and armed with new values and attitudes.

The executive stands in a web made up of relationships to the many individuals on whom he depends to achieve his goals. This network has been shifting: The number of individuals to whom he relates is decreasing, while the nature of their functions is changing. To cite just one example, while large-roster departments disappear, the manager is increasingly called on to deal with specialists of higher education and considerably more training than heretofore—another way in which the "new wave" is different.

The executive's ability to perceive the "human" aspects of his job under these changing conditions, to understand and work effectively with new types of fellow employees can be crucial. This chapter traces some of the major changes that have taken place—and concludes with a section devoted to sharpening the executive's ability to work with both new-style and traditional work groups and to heighten their efficiency and satisfaction.

New social values in business

The personnel-relations literature of the 1950s and early 1960s was studded with directives for managers seeking to master the "human factors" on the job. Starting in the mid-Sixties, however, basic cultural changes began to make the old ideas obsolete. Even the most dependable concepts and principles lost much of their point with the emergence of the new social attitudes and values.

For example, the ethics of hiring and firing employees have always been fairly simple. Employees are hired as needed and fired when their services are no longer required. But recent developments indicate that in the future, companies may be expected to employ people for social rather than purely business considerations.

The employer will be expected not only to create jobs but to provide the necessary training for the people hired to fill them. The executive's job of motivating and evaluating performance will be far different from before.

The attitudes of these "redundants," their level of education, their expectations and the economic implications of their presence on the work scene will not be the same as for the employee of today. Other developments also are affecting the manager's human-relations problems.

Humans and the advance of technology

Paradoxically, with acceleration of technological change, the spotlight has been drawn sharply to *man*. Much thought and printer's ink is being devoted to man's state in a mechanistic society. The recurring theme: Is man in danger of being dehumanized, alienated or rendered impotent in today's culture? Many spokesmen are convinced that the answer is yes. But some observers of the management scene see a different picture.

For example, Dr. Rensis Likert, director of the Institute for Social Research and professor of psychology and sociology at the University of Michigan, sees man as an increasingly important element in the world of business:

"All the activities of any enterprise are initiated and determined by the persons who make up that institution. . . . Every aspect of a firm's activities is determined by the competence, motivation and general effectiveness of its human organization. Of all the tasks of management, managing the human component is the central and most important task, because all else depends on how well it is done." [1]

Other experts say that man as a working animal is changing along with our technology. Certainly, work has taken on a different value for many people. In the years following the Industrial Revolution, people worked under the most physically distressing circumstances. Yet working in mills and mines at starvation wages was necessary for survival—and workers fought one another for the privilege of holding down a job.

Today, under very different conditions, two attitudes are crystallizing on the work scene:

"On to leisure." Some employees, generally those

---

[1] Rensis Likert, *The Human Organization, Its Management and Value* (New York: McGraw-Hill, 1967).

doing routine jobs, look upon work as a necessary interruption of their social life. They tolerate their jobs with an apathetic or indifferent attitude. Their main aim is to get by with the least amount of involvement.

"*Total commitment.*" For many others, particularly persons in highly skilled or professionally oriented occupations, the job is interesting, important and the main focus of their lives.

These attitudes, expressed against a background of a rapidly advancing technology and an affluent society, are major elements affecting the manager as a supervisor.

Onslaught of the machine

In the early days of automation—starting immediately after World War Two—Cassandras gloomily predicted that thousands of jobs would be eliminated by technological developments and the need for skilled labor reduced.

As recently as 1964, John Snyder, president of U.S. Industries, estimated that automation is a major factor in displacing 10,000 workers per week.[2]

But suddenly, only a few years later, the fear that jobs would disappear wholesale with advancing *cybernation* (the word coined by sociologist Donald N. Michael for *automation* plus *computerization*) was contradicted by government data.

A study by the United States Department of Labor[3] indicates that although demand for less-skilled workers will decline somewhat as a percentage of total employment, it will *not* decrease in overall numbers by 1975.

According to the study, if 1975 is a peacetime year and if unemployment stays at about three percent, civilian employment will probably reach 88.7 million by 1975, or 26 percent more than in 1964.

At the same time, the data makes clear that not all industries will share equally in the total employment growth and that there will be sharp shifts in the demand

---

[2] Quoted by R. H. Davis, "The Computer Revolution and the Spirit of Man," *SDC Magazine,* October 1964.
[3] *The Outlook for Technological Change in Employment Benefits,* Vol. 1, 1966; Superintendent of Documents, U.S. Government Printing Office, Washington, D.C. 20402.

for given skills within industries.

For example, fewer quality-control engineers will be needed, because of the development of automatic testing equipment. Yet other types will be required to design such equipment, sell it, install it and maintain it. Total demand for engineers is expected to rise by over five percent between 1964 and 1975.

Similarly, while automatic laboratory equipment will replace some technicians, others will be required to operate and maintain the new equipment. The sharpest employment increase projected for any single group— 54 percent—is for professional and technical workers.

The chart below, taken from the study, spells out the figures in specific industry categories:

TABLE 1

Employment of Wage and Salary Workers, by Industry, 1964, and Projected Requirements, 1975*

| | (in thousands) | | Percent |
	Actual 1964 Employment	Projected 1975 Requirements	Change 1964–75
Total	62,917	79,620	27%
Total government	9,595	14,750	54
Federal government	2,348	2,525	8
State and local government	7,248	12,225	69
Services and miscellaneous	8,569	12,275	43
Contract construction	3,056	4,190	37
Trade, wholesale and retail	12,132	16,150	33
Finance, insurance and real estate	2,964	3,725	26
Manufacturing	17,259	19,740	14
Durable goods	9,813	11,500	17
Nondurable goods	7,446	8,240	11
Transportation and public utilities .	3,947	4,425	12
Mining	633	620	**
Agriculture	4,761	3,745	–21%

* Proprietors, self-employed persons, and domestic servants are excluded. This accounts for the difference between BLS total projection of employment in 1975 of 88.7 million and the 79.62 figure here.
** Less than 3 percent.

Middle management—here to stay

Another chart in the study shows changes in total requirements in major occupational groups. A significant fact: Contrary to earlier fears, automation will not replace managers. In fact, the figures indicate that the managerial category will increase some 23 percent by 1975:

TABLE 2

Major Occupational Groupings, Actual 1964 Employment and Projected 1975 Requirements

	(thousands of workers)		Percent* Change 1964-75
	Actual 1964 Employment	Projected 1975. Requirements	
Total, all occupational groups	70,357	88,700	26%
White-collar workers	31,125	42,800	38
Professional and technical	8,550	13,200	54
Managers, officials, proprietors	7,452	9,200	23
Clerical workers	10,667	14,600	37
Sales workers	4,456	5,800	30
Blue-collar workers	25,534	29,900	17
Craftsmen and foremen	8,986	11,400	27
Operatives	12,924	14,800	15
Nonfarm laborers	3,624	3,700	*
Service workers	9,256	12,500	35
Farm workers	4,444	3,500	-21%

* Less than 3 percent.

Here again, however, demand for managers will be lower in some categories, higher in others. Office automation will limit the growth in demand for some middle-management positions, but the demand for technical managers will greatly increase. In this category are those needed to plan research projects, supervise data-processing systems and train workers in new skills needed for the new, complex machinery and techniques. And, of course, more managers will be needed to analyze the facts, figures and reports turned out by EDP systems.

The "new people" on the work scene

Social changes and economic growth have brought an influx of new types of employees into the manager's field of operations. The close-to-capacity operations that marked the two decades following the war, including the "Soaring Sixties," required recruiting individuals from every possible source. Personnel executives, employment agencies and executive recruiters operated in a seller's market. The scarcity of qualified people pushed wages up, created strong competition for available manpower and forced companies into using new recruiting and training techniques. To fill out personnel rosters, in some cases, companies paid bonuses to employees who could recommend friends or acquaintances.

Of the many "new people" who have emerged on the work scene, three groups promise to have the most significant impact on the human constellation surrounding the executive.

Nonwhites. In 1954, the Supreme Court triggered a social upheaval with its decision that segregated schools are unconstitutional. In 1964 Congress passed the Civil Rights Act, making it a federal offense to discriminate in hiring or promoting on the grounds of race, religion or sex. While the total situation is too complex to describe in detail here, these developments have had unprecedented effects on the business world.

The precipitous burst of opportunity for Negroes, Puerto Ricans and other groups found great numbers of individuals untrained and unqualified for the jobs available. The companies at the forefront of the move to help nonwhites advance themselves cooperated with Washington by joining the President's Fair Employment Practices Committee (predating the Civil Rights Act), but they found it difficult to recruit nonwhites. In fact, the demand so outstripped the supply that employment agencies specializing in nonwhite personnel found themselves pushed to extreme lengths in their attempts to satisfy even a minimum part of the demand.

A passing and temporary aspect of this problem forced industry into a kind of "tokenism." One or a few nonwhites were hired and placed in physically conspicuous points of exposure to make clear the company's good intentions. For example, in banks qualified Negroes were given desks "up front" where they had high visibility to the public at large.

This is not to say that the position of the American Negro has not been progressing. States one news weekly:

"The Negro's job situation is steadily improving. Negroes are moving into jobs that, not long ago, were all but closed to them.

"American Negroes, who make up about 11 percent of the nation's population, now hold nearly 14 percent of all the jobs in the federal government—and that figure is rising.

"In private industry, Negroes are filling an increasing number of white-collar jobs, going into skilled and semi-skilled occupations and into the professions and technical fields.

"Many firms are actively recruiting Negroes, on college campuses and elsewhere. Some employers say they would hire more Negroes for professional jobs if they could find qualified ones." [4]

The Social Dissenters. The number of 19–24-year-olds seeking jobs will be ample to meet requirements in 1975. The headache of tomorrow's managers with the younger groups will not be lack of supply. It's their *attitudes* that will pose problems for management and supervision.

The Sixties saw the entrance on the social scene of Youth as Rebel. Much-publicized and much-headlined, the Campus Revolt served notice to society at large that peaceful academia was a boiling stew of dissatisfaction and rebellion.

The beatniks appearing on the scene in the early 1960s made the colorful behavior of their predecessors, the bohemians of the 1920s and 1930s, as pallid as chamomile tea. For one thing, the bohemians represented a small minority of artistically inclined individuals. Beatniks appeared on *every* college campus and in *every* town to declare by dress, manner and viewpoint that established society had, in their view, "had it." They made clear their disapproval of its materialism, banality and lack of opportunity for—for *what,* it was not too clear. It was never clear as to what the beatniks were for, although what they were against was easily indicated by a wave of the hand at any aspect of society as it was.

Max Lerner's observations of the younger generation distinguished additional splinters among rebellious youth:

"In the last four or five years (that's about how long a 'generation' is in these days of accelerated everything), we have seen three subcultures emerging among the young in America: the 'New Left,' the drug culture and the hippies. All three have played a role in forming the far-out America of today. All three will pass and will

[4] *U.S. News and World Report,* August 21, 1967.

reemerge in other forms and combinations in the 1970s. But of the three, it is the hippies who reach deepest, because they have, in their own bizarre way, brought into the open a values revolution that has been in the making for decades.

"Mainly, it is a revolution against the achieving society—against the tyranny of the job, the pursuit of the fast buck, the clinging to property, the ties of marriage and family, the hunger for power, the demands of status, the jungle of machines, the big, impersonal corporate units, the institutionalized church, the legitimatizing of killing in war, the tensions of group interaction and struggle, the constant drive to produce and to succeed." [5]

The "drug culture" to which Lerner refers saw one of its most far-out proponents in Dr. Timothy Leary, once a Harvard teacher and subsequently an evangelist for the League for Spiritual Discovery. From an estate in Millbrook, New York, and in personal appearances on various campuses and student conferences, he preached his message of "turn on, tune in and drop out." Dr. Leary urged young people to appreciate the use of marijuana, LSD and other consciousness-expanding drugs which could help individuals to "drop out of society" and "drop into life." [6]

Admittedly, Leary's views represent an extreme of anti-establishmentarianism. But far-out as the drug cult or culture seemed, it was an indication of the alienation and apartness felt by an important, if small, segment of the youth population. And some reflection of this negative feeling necessarily intrudes on the work scene and sets the manager thorny problems of orientation and motivation. The plain fact is that one who feels like an alien in the workaday world will have difficulty in adjusting and functioning at acceptable levels of performance.

For the executive of today and tomorrow, the social dissenters represent two problems: First, their prevailing attitude is one of nonconformity, specifically, reluctance

---

[5] *The New York Post*, July 19, 1967.

[6] From a talk given to the National Student Association Congress, reported by the *New York Times*, August 18, 1967.

to conform to the traditions and standards of the work-aday world. Second, they may show apathy, indifference and carelessness—all difficult supervisory problems for management. The emergence of the social dissenters as large and well-defined social groups in the 1960s suggests that the problem will intensify and spread.

Facing such attitudes, the manager will have to develop methods of motivation and leadership that will minimize the tendency to be uncooperative. (The problem of motivating the "new employee" will be treated at length in chapters 8 and 10.)

Women on the work scene. The number of women at work has risen dramatically. Fourteen million women were in the work force in 1940, 23.5 million in 1960, and 25 million in 1962. By 1972, government manpower experts predict the total will reach 30 million.

It's significant that many women working today are mothers. In March 1966, one out of every three mothers of children under 18 years was in the labor force. In 1940, the ratio was one in ten. This has given rise to the term *fur-coat worker,* for often the working woman has a clear objective in mind: a mink stole for herself, an extra car for the family, a college education for her children.

The flood of women workers, however, has gone mainly into clerical, production and other lower-level jobs. With some exceptions, such as cosmetic firms, retailing, fashion and advertising, the traditional reluctance of business to promote women to high-level administrative positions has not significantly lessened.

According to *Nation's Business,*[7] in 1940, four percent of the executives in the United States were women. In 1950, the figure had risen only to five percent. The 1960 census showed practically no change.

The situation is very likely to change, however; specifically, Title VII of the Civil Rights Act now prohibits any company, employment agency or labor union from discriminating against an individual because of his race, color, religion, nationality or sex. Employers are also prohibited from segregating or classifying an individual in

---

[7] *Nation's Business,* July 1963.

connection with apprenticeship training and retraining programs or indicating preference in help-wanted ads. And both the Civil Rights Act and the Wage-Hour Law (equal pay for equal work) prohibit discrimination in salaries and wages paid to women.

An increase in the number of women in responsible positions has implications for the manager of tomorrow. For one thing, men's traditional "romantic" attitude toward women will fade rapidly. With women becoming more common and accepted members and colleagues on the work force, man's traditional susceptibility to the opposite sex is likely to be watered down. He can't afford to be as fascinated as his predecessor was by evidence of femininity or female pulchritude. For better or worse, the old tradition of secretary chasing and after-hours romance will diminish or else be accepted with great matter-of-factness in the new sophistication that lies ahead.

Training the new people

By and large, the minority groups, the social dissenters and, to some extent, women will be needed by business. But, often, the business world, with its routines, its standards and traditions, will be completely new to them. The implication of this fact for the businessman is that many new people he acquires as employees will not only have to be given job training but also will have to be educated into the ways and means of business behavior. As a matter of fact, the basic objectives and methods of business may have to be taught to them as general background in order to make their particular jobs make sense in an overall context.

One aspect of training for technical and complex operations will become more and more crucial. While a number of jobs will be extremely simplified and place little burden on the individual's physical and mental abilities, other tasks will require either judgment or high levels of skill.

Management jobs, characterized by an unstructured situation and decision-making requirements, will call for individuals of high intelligence. Will there be a sufficient number of these highly qualified people to fill tomorrow's needs? A comment by Professor George A. Miller of Harvard supplies one insight:

"We may already be nearing some kind of limit for many of the less gifted among us, and those still able to handle the present level of complexity are in ever-increasing demand." [8]

Three kinds of training

In the future, as now, businesses will have to do three kinds of training, namely—

1. occupational or skills training;
2. training geared to marginal workers, that is, training of disadvantaged people in minority groups to fill necessary routine and plan jobs;
3. management-development training to fit younger executives for new, more complex responsibilities.

Industrial training is shifting increasingly from behavioral science to behavioral technology, according to Dr. George S. Odiorne, director of the University of Michigan's Bureau of Industrial Relations, Ann Arbor.[9] "The dominant trend in industrial training today is the need to turn from general statements of values, needs, attitudes and feelings to more applied techniques which are specific and measurable by hard criteria."

He describes three important characteristics of the new behavioral technology:

Training should change behavior and not be concerned with personality therapy nor preachments about attitudes and values.

Behavior should not be treated as "activity which can be seen or measured." In good training, the behavior change sought should be identified by specifying the behavior desired when the training effort is concluded.

The evaluation of training success should be the measurement of the behavior change actually occurring.

---

[8] *Daedalus,* Journal of the American Academy of Arts and Sciences, Summer 1967.
[9] *Industrial Relations News,* September 10, 1966.

For the manager who's used to the old style of training, which was centered on informing rather than bringing about alterations in attitude and specific behavior, the new approach will require a radical adjustment.

The new loyalties . . .

The old concept of loyalty to the company faded sharply during the depression years. The inability of a company to play "Big Daddy" to employees, or even to survive, inevitably undermined the emotional structure that underlay the concept of company loyalty. The employee was loyal to a company that could sustain him and provide a protective paternal force in his life.

When the company itself had trouble surviving, the employee no longer trusted in its ability to protect him. By the end of the Great Depression, the concept of company loyalty was all but dead. When labor became scarce, starting with the post–World War Two booms, it was finally killed. Why be loyal to a company, paternalistic though it may be, if another firm will hire you tomorrow at a higher salary and greater fringe benefits?

In place of company loyalty, a new and better concept of *mutual respect* may be taking hold. Some companies are consciously fostering it with concrete programs and policies. If they prove successful, others are likely to follow. Here are the objectives of these companies' efforts:

1. The employee feels a sense of loyalty to his *group*. Work problems are presented by the manager as cooperative ventures, so that each member of the group feels that his presence and best efforts are essential to the success of the group.

2. The individual feels a sense of *professional* loyalty, a commitment to the occupational group of which he is a member.

. . . and the old conflicts

Traditionally, in a corporation consisting of line and staff, feuding, ill-feeling, suspicion and mistrust flourished between the individuals representing the line functions and those representing the staff functions. One of the effects of computerization and automation is to shatter the old line-staff relationship and structure. Many managers who used to stand squarely in line management now exercise functions previously thought of as staff responsibility: production engineering and maintenance, for example. Similarly, staff professionals—scientists, engineers—in many cases have acquired line responsibility and, at a minimum, work closely with line management on production problems. One result: The old antagonisms between line and staff are disappearing.

What will become of the human-relations problem?

Of all the areas of management development, the one that was most universal and which in most programs got major emphasis was that of dealing with people. The precepts and methods prescribed for dealing with people involved everything from "treating them well so that they will respond in kind" to being very matter-of-fact and simply assigning tasks and seeing to it they were performed to a satisfactory standard.

But in view of the different types of people emerging on the work scene, an entirely new atmosphere will grow on the work scene. Here is one expected result:

The professionalized employee

A concept developed by the author, based on the work-simplification approach by Allan H. Mogenson,[10] suggests the entry of a new factor in superior-subordinate relations. It is the concept of the *professionalized employee* (as distinct from the *professional* employee). It envisions that *every* employee setting foot on the work scene tomorrow will have had a certain amount of pretraining, gained in skills courses provided by the government, by trade associations or by previous employers. This training will equip the employee to move into almost any work situation and function almost immediately at a fairly high level of performance.

Somewhat parallel is the skill of a trained private

[10] Auren Uris, "Mogy's Work Simplification Is Working New Miracles," *Factory Magazine*, September 1965.

nurse. She can walk into any home where there is sickness and immediately perform the necessary functions. She makes the patient comfortable, sets the room in order, establishes a routine, drafts various members of the family for one task or another, and so on.

Similarly, when the professionalized employee enters a work situation, he will size up his overall assignment, collect the minimum information needed to order the equipment and facilities at hand, figure out his own hourly, daily or weekly program to accomplish work objectives, and so on.

Executives who have hired efficient secretarial temporaries have seen this type of behavior. The well-trained secretary can walk into a disordered office and, like the trained nurse, get things in order and start clicking on the jobs to be done pretty much on her own.

While the professionalized employee is not "a professional," his *training* will give him several professional qualities:

He will be trained to understand and master ordinary work routines—the starts, stops, recording of work progress, and so on.

He will be trained to understand the operation of a variety of standard jobs, such as monitoring automated equipment.

He will be given a set of rules that will help him deal with emergency or unexpected matters—including the setting up of communications lines to a supervisor, indication as to when to report exceptions, emergencies, and so on.

The well-trained professionalized employee will not only have absorbed the fundamentals of task accomplishment but will show an *internalization* of the discipline and self-regulation needed to operate efficiently. For the manager tomorrow, the appearance of the professionalized employee will mean the need for less on-the-job training and direct supervision.

Accordingly, there will be less communication between superior and subordinate on the routine areas of work. This *might* lead to a major lessening of contact and interaction. However, there is another, more fruitful possibility: that is, that the manager and the employee will have more to say to one another about the creative aspects of the work—the possibilities for modifying or improving procedures, machine operation and products that may have their origin in the front lines of business operations.

POINTS FOR EXECUTIVE THOUGHT AND ACTION

As the previous discussion suggests, the traditional problems of working with and supervising subordinates will be aggravated for the executive by an influx of a "new wave" of employees whose *attitudes* will differ markedly from customary ones. In addition, the advent of increasing numbers of women and minority ethnic groups seeking jobs and promotions to jobs previously denied them will further change the human constellation of which the executive is a part.

What can be done to maintain satisfactory levels of efficiency in working with today's and tomorrow's employees? A two-pronged approach is called for:

Flexibility. The executive must be willing and able to accept the new wave of employees and seek to increase his understanding and his ability to relate to them.

Utilization of proven procedures. There is a simple answer for a major part of the problem of employee efficiency. It lies in the large body of proven personnel procedures that have been developed over the years, that can help the employee adjust to his work surroundings and find personal and psychic rewards in his job.

Both these approaches will be presented in the Action Points that follow. The point of departure deals with the key matter of your personal flexibility, the ability you have to adapt to the new elements of the human constellation on the work scene.

How flexible are you?

The quiz questions below can help you assess your adaptability to new situations developing on the work scene. Answer the questions as accurately as possible. You'll find scoring directions following the quiz.

OK ? NG

1. How would you feel working under a woman boss? ☐ ☐ ☐

2. How do you feel you'd rate on a quiz titled "How Open-minded Are You Toward Minority Races?" (If the reader is nonwhite, simply substitute the word *other* in place of *minority*.) ☐ ☐ ☐

3. Do you think you would be able to judge a dispute between a white and a black person fairly and impartially? ☐ ☐ ☐

4. Would you agree to the implicit fairness of the following statement: "If I had two candidates for a job, one white and one black, with equal qualifications, I'd settle the hiring by tossing a coin"? ☐ ☐ ☐

5. How do you feel you rate in your ability to accept the new styles of the day— whether they be long hair for boys, short skirts for girls or other marvels still to come? ☐ ☐ ☐

6. What do you think of this executive's statement: "I think each generation must find itself, no matter what particular or peculiar paths it may take in that search"? ☐ ☐ ☐

To score your answers, give yourself 10 points for each OK, 5 points for each ? (which signifies doubtful or don't know), and *subtract* 5 points for each NG. Of course, the scoring is entirely rule of thumb, but you may care to rate yourself against the following scale:

60–50. You're wide open to the future and should fare well in adapting to any social changes affecting personnel on the work scene.

45–30. You're about average and should be commended for your honesty in giving obviously unfavorable answers to tough questions. Persistence in your realistic appraisals may well help you resolve problems involving the human element.

Below 30. You need practice in the acceptance of

people as they are. Make more friends in minority or "other" groups, make it a practice to talk to people you might naturally tend to avoid both socially and at work. Any other steps you can take to break away from traditional standards for judging individuals and groups, based on appearance or other superficial characteristics, will be helpful.

Proven procedures

The second element that is involved in successful utilization of the human constellation that surrounds the executive has to do with the practical aspects of the job scene. As an executive, your attention paid to physical surroundings and other such work factors can yield substantial benefits in terms of cordial relations and high levels of performance. Consider the following checklists in their relationship to actual work situations and present subordinates:

Physical Set-up

As far as possible, does each individual have a work station that is identifiably his or hers? □

Would it be worthwhile to discuss with individuals the extent to which they are satisfied or dissatisfied with the physical facilities at their disposal? □

Where they feel there's room for improvement, should you ask for their suggestions and implement them where possible? □

Hours of Work

The requirements of individual companies, departments and executives vary widely in the matter of time requirements. Some jobs are "nine to five." In other cases, particularly where individuals are involved in creative work, actual time on the job may be a secondary consideration. In between these two extremes, modifications that may be helpful to both employee and company are possible. Consider these questions that have to do with the time aspects of work:

Do people start at times that you feel are suitable to work requirements? □

Do you modify starting times to suit the convenience of subordinates where possible? ☐

Are rest periods, coffee breaks, and so on, provided at optimum points in the work cycle? ☐

Do you, through considerate and firm supervision, make sure that individuals don't unnecessarily prolong rest periods, lunch periods, and so on? ☐

Through the same means of considerate and firm supervision, do you see to it that subordinates stop work at the end of the day in orderly fashion? ☐

Facilities

Do you minimize the irritations and inconveniences that inefficient or insufficient facilities cause by—

making it easy for the coffee drinkers to get their "divine fluid" at scheduled breaks? ☐

providing pencil sharpeners that sharpen points instead of breaking them? ☐

providing centralized supply centers so that getting paper, pencils, rubber bands or any other supply items can be done expeditiously rather than starting off a wild-goose chase? ☐

maintaining washroom facilities to an acceptable standard of cleanliness? ☐

providing clean dining or cafeteria facilities, particularly where outside restaurants are inadequate or expensive? ☐

Inducting new employees

All management texts stress the critical nature of the new employee's first few days on the job. They are correct in doing so, since not only dissatisfaction but considerable turnover is the result of lack of consideration in welcoming a new employee. While some aspects of induction clearly reflect personnel-department policy and procedure, the individual executive often can influence and/or add to personnel-department practices.

Is the work station, desk or office of the new employee made ready for his arrival? ☐

Are all supplies and equipment available and in order? ☐

If the new employee is female, would it be appropriate to celebrate her first day on the job with a vase of flowers? ☐

Will the new employee's arrival be announced in advance to those in the department to smooth his acceptance by the group? ☐

Will the employee's immediate supervisor or senior employee see to it that the newcomer is "officially" introduced to colleagues and others with whom he will be working? ☐

Does the supervisor make a special point of seeing that the first day's work experience is a pleasant one—guarding against complications, frustrations, unexpected developments as much as possible? ☐

Can the new employee's welcome be reinforced by seeing to it that he doesn't fend for himself on his lunch hour? ☐

Does the supervisor try to wrap up the first day pleasantly by a brief chat with the new employee before quitting time? ☐

Special attention

A number of relatively minor moves, nevertheless, can recognize the individuality of employees. These don't cost much but they can make a huge difference in work atmosphere. Here again, in some companies these procedures are instigated by the personnel department. But regardless of who initiates them, whether Personnel or the employee's department, consider items like these:

Nameplate or name designation for all personnel, secretaries, clerks, and so on. ☐

Birthday and anniversary cards, either from the company, the individual supervisor or both. ☐

Flowers for female employees on their birthdays. ☐

Employees of either sex being taken to lunch by the supervisor on their birthdays, anniversary on the job, etc. ☐

Opportunity for participation

Less tangible but more potent factors that create a desirable work atmosphere emphasize not only the dignity and worth of the individual but also recognize his ability to think and contribute to the overall operation of his department. Accordingly, are employees encouraged—

to make suggestions and contribute ideas to the operation of the department? ☐

to share in planning in the work and other activities that need not be solely done by the executive or supervisor? ☐

to be informed of departmental problems and to discuss them either individually or in a group? ☐

to be delegated assignments that give them a chance to broaden their work horizons and to show what they can do? ☐

Opportunity for advancement

The chance to better oneself is more actively sought by some employees than others. Also, advancement may be more available to some individuals than to others. In view of the importance that some employees place on getting ahead, consider these possible moves:

Notifying employees of promotion opportunities with the department or company. ☐

Counseling with individual employees, advising them as to the moves they can make to qualify for higher or better jobs. ☐

Helping by company-devised training programs or activities that will both help the company maintain a satisfactory pool of skilled people and help those interested in self-betterment achieve this self-improvement within the company context. ☐

Would it be advisable for your company to develop a policy of paying for outside training relating to the individual's present or future job capabilities? ☐

And how about whole or part payment for any educational purposes, whether related to the individual's job or not? ☐

Any other moves you might make to improve the capabilities and develop the potential of your people—such as your personal training and guidance. ☐

EIGHT/LEADERSHIP AND MOTIVATION

"Man may be a reasoning animal," says a company president, "but the fact that he can reason doesn't mean that he will. From what I've seen on the job, he's illogical, unpredictable and very often unmanageable." In handling the human resource, the manager faces very different problems from when he's managing money or machines. Managing people for maximum results is hampered by the complexity of the human being.

Fortunately, human beings are also educable, persuadable, inspirable—and interested in being successful. The manager's task is to direct his people so that they apply their abilities toward the achievement of company goals. This has been the manager's job in the past, and it will continue to be in the future. The means by which he channels people's efforts to such an end will continue to be *leadership* and *motivation*.

As pointed out previously, the nature of the work group has been changing. Accordingly, the old concepts of leadership and motivation must be updated to suit new circumstances. The following pages will look at some of the newer management thinking and practice in these two key areas.

The "magic" of leadership

Age cannot wither nor custom stale the appeal of the idea of "leadership" for managers. There's good reason. Leadership has long been viewed as a kind of magic cure for many management ills:

Productivity too low? Good leadership could "snap employees out of it."

Errors and failures too high? Effective leadership could make subordinates aware of the quality requirements of their jobs.

Behavior out of line? A good leader could step in and not only create discipline out of chaos but inject a sense of involvement into employee work attitudes.

Most managers agree that the effective leader can indeed accomplish these highly desirable ends. But there's a catch. When it comes to describing "good leadership" for the practical purpose of selecting and training managers, it's difficult to get agreement. Opinions range all over the lot. What is good leadership? For that matter, what is leadership, in the management context?

Two approaches

In general, the traditional concepts of leadership fall into two broad categories:

The trait approach. This explains leadership in terms of *personality traits.* Ever since the dawn of the human race, people have been aware that leaders possess qualities that set them apart. Personal courage, for example, was often one of the traits ascribed to early tribal chiefs.

The trait approach has advocates in our own day. Some management authorities say that an effective leader must—

—be enthusiastic,
—know himself,
—be mentally alert,
—be self-confident,
—have a sense of responsibility,
—develop a sense of humor,
—etc., etc., etc.

No one can really quarrel with the *desirability* of these traits. The trouble is, how do you get the aspiring leader to develop them? Like a treatise on how to jump 20 feet up in the air, the most precise theoretical directions remain impractical.

If the would-be leader is not *naturally* enthusiastic, he can work himself into a nervous breakdown trying to develop an enthusiasm he doesn't feel. The insincerity of phony enthusiasm can even be disastrous.

In short, definitions of leadership in terms of personality traits are fine in theory, but not practical when it comes to developing leaders or exercising leadership.

The situationist approach. Some experts claim that the key to a manager's effectiveness as a leader lies in his ability to establish a situation in which people will naturally work toward company goals. This concept defines the good leader in terms of characteristic actions. For example, Norman F. Washburne, writing in *Nation's Business,* defines a good leader as follows:

A good leader initiates action.

He gives orders that will be obeyed.

He uses established channels within his group.

He knows and obeys the rules and customs of his group.

He maintains discipline.

He listens to subordinates.

He responds to their needs.

He helps them.

Although Washburne's ideas go a step further than the trait approach, they, too, are inadequate. The trouble with the situationist approach is that it's *descriptive* rather than *prescriptive*.

For example, it can be readily accepted that "a good leader initiates action." But *what kind* of action? *When* does he initiate it? And, most important of all, *how* does he do it?

Leadership—old style

The most serious weakness of traditional approaches to leadership is simply this: They're no longer "in phase" with today's business environment. They evolved out of an authoritarian era in business management, characterized by attitudes and relationships that no longer exist—at least not in the same way. As an extreme example of how leadership today differs from yesterday, consider the following bit of business memorabilia:

Back in 1872, Zachary U. Geiger, proprietor of the Mount Cory Carriage and Wagon Works, felt he owed it to his employees to spell out their duties and obligations.

Accordingly, he had a clerk post this notice prominently:

1. Office employees will daily sweep the floors, dust the furniture, shelves and showcases.
2. Each clerk will bring in a bucket of water and a scuttle of coal for the day's business.
3. Clerks will each day fill lamps, clean chimneys, trim wicks. Wash windows once a week.
4. Make your pens carefully. You may whittle nibs to your individual taste.
5. This office will open at 7:00 A.M. and close at 8:00 P.M. daily, except on the Sabbath, on which day it will remain closed.
6. Men employees will be given an evening off each week for courting purposes, two evenings a week if they go regularly to church.
7. Every employee should lay aside from each pay a goodly sum of his earnings for his benefit during the declining years, so that he will not become a burden upon the charity of his betters.
8. Any employee who smokes Spanish cigars, uses liquor in any form, gets shaved at a barbershop or frequents pool or public halls will give me good reason to suspect his worth, intentions, integrity and honesty.
9. The employee who has performed his labors faithfully and without fault for a period of five years in my service, and who has been thrifty and attentive to his religious duties, is seeked upon by his fellowmen as a substantial and law-abiding citizen, will be given an increase of five cents a day in his pay, providing a just return in profits from the business permits it.

Clearly, since Zachary U. Geiger's day, personal liberties on the job have greatly increased and the extreme dictatorial attitudes have practically vanished.

As the old styles fade

In the new climate shaping the business scene, the old foundations of authority—fear of being fired, acceptance of paternalism by employees, and so on—have practically crumbled. At the same time, an increasing sophistication among the rank and file generally dooms to failure any obvious attempts at being manipulative.

A new style of management leadership is emerging in response to three developments in the contemporary work situation:

Smaller work groups. In general, work groups are becoming smaller. Yesterday's manager who called his large group together and "bossed" it by the politician's hail-fellow-well-met tone is today an anachronism.

"Geography" of subordinates. In automated and computerized departments, the people a manager directs are often widely dispersed. Machine tenders, employees monitoring control boards, and so on, often work in isolation. The exchanges between a manager and his employees take place on a one-to-one basis. And the intermittent nature of the personal contacts means that the employee must operate on his own with minimal direct supervision.

Employees' changed leadership needs. As a result of higher education levels and a greater sophistication, employees are both less susceptible to and less in need of authoritarian leadership. Also, the fact that more and more individuals have engineering degrees and other kinds of advanced technical training means that they are equipped to handle specialized work situations and problems as well as the routine. In short, they feel less need for a "boss" to guide and direct their daily work.

Accordingly, the leadership exercised by tomorrow's manager will change both in *quantity*—it will decrease— and in *quality*. The manager will still have to provide direction for his subordinates. But it will not be the old bull-of-the-woods, beat-them-into-submission approach of the previous century. It will even be very different from the syrupy "charm school" leadership style smiled upon by the enlightened management experts of the '40s and '50s.

New solutions to the leadership problem

It's highly likely that several management concepts considered daring and impractical in the past decades will become accepted practices tomorrow because they are appropriate to the new work scene. For example, the participative-management concept is custom-tailored for work situations in which highly skilled and educated people work as a team to solve problems and make decisions. Similarly, Douglas McGregor's Theory X–Theory Y approach fits the need of the younger, highly trained worker for a work situation in which he is given leeway to exercise his capabilities.

McGregor's Theory Y assumptions are that people generally seek responsibility, have a positive capacity for exercising imagination, ingenuity and creativity, and can exercise self-control. (McGregor's assumptions probably have direct relevance to a much greater majority of the working population today than in the past.)

The concept of the leaderless group

Suppose that in the future, the "subordinate" requires no leadership, because his education and training make him capable of "leading himself." It's entirely possible.

In recent discussions with executives on the problems of directing scientific and technical personnel—an increasingly important segment of the working population—the author found a consensus on the importance of a concept referred to as "collaborative management."

In describing general-management procedures to which his scientists and technicians had responded favorably, a vice-president in charge of research for an optical company reported that his company's management concepts had progressed through three phases:

1. management by authority
2. management by objective
3. management by collaboration

This executive went on to say that the collaborative approach works especially well with individuals of strong ego, a high degree of professional expertness and a strong sense of logical procedures. A group of scientists do not need a "boss" to work productively with one another.

Another interviewee agreed and added that in order for the leaderless group to function effectively, open communication of a special kind was required: "I'm not talking here about the shuffling back and forth of paper, but of open exchange based on mutual respect and trust."

A third conferee noted that the approach had value when ". . . a purpose is clear but specific objectives may not be clear."

"Better communications improve the collaborative system and increase its workability," observed a fourth executive. In this connection, sensitivity training (the group approach to improving personal interrelationships) was highlighted as an extremely helpful technique.

Tomorrow: the sensitive leader

A growing segment of management believes that a manager's success in giving instructions, listening to complaints, checking on performance, and so on, will be only one part—and probably the lesser part—of his job as leader tomorrow. More and more, experts are suggesting that a manager's effectiveness will depend not on his skill in following some systematic procedure but on his *interpersonal relationships* with his subordinates. (Remember the point made earlier, that tomorrow's manager will more frequently need to relate to subordinates on a one-to-one rather than a one-to-group basis.)

The problem then becomes one of helping or teaching the manager to relate more effectively to his subordinates. It is to this problem that a controversial approach called "sensitivity training" is addressed.

Sensitivity training got its start about 1946, as a result of work done by psychologist Kurt Lewin of MIT. In that year, Lewin and others conducted a workshop at the State Teachers' College in New Britain, Connecticut, designed to help local leaders to understand and comply with the then-new Fair Employment Practices Act.

The workshop was divided into several groups, each with its own research observer. In the course of the sessions, Lewin became aware of two phenomena. People who had been part of the same group experience had differing perceptions of what had actually occurred. When groups discussed their own "perception of reality," some startling interactions took place. Here's one example, as recorded by the research observer:

"At 10:00 A.M., Mr. X attacked the group leader, and

then X and Mr. Y got involved in a heated exchange. Some other members were drawn into taking sides. Other members seemed frightened and tried to make peace. But they were ignored by the combatants. At 10:10 A.M., the leader came in to redirect attention back to the problem, which had been forgotten in the exchange. Mr. X and Mr. Y continued to contradict each other in the discussion which followed.

"Immediately, Mr. X denied and Mr. Y defended the correctness of their views. Other members reinforced or qualified the data furnished by the observers. In brief, participants began to join observers and training leaders in trying to analyze and interpret behavior events . . . participants reported they were deriving important understandings of their own behavior and the behavior of the group."

Lewin and his training staff felt they had hit upon a powerful process of reeducation. Group members, if confronted with their own behavior and its effects, might achieve highly meaningful insights about themselves, about the responses of others to them and about group behavior and group development in general.

What was created in 1946 is known today as "laboratory training" or "sensitivity training." It promises methods of altering the behavior of groups and individuals and increasing operating effectiveness. Clearly, it is of special import to those in leadership positions.

As far back as 1950, one observer of the management scene with special interest in management development, Chris Argyris of Yale, predicted that sensitivity training would become the most promising innovation in the area of managerial skills. The years seem to have confirmed Argyris's prophecy. The most enthusiastic management trainees today are those emerging from T-group sessions.

Recently, sensitivity training has undergone a fresh burst of growth. Many industrial psychologists and individuals with training experience have started T-group seminars. National Training Laboratory, one of the prime movers in the field, has terminated its affiliation with the National Education Association in order to expand its operations as an autonomous organization.

Much of what has been written in the popular press about sensitivity training makes it appear mysterious, "confessional" or just plain grueling. Here is a clarification of exactly what happens during a laboratory session.

The T-group experience

Participants in a typical sensitivity-training course spend about 60 percent of their time in T-group meetings. Each group includes a staff member, usually an industrial psychologist, who subtly guides the group. It would be a mistake to call him a leader, because he does little or no leading. At the first session, the staff man usually explains that the group will study behavior, that there is no agenda and that any learning that occurs will depend upon the group itself. With that, he stops talking.

What follows is anybody's guess. Since each unit is composed of different individuals, no group will operate in exactly the same way. Often a period of silence occurs —embarrassed, even awkward. Eventually, someone may suggest a topic to discuss, or the members will introduce themselves, or a participant will take it upon himself to try to lead the group. Whatever happens, the actions and statements of members are fair game for exploration.

It usually isn't long before the talk is freewheeling. One contributing factor, of course, is the desire of the participants to gain as much as possible from the training. Another is the relative anonymity of the setting— managers from many companies who've just met and who'll be together for only a brief period. As a result, the comments become open and personal.

Individuals who have participated in sensitivity training dwell at length on the vividness and depth of the experience. In fact, a more or less constant refrain from T-group participants is, "It's impossible to describe. You have to experience it to really understand what it's like."

To some extent, this is true. The T-group, with its ten or twelve participants and a psychologist-leader or trainer, is a microcosm, a small world with rules different from those "outside." As indicated, the usual amenities, like politeness and small talk, are absent.

In place of ordinary social conversation and small talk, participants begin reacting to one another in deep and significant ways. Complete openness is aimed for. After a preliminary period of caution, participants usually feel free to level with one another, voice their *true* opinions. This freedom to express what one really thinks and feels is based on trust. T-groupers know they will not be penalized for honesty. It's at this point the life of the T-group can be highly personal, revealing and instructive.

As one participant expressed it, "The few days I spent in a T-group gave me more information about my co-members than I had learned about people I had worked with for ten years." Because such close knowledge is gained, faults and virtues, strengths and weaknesses become apparent. And an individual sometimes gets a more accurate, even disturbing picture of himself than he's ever had before.

During the final week, the T-group members try to relate what they've learned about themselves, about each other and about group dynamics in general to their jobs back home. For many managers, the result is personal growth and improved on-the-job relationships.

It should be remembered that a T-group is also referred to as a *behavioral laboratory*. And what participants soon come to realize is that this phrase is *literally* accurate. They can *experiment* with behavior. They can say what they *really* think, unlike the rule in the "outside" world. For example:

Participant A (to B): There's something about you I don't like.

Participant B: Well, what is it?

Participant A: I'm not sure . . . something about your size. . . . Yes, that's it. . . . You seem so big, powerful. . . . I'm afraid we might get into a fight. . . .

With the skillful help of the leader, Participant A for the first time becomes aware that he reacts negatively to men who, because of their size, burliness or other physical aspect, suggest aggressiveness. With this insight, he is able to comprehend for the first time why he avoids (or works poorly with) men who seem to be threateningly aggressive.

Similarly, Participant B develops new insights. He learns how his appearance and behavior might affect other people and realizes why some individuals seem to become defensive in dealing with him. He can't change his appearance, but his new awareness helps him tone down his approach to people.

Note the benefits that emerge from this brief T-group interplay:

Participant A becomes aware of an *attitude of his* that affects his relationship with other people.

Participant B becomes aware of how some people *react to him* because of his physical appearance.

These two results taken together constitute the "sensitivity," the increased awareness of interpersonal relationships won by the T-group members. The advantages of this ability for the "new leadership" is clear.

The new motivation

Along with changes in the leadership relationship, individual attitudes and techniques in the field of motivation are also undergoing change. Essentially, managers are getting away from the phony, manipulative devices that have often tended to engender suspicion and mistrust in employees. The following advice from a so-called management advisory service, for example, would not be very effective today:

"Give out titles liberally. This doesn't cost any money. And employees appreciate a title and the status that goes with it. For example, instead of the title 'secretary,' you can give your secretary the title 'executive secretary.'"

This kind of advice, however, still represents an albatross dragging down today's manager in his working relationships. It's a past he must try to live down.

Motivation is being interpreted by today's managers in the sense of *creating conditions* that will draw forth top performance. Dwight D. Eisenhower described the process as, "getting people to do what you want them to do because they want to do it."

Why the applecart is upset

The problem is to discover what people really want. It's a tough one. A puzzled department head complains, "My people drive new cars, own color TVs and have money in the bank. An ordinary raise means little to them. What can we offer as an incentive?" He raises another problem: "Qualified people are in short supply. An employee who has anything on the ball can quit today and be on a new job tomorrow. This creates feelings of indifference, neutralizing most attempts to motivate and direct."

Another manager says bluntly, "Employees are so independent today that if you just look at them cross-eyed, they quit."

Today's employees have been described as the "don't care" generation. An exaggerated generalization—perhaps. Nevertheless, managers complain about carelessness, lackluster behavior, disinterest in company goals, work at a get-by level from persons obviously capable of much more.

New factors have indeed entered the motivation-performance equation. Three elements in particular are upsetting old applecarts:

1. *"Do-nothing" jobs.* In plants and offices alike, there are an increasing number of jobs where the worker simply watches or monitors a machine. It's difficult for the manager to measure performance, even more difficult for the worker to become enthusiastic about his work.

In the mixing department of a southern chemical company recently, an operator's attention wandered and a danger light, signaling a stuck valve, went unheeded. Result: a minor explosion requiring expensive repairs. Two weeks earlier, when a co-worker's attention had similarly wandered, too much powder was released into a mixing vat, forcing the dumping of an entire batch of a compound.

Monitoring jobs like these mainly requires concentration on automatic or semiautomatic machines. What happens? As a baking-company superintendent said, "The people feel no pride of craftsmanship, because they spend their entire time *looking*—at a machine—when they really want to be *doing*—tangibly contributing to the finished product." How to get the operator to pay attention to his machine, how to make him concentrate, is a major problem for the manager.

2. *"Desert island" assignments.* Many departmental operations increasingly require employees to work in isolation. In a Pittsburgh steel-processing plant, for example, one man operates a two-million-dollar piece of equipment—alone. He cannot see or hear his fellow workers or his supervisor.

"He has to do three routine operations when a blue light goes on," explains his boss. "But they've become conditioned reflexes by now, and that man doesn't feel or see what his fingers do anymore. I know that he's lonely and depressed."

"I have three drive-in tellers," said the personnel director of a Kansas City bank, "and whenever I walk into their booths during the day, they look at me as if I've walked uninvited into their homes."

Wherever people work in isolated stations, whether as monitor of a giant steel-processing machine or sorting letters in a mailroom, the supervisor has a problem in motivation, because the worker becomes less receptive.

3. *The crimping of upward mobility.* Hope for advancement is a traditional motivator. But the gap between employees and supervisory levels—the first rung of the management ladder—has become too great for even the above-average worker to bridge.

"Today's manager," states the vice-president of an electronics firm, "has to understand the mechanics of communication, how to write reports and how to read and absorb their content. The technical knowledge required of him is greater than a man can acquire as a machine operator. The men under my supervision who run machines know all this and, though I came up through the ranks and became a supervisor fifteen years ago, they know that's probably out for them."

This kind of realization can have a souring effect even on highly paid people. For example, in a West Coast machine works, the 25 percent of personnel that accounted for the firm's high rate of absenteeism in 1967 were mainly highly paid tool-and-die workers. And in a midwestern insurance company, the company's data processors troubled their supervisors with frivolous complaints ranging from alleged drinking-fountain malfunctions to claimed inequities in the assignment of overtime. Company officials in both instances attributed the discontent largely to the feeling that employees have "no place to go" in their career development.

A generation ago, men *knew* that hard work would get them on the next rung of the career ladder. This is less true today and will be even less true tomorrow.

In the preceding pages, the problems and difficulties facing the manager in his twin roles of leader and motivator of personnel have been stressed. The action points that follow suggest specific practical steps that can help managers become more effective in the leadership and motivation areas. Also, a procedural approach that both is time-tested and seems to have particular pertinence in today's somewhat confused leadership situation is described in chapter 10. (See Selective Leadership.)

POINTS FOR EXECUTIVE THOUGHT AND ACTION

The executive who knows how to motivate subordinates and, more generally, how to fill the role of leader for his staff or work group possesses one of the most sought-after skills in management. It is precisely this ability of which management is speaking when the statement is made, "We are looking for executives who can manage people as well as things," or, "The management of people on the job is the highest executive skill."

It should be repeated here that leadership and motivation are strongly interrelated concepts. And, to some extent, today the concept of leadership has been superseded by that of motivation. In other words, the relationship between the two concepts is expressed in the sentence "The effective leader today is the man who knows how to motivate his people."

A special study by the Research Institute of America[1]

---

[1] Research Institute of America, Inc., *The New Motivation, a Special Report* (New York: 1967).

provides a set of recommendations that managers, today and tomorrow, can follow in dealing with the motivation problem. The study is directed to the *supervising executive*. It is he who is directly involved with problems of leadership and motivation, whether his subordinates do work that is monotonous and boring or, at the other extreme, challenging and requiring a high level of creativity. Here, then, within the context of leadership and motivation, is a step-by-step procedure for improving employee performance:

When the manager is confronted by a problem of unsatisfactory performance, he should—

1. *Consider motivation second.* Whether it's lateness, excessive errors or what you will—the manager must *not* assume the erring employee is a motivation problem. First thing to check is the physical aspects of the situation. For example: The Western Electric Company, in its Kansas City, Missouri, works, was troubled by poor performance. Instead of concluding that poorly motivated employees were at the bottom of the difficulty, a team of specialists got together and eventually developed three "solutions":

A padded posture chair to overcome back pains and muscle soreness; special pliers to reduce wrist and forearm fatigue; filters on bench lamps to reduce eyestrain caused by glare in work areas.

Did the helpful items improve performance? Performance did actually improve, but some observers suggested that the show of interest was most important.

2. *Avoid the need for punishment or penalties.* Regardless of how well or poorly punishment used to work as a motivating device, it has clearly lost its edge today. Steps like these can help avoid the need for pressuring employees into "correct" behavior:

Define performance standards and criteria clearly enough to guide subordinates yet broadly enough to allow for initiative and risk taking.

Communicate an understanding of the performance expected and how it will be measured. This understanding often requires two-way discussions between manager and subordinate.

Measure performance. There are few—if any—jobs not capable of some objective measurement.

Be consistent in the practice of rewarding good performance; come down hard on repeated ineffective performance. The consistent manager is always more effective than the one who seems to act on whim.

3. *Make it clear that advancement may mean promotion—but it doesn't have to.* Interest in the job is always enhanced when an employee feels he's "getting somewhere." (This reaction directly reflects Maslow's self-fulfillment idea.)

Some managers mistakenly feel that lack of promotion possibilities for an employee necessarily leads to the feeling that he's in a dead end—and that he is demotivated accordingly.

Fortunately, the facts are otherwise. There are several things that can be done to neutralize a subordinate's "I'm in a rut" feeling. Keeping in mind the special conditions of each case, the manager can see which of these recommendations apply:

Are there actual chances for promotion or transfer?

Sometimes there are openings *outside* the present department that might suit the more deserving people. Search an employee's work record. His present job may have thrown him off an old course. He may have past work experience that can be reapplied. Discussion about his interests may reveal additional possibilities.

Can his job be expanded?

Without any loss of efficiency, other operations might be incorporated into his job. They may be steps that either immediately precede or follow the employee's regular task. Or they may be entirely unrelated but still make use of his special abilities.

Can his work methods provide a challenge?

Without changing the job, a manager may still be able to increase an employee's efficiency, raise quality performance, or both. This may provide a sense of progress in the job without promotion to a new position. A particularly worthwhile application of this idea is to get the employee into the act, get him involved in bettering his own job procedures. This can yield a double pay-off: He has the challenge of the task and the likelihood of achieving a desirable objective.

Make him realize that he's doing a useful job.

The employee who can't move up will be more content to stay put if he knows that he's accomplishing something worthwhile. He, more than any other type of worker, needs a constant reminder that his work is necessary. Give him—

—an understanding of his relation to the company, how his job fits in;

—an understanding of how the company serves the community or the nation.

Time spent by the manager discussing these matters with the employee will reinforce his self-esteem.

4. *Create a feeling of involvement.* "When a man seems to have lost his capacity for productive, creative work," says Dr. Chris Argyris of Yale, "management often decides that the employee is lazy and not responsible. But it's not necessarily so. Poor job performance is more often due to lack of involvement than to laziness or incompetence."

The fact that his superior cares about an employee can be reflected in a number of approaches, all of which tend to create involvement:

Ask for his thinking. No subordinate wants to feel like a robot doing a routine job, someone who merely follows orders. When he gets feeling that way, he's bound to lose interest, become indifferent. Consultation with him tends to stimulate job or task interest.

Communicate management thinking. Communications are a two-way street. The better an employee understands management thinking, the more likely he is to share its outlook and values. The manager should communicate his feelings and views to the employee.

Set standards. Unless the employee is familiar with the standards he is to meet, he'll become careless and indifferent. Preferably, standards should be high enough so that they present a challenge. The manager should establish goals through discussion that the subordinate agrees are attainable.

Praise and criticize. Praise and criticism are strong indications that management cares about what an employee is doing. Both are needed, both create a sense of involvement.

Finally, management must convey a sense of its own excitement and enthusiasm about the job and the company. Caring is contagious—and it's up to the manager to spread the benign disease.

5. *Consider the antidote for alienation and isolation.* Alienation has become so central a problem for our time that some sociologists have termed it the "alienated age." The feelings of alienation toward work were already noted by Mayo back in the 1930s. Solutions for alienation with a capital *A* should not be expected here. But for the alienation and isolation of the individual that grow out of the immediate circumstances of his task, remedies are possible. For example:

Where employees work at stations apart from others, the problem may resemble the sensory deprivation that besets soldiers manning underground missile posts. The military men worry—and rightly—about one man alone with a push button that can launch a fantastically destructive missile. One solution: redundancy—placing a second or even a third man in the post. For industry, the pressures of competition usually prohibit such duplication. However, there are other possibilities:

Add a creative element to the job. The purpose is to give the employee more to keep him occupied and prevent boredom. One manager reports very good results by getting his people to develop additional or improved uses for their equipment.

Extra privileges. A Stamford, Connecticut, manufacturing plant has used privileges successfully. Free coffee and doughnuts are provided twice a day. Also, employees are permitted to use transistor radios and other harmless distractions that can make monitoring less arduous. In addition, the manager's reasonably frequent contacts with isolated employees can give them that "in touch" feeling. Another company uses the practice of having experienced employees train newcomers.

Pressing for results

Finally, and in general, three guidelines can help keep the manager on track:

Realistic goals. Managers must be willing to adjust their sights to the possible. For example, the manager must judge which employees can be inspired to deep involvement in their jobs and when to settle for "a fair day's work."

A positive environment. To get top performance from employees, the atmosphere of the department and the manager's attitudes should encourage personal involvement, the element of challenge, personal responsibility and growth.

The absence of negatives. In the strange arithmetic of motivation, one negative can wipe out a dozen positives. Managers often nullify their own efforts by overlooking the impact of Herzberg's demotivators: minor grievances, oversupervision, petty annoyances in the working situation, and so on.

Realistic approaches that concentrate on productivity rather than morale, on employee involvement rather than "happiness," on the capabilities of individuals rather than on some abstract standard of general performance —these can bring the manager's highest reward, individuals whose satisfaction with their work is reflected in how well they do it.

PART THREE/TOOLS

To an increasing degree, the executive is becoming a tool user. The adding machine, the slide rule and the tape recorder are becoming common. The computer, of course, is a major innovation in the executive tool kit. To the computer can be added new methods of information gathering and communication.

Executive tools for planning and decision making have also been increasing in number and importance. Operations research, PERT, problem simulation—these are just some of the tools increasingly available to the contemporary executive. They must be mastered or they pose the threat of obsolescence to the manager, on whatever echelon he may be.

Aside from the tools and techniques of his own premises, a new array of aids and assists are now available to the manager from outside services. Consultants of a dozen different stripes and varieties are at his beck and call. Services, from psychological testers to temporary office and factory help, can be summoned by a phone call. Gaining familiarity with and improving one's skill in using these services is the theme in this section.

NINE/THE EXPANDING EXECUTIVE
TOOL KIT

"Man is a tool-using animal . . . without tools he is nothing, with tools he is all," said Thomas Carlyle.

The traditional executive was a non–tool user. He gloried in his ability to wheel and deal, equipped only with a native shrewdness and quick reflexes. In yesterday's business world, the tool user was at least a humble mechanic, at best a "technical man." Engineers, industry-oriented scientists and statisticians were the people the executive thought of as tool users.

Today's manager first borrowed tools from the technicians, then innovated on his own to deal with the increasing complexities of the management job. For example, he acquired for his personal use adding machines, slide rules, charts—tools of the accountant and engineer.

Yet the modern management tool kit includes not only physical devices but *systematic approaches*. The latter *multiply* the abilities of the manager to cope with his tasks and problems. The manager's use of tools will increase as company operations become more extensive and complex. Tools—in the larger sense of the word— mark the progress of the executive toward a greater professionalism. It is to the executive's tool kit, each year adding new items, that the following chapter is devoted.

The three basic types of tools

There are three areas in which management tools will become more refined:

Administrative tools. From the telephone to the dictating machine, devices, mostly physical, will help the manager deal with his paper work and communications problems.

Operations-managing tools. PERT and operations research are two devices in this category; they represent tools in the larger, more figurative sense of the word.

Man-managing tools. For many managers these are the leading edge of management innovation. Included are "Management by Objectives," the "Managerial Grid," "Zero Defects," and so on.

The administrative tools

The tools in this area are mostly physical devices, and they often represent advancing technologies in other areas (for example, the tape recorder is a product of electronics progress). Few executives use all, or even most, of them. Nevertheless, taken as a whole, they represent instruments, devices, gadgets—old and new—that managers have found of assistance in doing their jobs.

Files. Most of the equipment and systems for record keeping are designed for general-office use. But the manager, too, has need of facilities for record keeping. He may use a simple vertical file or one of the ingenious devices that fit inside a desk drawer.

Recent technological developments provide the executive with more sophisticated means of filing data: for example, electronically recorded information on disks or tape wedded to a computer ending in a graphic display terminal. Sitting on the executive's desk or an adjoining table, a TV-like box displays on a cathode-ray tube information stored in the system and retrieved at random on command—a numerical code actuated by a small keyboard. Sales managers can have regional and individual performance records available mere hours after the fact. Individual personnel records can be brought to a personnel executive within seconds.

The *Thomas Register of American Manufacturers,* ordinarily a seven-volume directory, has been made available in microfiche, that is, sheets of film four by six inches, each carrying reduced images of a number of directory pages. Combined with a viewer or slide projector, the record is readily available. A growing number of companies use microfiche as well as microfilm for maintenance manuals, engineering records, and so on—giving the executive the benefit of minimum storage space with convenient retrieval.

Charts and graphs. All types and sizes of these are available for organization control, production control and quality control; for a quick picture of absenteeism, safety, budgets, waste and costs; for keeping track of orders received, processed and shipped, overtime, stock needed, and so on.

Phone adaptations. Available are conference phones that sit on the desk and require no handling; phones linked up for three-way or group talks; phone side switches to tell the switchboard whether the executive is in, away or available by auto-call; timers to limit long-distance calls.

A recent development is a *portable* executive telephone. This device is similar to a car telephone or a marine radiotelephone. It is carried in an attaché case and weighs about ten pounds, including antenna and rechargeable batteries. A light on the case flashes when there's an incoming call. Obviously, it provides flexibility to the executive who must travel out in the field, away from ordinary phone contact.

Blackboards, easel charts, flannel boards. These can be used behind the desk as well as in conference rooms for problem solving, illustration, etc. They can help a manager in his planning and in setting forth a plan or problem to his group.

Slide rules, adding or calculating machines. "I run up a column of figures a dozen times a day" is a fairly typical statement from a top-level executive to explain his use of such equipment. They assist in anything from adding up the month's production to figuring out a salesman's commission.

Cameras. Movie, candid and still types are often used to get visual evidence of a damaged shipment, inventory on hand, poor safety practices and many other facts. Instant self-developing cameras, such as the Polaroid, are of particular value.

Calendars. Different kinds for planning operations and

recording appointments are available and in use on the business scene. They come in paper or metal, to be hung on the wall, placed on the desk or worn on the wrist.

Projectors. Slide or movie projectors are becoming more common in executive offices. As an adjunct to conferences or as a briefing or training device, their rich possibilities are still not completely explored. The overhead projector makes it possible to project material and have the user modify—draw on or erase—the images. Sound-slide films add audio content.

Dictating machines or recorders. The use of a dictating machine for letters, reports, and so on, is standard. But executives have found that putting a conference "on tape," for example, provides a verbatim record that at times is highly desirable. Sophisticated equipment makes it possible for today's manager to pick up a phone and dictate onto a remote recorder which will later be transcribed by employees in a typing pool. The possibilities for each tool itemized above are by no means exhaustive or frozen. New uses or adaptations appear continually. Ingenuity in seeking out new uses makes for continuing improvement in managerial effectiveness.

Two examples of executive tools will be used to illustrate the executive tool-using potential:

1. The executive as shutterbug

Ever since 1829, when Daguerre first exposed an iodized silver plate to mercury-vapor fumes and created the first photograph, the camera has sprouted new uses. The photo-equipment manufacturers have done a good job of publicizing the business potentialities of the camera. Polaroid equipment, with the unique feature of getting from the clicking stage to the finished print in 30 seconds, offers some special advantages. But any camera, handled with a fair degree of competence, may prove a valuable addition to the executive tool kit.

Here are some of the business uses to which cameras have been applied:

Work methods. The Allis-Chalmers Company, in its Boston plant, photographs tooling setups for short-run jobs. If the job is ever repeated or the question arises as to how a particular job was turned out, photographs supply a visual record and guide.

Physical plant changes. A change in layout or alteration of a structural detail can be made specific by use of the camera. A photo of the original condition is the starting point. Then a grease pencil in the hands of an executive makes it possible to sketch the change right on the print.

Job instruction. Alden Products Company of Brockton, Massachusetts, uses photos of tricky operations, pasting them to the machine of the employee as a guide.

Damage claims. Heads of traffic departments use photos of damaged shipments as they arrive at the receiving platform. This enables the department to evaluate the damage and call the carrier's claim inspector.

Progress reports. Whether it's a new plant being erected or a machine gradually taking shape in the engineering department, daily, weekly or monthly photos afford a visual record of progress.

It may not be practical for big construction, but in the case of a new design that ends up with an unsatisfactory result, shuffling back through the photographic record may show where undesirable elements began to creep in.

Before and after. Whether it's office rearrangement, changing layout of a production area, trying out a new cleaning agent, there's always a chance that before and after pictures can prove useful. In some cases, where results are visual, these photos can report better than the proverbial "ten thousand words" just what has been accomplished.

Decision making by eye. In some cases, one may choose among alternatives that can be reported visually:

Site planning. Krebay Construction Company of Indianapolis shoots proposed building sites. Back in the office, executives use these photos to help in estimating costs, distribution, and so on, of one way as compared to another.

Store relocation. The executive of a chain-store organization who must select desirable store properties may use photos to refresh his memory, as well as to evaluate the physical advantages and disadvantages of one store as opposed to another.

Housekeeping and safety. An executive responsible for safety or the physical maintenance of a shop or plant can use pictures to make his findings stick with supervisors. Photos of bad conditions could back up his complaint and eliminate argument. And photos of satisfactory findings would make an effective item for the bulletin board along with a letter of commendation.

In general, whether it's a work scene, an operating condition, or whatever, good photographs can help tell the story, refresh the memory and act as a permanent record.

The techniques next to be discussed are of fairly recent origin and represent the application of scientific concepts and methods to practical management. In their advanced form, they are not simple and may require highly trained specialists for proper application. Generally, they represent the most sophisticated instruments in the management tool kit—for they are tools for planning and decision making.

2. Operations-managing tools

The growth of an organization and of its operations brings with it problems of logistics involving materials, equipment and men. This deployment of facilities must be handled by the manager, and an *ad hoc* approach will not do. Materials must be ordered in advance and delivered to the exact points of operation as and when needed. Equipment must be available in the condition and of the capacity that customers' orders require.

In the production of a complex product like a submarine or space rocket, the one essential element, after the development work has been completed, is that the planning of the overall operation be so integrated that the thousands of individual operations proceed in an orderly fashion and culminate in the efficient assembly of the final product. Without such systematic planning, it would be practically impossible to produce as complex a product as today's four-engine jet planes or a computer.

A tool that makes systematic planning possible will now be discussed.

PERT/CPM

There are various names for this management tool: the U.S. Navy calls it PERT, an acronym for "Program Evaluation and Review Technique." The navy used the approach to expedite its initial *Polaris* missile program.

The technique is also known as "Critical Path Method" (CPM) or "Critical Path Scheduling" (CPS). Regardless of label, the idea is basically simple. It can be used to hasten the construction of a submarine missile, to overhaul a plant or to make bread. Essentially, it helps organize a series of interrelated operations so that time and cost can be *optimized*.

For complicated operations, it takes an engineer with a computer and knowledge of linear programming to apply the critical-path method. But the basic principles may be applied to simple tasks. To some extent, it's like the housewife's approach to preparing a multicourse meal. She uses several burners and the oven simultaneously, starts the things that take longer first and ends up at dinnertime ready to serve.

A recent application of the critical-path method drew international attention.[1] Colonel Edward Churchill, the man who supervised the building of Canada's famed Expo 67 on its hundreds of acres of fairgrounds, and its numerous structures and facilities, was told the project would take five to seven years to complete.

"I went into it all with a feeling of absolute fear," confessed Churchill. What calmed him down was the enlistment of a computerized control system called "the critical path." A computer digested data about every phase of Expo construction, set deadlines for each and then warned when delays in one phase—say, the installation of sewers—would jeopardize the completion of another phase—the planting of hyacinths. With the assist of CPM, the job was completed in four years.

For purposes of illustrating CPM in action, let's look

---

[1] Reported in *Newsweek*, May 1, 1967.

at a simple operation involving the transfer of materials within a department. The department head, using CPM, would proceed in this fashion:

1. *List everything that has to be done.* The problem or task is to transfer cartons of stored material from one room to another. These are the things the manager would have to arrange for:

Get a hand truck.

Get two employees to do the moving.

Make sure new area can take the load.

Move cartons to the new location.

Sort and label the cartons.

Check amount of material to be moved.

OK by supervisor.

Stack cartons using the new system.

2. *Put the jobs in sequence.* Go over the list of job steps and put them in the sequence in which they must be done.

In the list above, for example, the first step would be to make sure that the new area is big enough to accommodate the material to be sorted.

3. *Estimate time for each step.* The time may be expressed in minutes, hours or days and indicated alongside each step on the sequence of operations you've listed. Now the list looks like this:

A. Check amount of material (0.8 hour).

B. Check capacity of new area (0.4 hour).

C. Get truck (0.2 hour).

D. Get employees (0.1 hour).

E. Move material (5 hours).

F. Sort and label (2 hours).

G. OK by supervisor (0.5 hour).

H. Stack (3 hours).

4. *Make an arrow diagram.* The CPS chart, or "network," as it is sometimes called, is a key step. It helps show how the various parts of the job interrelate. And, finally, it helps work out the critical path itself. The chart may be drawn in the fashion shown below.

An arrow is used to indicate each step in the operation. The length of the arrow doesn't matter. But the *direction* of the arrow shows you how the step relates to the rest of the job.

The diagram is constructed by asking three questions of each element in the sequence:

What immediately precedes this element?

What immediately follows it?

What other elements can be done at the same time?

Here's how a complete CPS chart for the carton-moving operation might look:

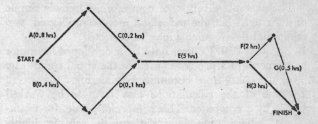

Note some of the things the chart tells at a glance. First, step E, the actual moving, can't take place until after steps A–D are completed.

Second, it shows the general scope of the operation.

Third, it helps determine the critical path.

The critical path is the *total of the longest consecutive jobs.* In the chart shown, the critical path is shown by the heavy line. Knowing the critical path, the manager is now in a position to do several things:

Estimate the total time for the job. In our example, it would be nine hours.

Spot bottlenecks. Every operation on the critical path is, theoretically, a bottleneck. Operations *not* on the critical path (these are called *slack paths*) may generally be done at the same time as those on the critical path.

Since they take less time, it is the critical path that limits the schedule.

Expedite the schedule. The manager has two alternatives: *(a)* Steps on the slack paths may be performed as much as possible at the same time as those on the critical path; *(b)* shorten critical-path operations by making them crash activities, i.e., putting more men or equipment on the job, devising a more efficient method, etc.

Used properly, CPS also helps keep costs down. One could, for example, devise two alternative CPS charts representing two different ways of getting a job done. Comparing man-hours, possible overtime and other cost elements, and comparing completion time of one method against the other, one can come up with figures that tell whether a "normal" production or a speeded-up schedule is more desirable from a cost standpoint.

The example given is, of course, an extremely simple one. As tasks become more and more complicated, two additional developments may be expected:

1. Separate PERT charts have to be developed for major segments of a project to prevent the visual complexity of the chart from becoming bewildering.

2. Some of the calculations may have to be worked out by a computer. This is especially true, for example, where time interrelationships become highly complicated.

There are two basic objectives to which PERT may be directed. One focuses on minimizing *time,* the other on minimizing *cost.* A PERT/time network concentrates on the time-scheduling aspects of a project. A PERT/cost network focuses on the costs of the network elements.

In PERT/cost calculation, a single cost may be estimated for each activity. Another approach is to use three cost figures, "optimistic," "pessimistic" and "most likely." These are then combined into an "expected cost."

As is often true in management, an idea introduced in one industry or function is borrowed and adapted for other applications. Accordingly, it is not surprising that the PERT approach has been used in everything from organization planning to personnel development.

In their book on network systems[2] Russell D. Archibald and Richard L. Villoria point out that CPM need not be applied only to planning, scheduling and control of one-shot projects. According to these authors, CPM

[2] Russell D. Archibald and Richard L. Villoria, *Network-Based Management Systems,* (New York: John Wiley & Sons, 1967).

can be used to improve routine operations, such as the manufacture of standard parts, and for analytical tasks, such as identifying a paper-work bottleneck.

Operations research

While PERT is essentially a method for optimized scheduling, operations research addresses itself to broader problems involving the utilization of capital and human resources.

In 1962, the Council of the Operational Research Society of the United Kingdom published the following official definition of operations research:

"Operational research is the attack of modern science on complex problems arising in the direction and management of large systems of men, machines, materials and money in industry, business, government and defense. The distinctive approach is to develop a scientific model of the system, incorporating measurements of factors such as chance and risk, with which to predict and compare the outcomes of alternative decisions, strategies or controls. The purpose is to help management determine its policies and actions scientifically." [3]

In actual practice, OR is often applied by interdisciplinary teams. These OR teams or staffs include mathematicians, engineers, chemists, business administrators, economists, statisticians and other scientists whose specialties reflect the subject areas in which the problems originate.

In working toward the solution of problems, an OR team generally proceeds through three steps:

1. Describing the system that encompasses the problem. For example, assume the management of a small chain of department stores wants to develop an inventory policy that is best for each store location. An OR group will collect all the factors of goods sold, rate of turnover, storage space available, and so on.
2. Constructing theories (or "models") that account for the data developed in the first step. In the case of the department stores, the "model" would seek to

---

[3] "Operational Research Quarterly," vol. 13, no. 3, 282 (September 1962).

represent the activities of each store.

3. Using the model to predict future activities that are the results produced by changes in the systems or models.

How should Smith invest?

An extremely simplified example illustrates one aspect of OR in action:

Jim Smith has the opportunity to invest $1000 in either of two companies. Company A will return $2000 at the end of the year, but there's a 25-percent chance of no return. Company B will return $3000, but there's a 50-percent chance of no return. In both cases, the investment is secure. Which company should Smith invest in?

Even in this simplified problem, one sees three basic aspects of decision making and OR. First, every decision is a gamble—that is, it involves *risk*.

Second, a rational decision requires that all factors be *quantified*. Jim Smith, for example, must quantify the risk, the payoff and the potential loss.

Third—an important point to remember—the scientific approach provides the *rational decision* and not necessarily the one the executive will, or should, make.

Using OR principles, Jim Smith solves the investment problem by determining the *expected value* of the investment in Company A versus the investment in Company B. The expected value of A is $1000 potential gain times 0.75 (probability of success), or $750. The expected value of B is $2000 potential gain times 0.50, or $1000. Apparently, Company B is the better investment.

Quantification is an essential aspect of OR calculation. Qualities, or elements not ordinarily thought of in quantity terms, must nevertheless be expressed by some numerical value. For example:

Manager Bob Brown is hiring a new secretary and has narrowed the field to two girls, Miss A and Miss B. Such factors as salary expectation, experience and education may be fairly easy to quantify. But how about the element of physical attractiveness? Since it's going to make a difference to manager Bob Brown, he sets a value on each girl's personal appeal. (He rationalizes this fact by assuring himself it's helpful to his morale to work with an attractive secretary rather than one who sets his teeth on edge.) He can make this quantification in several ways. For example, he may say that Miss A is twice as attractive as Miss B, and in formulation will rate her $2\ p$. (for pulchritude) ; and Miss B is rated at p. Or he might do it on the basis of percentage rating. In similar fashion, intangibles, such as customer goodwill, employee morale, effect on company image, can all be assigned numerical values in OR computation.

Uses for OR

Both the potential and the problems associated with operations research have come in for closer examination in recent years. A key paragraph from a recent book points out these two aspects of the management science:

"It is becoming increasingly apparent that, at a deeper level, operations research has to do with the organization of social decision making: the information, the manipulation of data and the methods of evaluation that are used to maintain or change the activities people undertake. It also begins to be clear that operations research has had a profound influence on the nature of decision-making process. This influence is possibly greater and more subtle than any of us are yet in a position to judge, even though much of what we read in this volume suggests many deficiencies in the use of problem-solving models. Indeed, these very suggestions that operations research could be used more effectively are indicative of the changes that have occurred. The way in which people think about decisions and the institutional context in which they operate have been changed because the OR worker has devoted his attention to the meaning and implications of the total processes." [4]

Business has found many specific areas of application for the OR approach. Russell Ackoff [5] has listed seven

[4] David Hertz and Roger T. Eddison (eds.), *Progress in Operations Research* (New York: John Wiley & Sons, 1964).

[5] R. Ackoff, "The Development of Operations as a Science," *Journal of Operations Research*, June 1956.

types of processes in which OR can be useful:

Inventory processes, involving decisions as to how many units to produce or purchase, and when, where carrying costs must be balanced against the costs of various alternatives.

Allocation processes, in which the overall effectiveness of allocating available resources in various ways must be determined.

Waiting-line processes, involving waiting costs associated with delays of units to be serviced or of service equipment.

Routing processes, to fix routes of optimum efficiency.

Replacement processes, where maintenance costs must be balanced with the costs of new equipment.

Information-collection processes, involving relative costs in the gathering of relevant data for decision making.

Competitive processes, to determine how "vulnerable" the results of a given decision may be to any subsequent decision by an adversary (often explored by "game" techniques).

When the OR technique is teamed with the computer, mathematical models of a real system may be constructed and manipulated. In the course of the manipulation, data may be fed into the computer and output developed that gives the business executive some idea of the consequences of alternatives.

Offshoots of operations research

A common example of the mathematical model developed in operations research is the so-called *business game.* This is a simulation in which, working with a previously programmed computer, the executive can experiment with various inputs. For example, the effect of increasing an advertising outlay at a given level of output in a stated marketing situation, and the likely result in sales and profitability, can be calculated. Essentially, what simulation of this type makes possible is the supplying of meaningful answers to the question, "What would happen if . . . ?"

Developed with the help of a computer, the "business

game" gives managers an opportunity to manipulate either real or theoretical company operations so that the total system can be adjusted for optimum results.

Also in the area of operations-managing tools are flow charts and decision trees—the latter a technique that mathematically factors the degree of risk into a business decision. With the "odds" included, the executive can make meaningful comparisons among alternative decisions and courses of action.

A number of specialized technologies, essentially operations-managing approaches, have developed in recent years—quality control, materials handling, purchasing, and so on. Each of these specialized management functions tends to develop its own array of tools. For example, "value analysis" has been one such innovation in the field of purchasing.

POINTS FOR EXECUTIVE THOUGHT AND ACTION

The contents of the preceding chapter lend themselves directly to "how to do" considerations. For example, check through the list of applications given for the use of the camera by the executive. Are any of these appropriate for some present job problem, one you may have in the future?

The same spectrum of uses is possible for other executive tools mentioned, from the slide projector to the tape recorder. Are there any applications of some of the standard tools that you could apply to good advantage in your work?

The example given of a PERT application is a simple one that may have many parallels in your day-to-day operations. Of course, you may already be familiar with this tool and may have used it in much more sophisticated ways. But if not, think over some of the operations for which you are responsible. Could the use of PERT principles help you do the job more efficiently?

You may be interested in giving yourself a quick one-minute quiz on just how adaptable you are to the tool approach. The following—some, slightly facetious—questions will help you score yourself on this quality:

How tool-minded are you?

Yes   No

1. Would you rather drive a spike with a sledge than your fist? ☐ ☐

2. As you know, a tool extends the human capability. Do you agree that there's nothing sinful or threatening to the natural order of things in being a "technical" executive rather than one who tries to get by on purely nature-given endowments such as intuition, native intelligence, and so on? ☐ ☐

3. Do you agree that it's worth spending the time to master a given management tool in order to gain the added capability it promises? ☐ ☐

4. Of the following tools, do you use three or more on the job: tape recorder or dictating machine, adding machine or calculator, camera, charts or graphs, typewriter, slide rule? ☐ ☐

5. If you already have used PERT or some of its variations, just answer this question yes. If not, will you in the near future make the effort to see whether you can use the PERT approach on one of your projects? ☐ ☐

6. Next time you struggle with a problem involving such factors as morale, cooperativeness, goodwill—or a secretary's personal attractiveness—will you try to quantify these to help develop a decision or plan of action? ☐ ☐

Scoring: Give yourself 10 points for each yes. Then rate your total score against the following scale:

50–60	You're as tool-minded as tomorrow.
30–40	You're pretty good in the tool department. Now just expand your interest and capability in wielding tools; experiment with those you haven't considered.
Below 30	You're painfully honest. But how about rereading the preceding chapter and taking its principles closer to heart?

TEN/MAN-MANAGEMENT TOOLS

Archimedes said, "Give me a lever long enough and I will move the world." Today's human-relations-oriented manager paraphrases the ancient Greek: "Give me a motivation strong enough and I will get my people to move the world."

In answer to the search for ways of improving the performance of individuals on the work scene, the behavioral scientists have forged a variety of tools, most of them essentially motivational in character. This chapter focuses on the man-managing tools available to the executive, expressly designed to make subordinates more productive and creative. It may be regarded as a sequel to chapter 3, since the concepts to be treated derive either directly or indirectly from the disciplines of the behavioral scientists. But while the discussion of chapter 3 was essentially historic, the tools described here are presented in the practical context of helping the executive to perform his day-to-day job.

Tools fit the times

In the decades following the Industrial Revolution, labor was thought of as a commodity and the working individual was thought of as a "hand." Management's approach to the employee was blunt and authoritative. As the integrity and dignity of the individual increased in our society—and as his personal liberty grew—management was forced by the logic of events to treat the employee with more respect and more circumspectly.

In more recent years, the necessity has taken on the added virtue of effectiveness: Enlightened ideas of motivation have been adopted because they promise to be the best means of maximizing utilization of the human resource.

The man-managing tools to be considered here have been selected because they are currently of major interest. The subject of brainstorming is included to illustrate an important characteristic of this entire tool genre. The list:

1. management by objectives
2. the managerial grid
3. selective leadership
4. zero defects
5. brainstorming

1. Management by objectives

When a subordinate asks, "How am I doing in my job?" what yardsticks can the manager use in formulating his answer? Is it possible to make a subordinate self-motivating?

These are some of the questions that MBO seeks to help the manager answer, and more definitively than in the past. Basically, management by objectives is a simple concept: job performance and achievement guided by results desired. There are two types of application:

Unit performance. The method may be used to set goals and evaluate results for departments, divisions or whole companies.

Individual performance. The MBO idea may be applied to the work of individual executives, managers and employees. It is in this latter application, as a tool for motivating and measuring individual performance, that management by objectives takes on special value, helping the manager deal with his subordinates.

Essentially, MBO is a substitute for, and successor to, traditional merit-rating and performance-appraisal methods. Back in the "dark ages" of management, before the Thirties, most supervisors took the measure of their employees intuitively. They would give the employee day-to-day work goals but no larger objective. When the time for evaluation came, the supervisor would deliver an off-the-cuff opinion about the subordinate: Yes, he was doing a good job or, no, the performance didn't merit a raise, a promotion—or even continued employment.

But the off-the-top-of-the-head appraisal technique was undependable. Intuition couldn't be trusted when it came to men's careers and their company's success. And so evaluation by personality trait came into being, a decided advance over intuitive evaluation.

The basis of this "personality evaluation" was a belief that a set of traits—initiative, judgment, cooperativeness, etc.—was a good indication of an individual's performance. The manager, by rating traits important to the employee's job (for example, "creativity" might be included in an engineer's appraisal but not in a file clerk's), would arrive at an overall judgment of performance.

Although trait evaluation is an improvement over less systematic methods, it has limitations. For example, the method looks back at the kind of *effort* the man has expended rather than at the *results* obtained.

Nevertheless, trait appraisal was popular—and still is in many firms—because, obviously, there is some connection between input and output, between effort expended and results achieved, between individual attitudes and company profit.

But, in 1954, Peter Drucker and other management experts began questioning the validity of measuring performance by trait. Their doubt: The measure is too indirect. An individual might know his function perfectly, be cost-conscious, have good judgment, and so on, and yet not make any significant contribution to departmental or company results.

As a remedy to basic objections like these, MBO seemed to have particular promise.

In 1957, the top management of General Mills of Minneapolis applied the management-by-objectives concept throughout the company.

People from frontline management echelons upward set job objectives for themselves after their immediate superiors presented them with statements of their accountability. "An accountability" is a *result* that the company expects for the satisfactory performance of the

job. Each job at General Mills has from three to ten accountabilities. Accordingly, each manager of the company is annually presented with a list of three to ten
results that he must accomplish—whatever the means he
chooses to accomplish them.

A company spokesman gives an example: "I'm responsible for insuring that our salary structure compares
favorably with our competitors'. A frontline manager
might be held accountable for maintaining an effective
work force."

After the frontline manager has drawn up his statement of accountabilities, he writes out certain specific objectives; for example, "To improve the performance of
employee John Doe by January 1." The manager creates
as many of these goals as he thinks necessary to satisfy
every accountability the company has placed upon him.

When he finishes, he meets with his superior to discuss
whether the accomplishment of these objectives will satisfy the accountabilities. If need be, he modifies his objectives, adds more or changes some.

The method can be summed up in three steps:

Superior and subordinate work out realistic performance
objectives.

They agree on the means for achieving specified results.

At the end of the agreed-on period, actual results are
compared to expected results.

The manager commits himself to specific, measurable
action with specific time limits. In so doing, he obviously
takes the risk that he will fail *and that his superiors will
know he has failed.*

General Mills reports satisfaction with his application
of the concept:

*"Management by objectives continuously stretches the
capabilities of every one of our managers and makes him
grow in value to us," says the company spokesman. "In
the old days, a man had only a general idea of what was
involved in his job. 'So long as I stay out of trouble, I'll
survive,' he'd think and hope that what he was doing
was right. Now he—and we—don't have to guess."*

As used by General Mills and other companies, management by objectives is confined to the management echelons. But the concept is of particular interest because it may offer help for one of the manager's thorniest jobs: evaluating his subordinates.

Of course, management by objectives has often been used under other labels or under no label at all. For example: The performance of salesmen has traditionally been measured by results. A salesman will be assigned a quota—he may have to bring in X number of new accounts in a given period, renew Y accounts, and so on. He will then be appraised on his success in achieving these objectives.

But the new trend is to apply MBO to measure job performance where goals are not as easily quantified.

Of course, MBO can't cure all the problems of evaluating performance. The personalities of employees will still need to be taken into account, especially when they interfere with work. Employees will still take issue with supervisory evaluations. And, for that matter, some managers will still fail to shed their subjective judgments.

Observers of MBO in action have noted these additional problems:

Heel-dragging participation. In one company that tried to pursue an MBO program, resistance showed up during the orientation workshops. Some recalcitrants were insecure managers, afraid to give up the comfortable old ways. Others were afraid to be under the spotlight of having to tell their superiors what results they would achieve. And there were others who had been on plateaus. They weren't happy about having to stretch themselves —which MBO forces on a manager.

The participation of some managers was only half-hearted. As one executive observed: "They would get a business call and have to leave. Or they would prolong the talk about the need for objectives so as not to have to write any. We encountered many delaying tactics."

The setting of low standards. In discussions with his boss, the subordinate sometimes committed himself to objectives that involved no challenge, hoping thereby to overachieve.

One executive reports on these situations, "Men would become embarrassed, found difficulty talking about their conceptions—or misconceptions—of the job. Or a superior and a subordinate would both get embarrassed because both had misunderstood the subordinate's job. Sometimes the subordinate and his boss would realize, simultaneously, that the boss had failed as a manager— because he had not communicated what was expected of the subordinate."

The problem of quantification. The difficulty in quantifying objectives can be a big stumbling block. For example, an executive of the Internal Revenue Service's New York office commented, "We tried to implement MBO for our group supervisors. But we found it difficult to set an objective for morale and attitude, which are the two most important contributions of our people." There are other jobs for which morale, willingness, call it what you will, is important. This can be a soft spot in management by objectives.

Clearly, the value of MBO is largely comparative. But it is still superior to past methods for goal setting and performance measure. Until a better tool comes along, it is likely that MBO will continue to be adopted by more companies in the future.

2. The managerial grid

The behavioral scientist's basic premise is that the individual does not exist in isolation. He is part of a whole situation—a work culture—and management can do a better job of effecting permanent change in both the individual and the organization by attempting to change the whole situation rather than just the individual.

Dr. Robert R. Blake and Dr. Jane S. Mouton, professors at the University of Texas and associates in the management-consulting firm of Scientific Methods, Inc., Austin, Texas, have developed an approach based on a so-called organic theory of change.[1] They reject a static,

[1] Robert R. Blake and Jane S. Mouton, *The Managerial Grid* (Gulf Publishing Co., 1964).

mechanistic view of the organization, seeing it, rather, as a developing set of interdependent *networks of people*. Their main emphasis, therefore, is on improving work relationships.

Dr. Blake and his associates feel that the most effective type of management is that of an integrated team operation, from the standpoint both of production and of an organization's ability to adapt swiftly and appropriately to rapidly changing conditions.

The "managerial grid" approach (see the illustration)

THE MANAGERIAL GRID

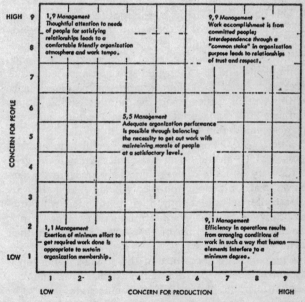

has two basic premises: (*a*) A manager or management can be measured according to two variables—a concern for people and a concern for production; (*b*) the best management is team management. If one accepts these premises, then the grid can be useful in analyzing the manager's efforts as well as those of his subordinates.

On the grid, "concern for people" is measured vertically on a line divided into nine sections; "concern for production" is measured horizontally on a line similarly divided. The resulting grid has 81 "positions" which can be used to delineate various styles of leadership. Here are major styles discussed by the authors:

Task management. Down in the lower right-hand corner of the grid, one finds 9,1 management. It is characterized by strong emphasis on the *task* to be performed. People in themselves are of little consequence except to the extent that they impede or further production. They are there to be used, somewhat like machines, and they should be replaced if they don't function effectively.

This type of leadership is strictly authoritarian. Subordinates are expected to carry out their orders unquestioningly and all conflict is suppressed. As a result, subordinates tend to lose initiative, their creative approach to problems, and any increased skill and knowledge they develop is likely to remain untapped. One consequence of this type of leadership is the "gradual shift of many working and managerial persons in the direction of a 1,1 accommodation."

Country-club management. Country-club management, located at 1,9 in the upper left-hand corner of the grid, is the very opposite of task management. Here the emphasis is all on people, the theory being that if they are kept contented and happy, high production will automatically follow. But whether production follows or not, the attitudes and feelings of people "are valuable in their own right. They come first."

One possible consequence of this style of leadership is that production will suffer at the expense of harmonious human relations. But even here, conflicts are likely to be smoothed over and buried rather than resolved. And when this type of organization is called upon to increase efficiency, it is frequently unable to respond. As a result, over the long haul, it tends to succumb to competitive pressures.

Impoverished management. Impoverished management, located in the lower left-hand corner of the grid, couples low concern for production with low concern for people. This type of manager does just enough to get by. To all intents and purposes, he is "out of it." He avoids involvement and concern because this "can only lead to deeper frustration and discouragement."

An organization is seldom managed this way, because, as Mouton and Blake point out, "a business operated under 1,1 concepts would be unable to survive very long." But an individual can sometimes persist for quite a long time as a 1,1 manager in a bureaucratic or country-club atmosphere. However, it's a situation of failure, not only for the individual but for the company, since it involves the loss of a "potential productive contribution."

Dampened-pendulum management. In the middle of the grid at 5,5 is located the middle of the road or dampened-pendulum type of management. It avoids swinging to the extremes of 9,1 or 1,9. The 5,5 manager is aware of a conflict between people and production and tries to effect a happy compromise, to play it safe by not over-emphasizing one or the other. Real problems are apt to be muted, and the climate is frequently paternalistic.

While 5,5 management is likely to be superior to any of the extremes mentioned so far, it, too, has its limitations. According to the authors, "5,5 provides a poor basis for promoting innovation, creativity, discovery and novelty. All of these are likely to be sacrificed by the adherence to tradition and 'majority' standards of conduct. Long term, then, the 5,5 or status quo, results in a gradual slipping behind as more flexible, progressive organizations take advantage of new opportunities or better management practices."

Team management. The obvious goal of good management lies in the upper right-hand corner of the grid at 9,9. Here there is a high concern for both people *and* production. The result is a team approach to management where the "needs of people to think, to apply mental effort in productive work and to establish sound and mature relationships . . . with one another are utilized to accomplish organizational requirements."

Some of the gains attributed by the authors to a

change toward 9,9 management are: *(a)* increased profitability, *(b)* improvement of intergroup relations, *(c)* more effective use of team action, *(d)* reduced frictions and increased understanding among individuals, and *(e)* increased individual effort and creativity and personal commitment to work.

In short, under team management, "the needs of individuals to be engaged in meaningful interdependent effort mesh with the organization requirements for excellent performance."

The managerial grid is a tool to help analyze one's managerial style, the styles of other managers or the total management of a company. It's a way of structuring one's thinking about styles of management and, as such, both an analytical and a constructive tool.

Related to the managerial grid in that it also provides deeper insights into management is "selective leadership." This approach, though older than the managerial grid, continues to have adherents in the management world and, for personal reasons, has special value in the eyes of this author.

3. Selective leadership

Should a manager approach an experienced subordinate in the same way as a novice? Should one manage a group of laborers the same way as one might a group of scientists? What difference—if any—does the personality of a subordinate make in his boss's approach to him?

In the early 1950s, this author developed a systematic approach to leadership. The business community accepted it as a long-felt answer to a basic need (as evidenced by multiple printings of the volume setting forth the concept and translations into six languages).[2]

The concepts and practices that make up selective leadership derive from key experiments by psychologist Kurt Lewin at the University of Iowa. To explore the nature of leadership, Lewin set up experimental groups

---

[2] Auren Uris, *How to Be a Successful Leader* (New York: McGraw-Hill, 1953). Paperback edition published under the title *Techniques of Leadership,* 1964, also by McGraw-Hill.

of two sorts:

One type was dominated by an "autocratic" leader. He determined policy, decided what was to be done and how, assigned tasks and chose work companies for each member. He was highly personal in his praise, criticism and general comments.

The second type was led by a "democratic" leader. He brought up matters of policy for group discussion, encouraged group members to choose their own work companies and was highly "objective" in his comments.

Then came an unexpected development: Observers noticed that an individual playing the role of democratic leader created an atmosphere different from that of other democratic leaders. He exercised virtually no control over the group; he permitted group members to shift for themselves; he let them tackle problems unaided as best they could. The group's response to this technique was so different from the reactions of other democratic groups that Lewin set up a third kind of group under leadership which he termed "laissez-faire."

Significant differences emerged in atmosphere, behavior, feelings and accomplishments:

Autocratic. Group members were quarrelsome and aggressive. Some individuals became completely dependent upon the leader. When the leader was absent, activity tended to stop altogether. Work progressed at only a fair rate.

Democratic. The individuals got along with one another on a friendly basis. Relations with the leader were freer, more spontaneous. The work progressed smoothly and continued even when the leader was absent.

Laissez-faire. Work progressed haphazardly and at a slow rate. Although there was considerable activity, much of it was unproductive. Considerable time was lost in arguments and discussions between group members on a purely personal basis.

Actually, each method has built-in strengths and weaknesses; *each* method has its value. The three methods developed in the University of Iowa investigations provide the framework of the selective-leadership approach, welding the Lewin concepts into a unified and systematic method.

Using the selective-leadership approach, the manager *selects* the most appropriate of the three tools:

Autocratic leadership. The leader mainly seeks obedience from his group. He determines policy and considers decision making a one-man operation—he, of course, being the one man.

Democratic leadership. The leader draws ideas and suggestions from the group by discussion and consultation. Group members are encouraged to take part in the setting of policy. The leader's job is largely that of moderator.

Free-rein leadership. (Lewin's laissez-faire method.) The leader functions more or less as an information booth. He plays down his role in the group's activity. He exercises a minimum of control.

These definitions provide the basis for a systematic approach to leading people. Autocratic, democratic or free-rein methods may be considered as *three tools* of the management leader. Contrary to common belief, the three approaches are *not* mutually exclusive. No one has to choose among using autocratic, democratic or free-rein methods. That would be like telling a golf player he must choose between using a driver or a putter; in the course of a game, he will use *both*.

Note Manager X in action:

He *directs* (autocratic method) his secretary to make a report.

He *consults* (democratic method) with his employees on the best way to push a special order through the shop.

He *suggests* (free-rein method) to his assistant that it would be a good idea to figure out ways in which special orders may be handled more smoothly in the future.

This type of leadership suggests that mastery lies in knowing *when* to use *which* method. In short, selective leadership is a logical adaptation of autocratic, democratic and free-rein techniques to appropriate situations.

Once the three basic approaches are understood, it remains only for the manager to learn to suit the appropriate approach to a given situation. For example, the personality factor is taken into account in this fashion:

The hostile subordinate. With an individual of this type, the *autocratic* method is likely to be most effective. While he resents authority, he respects it at the same time. Accordingly, his hostility must be met by a show of authority. The autocratic approach has the effect of channeling his aggressions, confining his energies to constructive ends.

The group-minded individual. The subordinate who is team-minded, who enjoys "team play," will probably function best if led by *democratic* techniques. He needs less direction, regards work as a group job and is willing to accept group goals as personal ones.

The individualist, the solo player. He usually thrives best under the *free-rein* type of leadership. He likes to develop his own methods and ideas; the more he is given his head, the greater freedom he has to mobilize his creativity.

In addition to adapting to the personality factors of a situation, selective leadership also takes into account the nature of the response the manager seeks in any given context. For example:

Compliance. If the subordinate or group is working along routine lines, with well-established goals, the *autocratic* method is appropriate.

Cooperation. A rush order may put a group under pressure to perform above standard. Calling the group together, describing the nature of the crisis, asking for help and suggestions are *democratic* techniques that will best help meet objectives.

Creativity. Productivity can be stimulated slightly by autocratic means, considerably by democratic approaches. But creativity poses different problems. When novel ideas are sought and imagination is needed, the *free-rein* approach is usually most effective.

So much for the selective-leadership concept. The next man-managing tool to be discussed, unlike the previous ones, is aimed at the total work group of a company. It developed out of the need for higher and higher quality performance because of the extremely close tolerances in aircraft and spacecraft manufacture.

4. Zero defects

"Zero defects" made a glamorous entrance on the management stage. It caught the imagination—and the backing—of thousands of managers who were on the alert for ways and means of improving quality. Objectives were clear: the complete elimination of defective operations, a reject rate of 0 percent.

Originated at the Martin Company's Orlando Division in 1962, ZD sought to achieve quality perfection by enlisting the cooperation of all employees. ZD, says Martin's director of quality, was a massive program of motivation. "We superimposed it on our normal inspection process," continued the director, James F. Halpin, "so that we weren't just looking for errors. We wanted to prevent mistakes." Thus, "Do it right the first time" became ZD's slogan.

In a zero-defects program, as created by Martin and adapted by hundreds of other companies, every man and woman on the roster is told of the importance of product quality, made aware of his personal role in quality and shown opportunities for reward in exchange for quality performance.

Many large companies like Martin, General Electric and Lockheed have adopted a zero-defects program to back up their conventional quality-control work. The idea, in the words of one manager, is "to make a dramatic and continuing effort to convince every employee of the importance of product quality and make him fully aware of his role in the company's total performance."

Successful zero-defects programs combine theatrical ballyhoo and down-to-earth persuasion. Typically, they are kicked off with speeches by the company's top executive, posters and pamphlets, pledge cards signed by employees and contests designed to reward individuals and departments that achieve error-free production.

The following are just two of the many techniques that have been effectively used in some of the current zero-defects programs:

Reexamining all written work instructions to make sure that they are expressed in language that is easy to understand and requires a minimum of interpretation.

Setting aside a period every week when the men in a department get together with the foreman to talk over suggestions or ways of cutting down rejects.

Of course, techniques like these are already used in many companies as a matter of routine. But the process of organizing them as part of a program that generates excitement seems to make them dramatically more effective. General Electric, for example, claims that a zero-defects drive at its Lynn, Massachusetts, plant turned up 4500 possibilities for cutting errors, and about 4000 of them were put into effect.

After only three or four years of wide acceptance and popularity for zero defects in management circles, an interesting development took place. Critics and detractors publicly voiced the feeling that zero defects, the approach that was getting all-out treatment from so many quarters, was not what it was cracked up to be. They said:

Zero defects is mostly hoopla, an employee-relations circus.

It overemphasizes the contributions that employees really can make to quality control.

It's a poor substitute for good engineering.

It turns operators into inspectors, and inspectors who carry their mistakes home in their lunch pails.

That a particular man-managing tool developed apparent flaws is interesting but not of any special significance—except to illustrate one fact. A rise and fall in popularity is *typical of this category of tools*. This is most clearly seen in the fate of another technique that was yesterday's darling, but today is rarely mentioned and still less used.

5. Brainstorming—birth and death of a concept

A few years ago, every company that was "up" on the

newest in management techniques conducted brainstorming sessions to solve its problems. Essentially, brainstorming was the brainchild of Alex F. Osborn, cofounder
of the giant advertising agency Batten, Barton, Durstine
and Osborn, and had its beginnings in the early 1930s.
But it was not until 1953, with the publication of Osborn's *Applied Imagination*,[3] referred to by some as the
"bible of brainstorming," that the virtues of the technique began to echo through management's paneled halls.

Organization after organization went all out for the
idea gusher represented by the Osborn approach. Looking back, it's easy to understand why. As American enterprise became increasingly technical in character, company
after company began a search for new ideas to hasten
the development of products, processes and procedures.
What a godsend to come at last upon a simple, easy
method! No need any longer to probe the complexities
of the psyche, to look into the causes of creativity. Brainstorming was *the* answer.

The proponents of brainstorming gave "the word" in
a few simple sentences:

Get yourself a conference room, a conference leader and
a group of conferees.

Pick a problem, preferably one that is particular rather
than general. Osborn suggests, "A problem like 'how
to introduce a new synthetic fabric' is too broad. This
should be broken down into at least three subproblems,
such as: *(a)* 'ideas for introducing the new fiber to
weavers and mills,' *(b)* 'ideas for introducing the new
fiber to dress houses and cutters,' and *(c)* 'ideas for
introducing the new fiber to retailers.' "

Once the problem has been set before the group, instruct
the conferees not to hold back, to speak up as soon as
an idea comes to mind.

Tell the conferees to suspend critical judgment, not to
use any "killer phrases," sounds or signs that might
indicate disapproval.

Strive for quantity; the more ideas the better. "Quantity helps breed quality," say the brainstormers.

---

[3] Alex F. Osborn, *Applied Imagination* (New York: Scribner's, 1953).

However, the hope that brainstorming would become the major tool for promoting creativity and solving problems slowly faded. Two things cut the props from under the movement. The first was an assault from academic circles suggesting that brainstorming was merely a gimmick that produced no more or better ideas than a well-disciplined individual could produce on his own. Then companies which had been employing the technique, once their suspicions were raised, decided that the brainstorming apparatus was more trouble than it was worth.

The point is that what happened to brainstorming, and is happening to zero defects, is more or less a typical development in the area of man-managing tools. The "life cycle" of a management idea of this type has been analyzed and charted:[4]

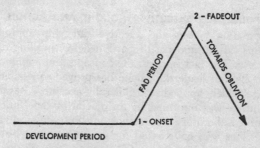

The three phases indicated may vary in length, but points 1 and 2 are standard:

1. *Onset.* The fad or popularity period is brought on by a favorable study or report. A company applies the idea and claims favorable results. The word gets around, one way or the other. The attention of management is caught and the fad takes hold. The "infection" is spread by articles, seminars, meetings.

2. *Fade-out.* Critics arise who begin taking potshots at the concept on theoretical or practical grounds or both. The "antis" show the faultiness of the idea. The shiny new concept begins to tarnish in the public's eye.

In short, the tools considered in this chapter—man-

[4] Auren Uris, *The Management Makers* (New York: Macmillan Co., 1962).

agement by objectives, and so on—can be said to represent the art of management. And, like art, these developments enjoy a waxing and waning of popularity, often regardless of any positive or objective values they may have.

Therefore, one may look forward to the appearance and disappearance of man-managing tools over the next decades, as the spotlight of management interest and sense of need shifts. And the behavioral scientists, whose studies and inspirations are often the seed of these approaches, will undoubtedly continue to supply the ideas and concepts that unfortunately cater to a kind of management hypochondria and a yearning for a miracle panacea for a frustrating ailment—the aches and pains of managing people.

POINTS FOR EXECUTIVE THOUGHT AND ACTION

As a developer of the selective-leadership approach, perhaps this author can be pardoned for dwelling on it at length. The fact is, of all the concepts and approaches in the field of leadership, none has proved so flexible or been so widely applied and generally accepted. Recently the author was informed by an official of the National Training Laboratory that participants in sensitivity-training sessions who have asked for guidance in the leadership field are advised to read *How to Be a Successful Leader,* the book in which selective leadership has been described at length.

Accordingly, with the hope that the insights provided can be of direct and practical benefit, two self-rating quizzes, "What type of leader are you?" and "What kind of follower are you?" are provided here exactly as they appear in *How to Be a Successful Leader* (and its paperback counterpart, *Techniques of Leadership*).

What type of leader are you?

Are you naturally an autocratic, democratic or free-rein leader? The following quiz can reveal to you in approximate terms the type of leader you naturally tend to be:

Yes No

1. Do you enjoy "running the show"? ☐ ☐

2. Generally, do you think it's worth the time and effort to explain the reasons for a decision or policy before putting it into effect? ☐ ☐

3. Do you prefer the administrative end of your leadership job—planning, paper work, and so on—to supervising or working directly with your subordinates? ☐ ☐

4. A stranger comes into your department and you know he's the new employee hired by one of your assistants. On approaching him, would you first ask *his* name rather than introduce yourself? ☐ ☐

5. Do you keep your people up to date on developments affecting the group, as a matter of course? ☐ ☐

6. Do you find that in giving out assignments, you tend to state the goals, leave methods to your subordinates? ☐ ☐

7. Do you think that it's good common sense for a leader to keep aloof from his people, because in the long run familiarity breeds lessened respect? ☐ ☐

8. Comes time to decide about a group outing. You've heard that the majority prefer to have it on Wednesday, but you're pretty sure Thursday would be better for all concerned. Would you put the question to a vote rather than make the decision yourself? ☐ ☐

9. If you had your way, would you make running your group a push-button affair, with personal contacts and communications held to a minimum? ☐ ☐

10. Do you find it fairly easy to fire someone? ☐ ☐

11. Do you feel that the friendlier you are with your people, the better you'll be able to lead them? ☐ ☐

12. After considerable time, you dope out the

Yes   No

answer to a work problem. You pass along the solution to an assistant who pokes it full of holes. Would you be annoyed that the problem is still unsolved rather than become angry with the assistant? □ □

13. Do you agree that one of the best ways to avoid problems of discipline is to provide adequate punishments for violations of rules? □ □

14. Your way of handling a situation is being criticized. Would you try to sell your viewpoint to your group rather than make it clear that, as boss, your decisions are final? □ □

15. Do you generally leave it up to your subordinates to contact you as far as informal, day-to-day communications are concerned? □ □

16. Do you feel that everyone in your group should have a certain amount of personal loyalty to you? □ □

17. Do you favor the practice of appointing committees to settle a problem rather than stepping in to decide on it yourself? □ □

18. Some experts say differences of opinion within a work group are healthy. Others feel that they indicate basic flaws in group unity. Do you agree with the first view? □ □

Your score

To get your score, indicate the number of yes answers you had for the following groups; that is, circle the question numbers 1–18 to which you answered yes.

    I: 1, 4, 7, 10, 13, 16
   II: 2, 5, 8, 11, 14, 17
  III: 3, 6, 9, 12, 15, 18

If you had the most yes answers in Group I, chances are you tend to be an autocratic leader.

If your total of yes answers was highest in Group II, you probably have a predisposition toward being a democratic leader.

If Group III is the one in which you show the greatest

number of yes answers, you are probably inclined to be a free-rein leader.

Evaluating the results

Regardless of what score you made, don't think of it as either good or bad. For one thing, the test was not designed to grade you on a good-bad scale. But even more to the point, the condition itself, the degree to which a person tends toward one of the three basic leadership approaches, should not be thought of in terms of good or bad.

The test helps you establish a starting point for your thinking. It provides a base from which you can take a fresh look at your leadership practices from the viewpoint of your own emotional needs.

Accordingly, your score is neither a judgment on your past performance nor an omen of the future. The fact, for example, that in the past you've generally operated as a democratic leader while the test results indicate a leaning toward autocracy doesn't mean you've been "wrong." Nor would this result mean it's desirable for you to switch to autocratic methods.

What the test can give you is food for thought and, subsequently, a basis for making alterations in your leadership behavior, if this seems desirable.

What kind of follower are you?

You won't find it easy to arrive at judgments of your subordinates on which to base your leadership approach. People are complex. In the final analysis, they often defy the cleverest system of tags yet devised. Changes in the objective situation also can cause variations in both their attitudes and behavior.

But it is possible to gain a great deal of insight into this problem by considering *your own feelings* about leadership. Whether or not you now work under a superior, you probably have done so in the past. Analyzing your own feelings and reactions to leadership can give you the best possible approach to understanding your subordinates.

Answer the following questions, keeping in mind what

you have done, or feel you actually would do, in the situations described.

Yes No

1. When given an assignment, do you like to have all the details spelled out? □ □

2. Do you think that, by and large, most bosses are bossier than they need be? □ □

3. Would you say that initiative is one of your stronger points? □ □

4. Do you feel a boss lowers himself by palling around with his subordinates? □ □

5. In general, would you prefer working with others to working alone? □ □

6. Would you say you prefer the pleasures of solitude (reading, listening to music) to the social pleasures of being with others (parties, get-togethers, etc.)? □ □

7. Do you tend to become strongly attached to the boss you work under? □ □

8. Do you tend to offer a helping hand to the newcomers among your colleagues and fellow workers? □ □

9. Do you enjoy using your own ideas and ingenuity to solve a work problem? □ □

10. Do you prefer the kind of boss who knows all the answers to one who, not infrequently, comes to you for help? □ □

11. Do you feel it's OK for your boss to be friendlier with some members of the group than with others? □ □

12. Do you like to assume full responsibility for assignments rather than just do the work and leave the responsibility to your boss? □ □

13. Do you feel that "mixed" groups—men working with women, for example—naturally tend to have more friction than unmixed ones? □ □

14. If you learned your boss was having an affair with his secretary, would your respect for him remain undiminished? □ □

Yes No

15. Have you always felt that "he travels fastest who travels alone"? ☐ ☐

16. Would you agree that a boss who couldn't win your loyalty shouldn't be a boss? ☐ ☐

17. Would you get upset by a colleague whose inability or ineptitude obstructs the work of your division or company as a whole? ☐ ☐

18. Do you think *boss* is a dirty word? ☐ ☐

To get your score, indicate the number of yes answers you had for the following questions:

  I: 1, 4, 7, 10, 13, 16
 II: 2, 5, 8, 11, 14, 17
III: 3, 6, 9, 12, 15, 18

Analyzing your score

If you had the most yes answers in Group I, chances are you prefer autocratic leadership.

If your total of yes answers was highest in Group II, you probably have a predisposition toward democratic leadership.

If Group III is the one in which you show the most yes answers, free-rein leadership is your preference.

If your score shows no preponderance of yes answers under *any* one of the three groups, the indication is that you're unusually flexible—so much so that you could adapt equally well to any type of leader. Another possibility is that your experience or predisposition is such as to make the role of follower more difficult for you than for most people.

Your experience with this quiz can be of considerable help in suiting your leadership to the emotional needs of your subordinates. Relate your score to your attitude toward authority and you'll get some idea as to how *many of your people feel about you*.

ELEVEN/THE EXECUTIVE AS COMPUTER USER

Contemporary news media verify the extent to which computers have pervaded our society—in business and out:

The weekly Dow Jones newspaper, *The National Observer*, on September 11, 1967, front-paged a story, *Wooing Voters with a Computer*. The item states:

"Winthrop Rockefeller keeps a secret weapon in room 440 of the Tower Building here. It's an IBM 1401 computer whose attachments include a 1402 reader, a 1403 printer, two 1311 disk drives, a document-roll input and a document converter. Mr. Rockefeller's aides freely admit that without the computer (and all those exotic spare parts), he would never have been elected governor in 1966. And it's partly because of the computer that he's a heavy favorite to be reelected next year."

(Apparently, it was the computer's analysis of the electorate that enabled Rockefeller's organization to plan and pursue campaign objectives most precisely.)

The Columbia Broadcasting System devoted two weekly segments of its TV feature *The 21st Century* to the impact that the computer is having on everything from education to space flight.

The business pages of the *New York Times* of May 4, 1967, reported a talk by Russell H. Colley, a New York management consultant, to European audiences, the gist of which was, "The electronic computer will have the greatest impact on advertising since its electronic cousins, radio and television."

The importance of such phenomena as the three just mentioned is that they are not isolated instances but rather a representative sample. Every week dozens of major stories about one or another application or advance of computers fill our newspapers and business journals and ride the airwaves.

What's the problem?

Admittedly, it isn't difficult to make a strong case for the wide application and the important future of the computer. However, that fact simply underlines the problem: Granted that the computer is a crucial tool for the executive, how does he catch up with this galloping phenomenon? How does he go about getting answers for his simplest but most personalized questions about the implications the "thinking machine" has for him and his job?

Offhand, one might think such questions would find easy answers. Rivers of printing ink have been spilled in the cause of disseminating information about computers, presumably to tell the public what it wants to know. Books, magazine features, monographs, films pour down on the public; yet, somehow, the thirst isn't satisfied. There seem to be three reasons:

The subject *isn't simple*. The computer isn't like a typewriter or tape recorder. Even in its simplest form, it is complex in its actual workings. It is difficult for the average individual to conceive what is going on when the tapes spin and the punched cards flow.

The field is in a *state of flux*. Each year finds new refinements and new equipment added to a rapidly growing catalog. And the additions mean new capabilities, new services—added to a list that has already grown long.

Experience in applications *varies*. One learns from interviewing the experts—management consultants, executives with firsthand familiarity with computers—that there have been failures as well as successful applications, that some types of equipment have been erroneously installed, that competition among manufacturers will sometimes result in unsuitable applications for the sake of a sale. Accordingly, two conflicting pictures clash: on one hand, the practically omnipotent computer; on the other, the abused, unsuccessful machine. How to make sense out of the contradictory evidence?

And there is a fourth reason that, although subtle, may actually be the most important influence of all. The entire subject of computers has developed an emotional aura that in some cases has paralyzed or at least distorted management observations and evaluation.

"I've found managers—even those at the top—developing a strong allergy to computers," says one authority. The manager who feels his job—or his business way of life—threatened by an EDP installation can't be expected to view it objectively.

A simplified approach

Since we have stressed at some length the difficulties of the subject, it follows logically that only the most limited objectives are intended for this chapter. Certainly, comprehensiveness is not the aim. The approach to be used was suggested by a vice-president of operations of a large chemical company. He has seen both failures and success in the use of electronic data-processing systems and equipment and consequently has developed rather iconoclastic views.

"So you're going to write about the use of computers," said the vice-president of operations. "What makes you think you will be any more successful than the others?"

The vice-president has a point. One can read through mountains of management literature and emerge with only the foggiest idea of what a computer is, how it operates, what its significance is for the business community and, finally, how it affects or *can* affect the manager in his day-to-day job.

One trap into which "the others" tend to fall is the temptation to "tell all." Obviously, within ordinary limitations, it's impossible to do justice to so vast and dynamic a subject. Accordingly, in the paragraphs and pages ahead are 12 questions and answers that seek to cover key aspects of the subject. These questions have in large part originated from conversations with managers who have suggested individual questions that to them represent the most puzzling or most interesting aspects of the computer.

Question 1: Can you provide a brief thumbnail history of the computer?

Answer: There are two main types of computers. The one generally meant and under discussion here is the *digital* computer. The *analog* computer is a different type of machine with different capabilities. The analog computer measures relationships, solves equations and presents the solution as a continuous record, since it is *analogous* to the condition or situation to which it relates.

A digital computer, on the other hand, is a high-speed machine that counts electronic impulses. But although this is what it does essentially, when the electronic impulses are given specific values which can be manipulated according to a given program, the result is a high-speed ingestion of information and an output of "answers" relating to scientific, business or other problems.

The computer first came on the scene in 1944. Before that, a few slow, bulky and unreliable machines were built with mechanically related parts. A breakthrough was made in 1944 when an electronic machine was developed by Howard Aiken at Harvard University. This machine, developed for the International Business Machines Corporation, used punched cards. Although its theory was sound, its bulk and the undependability of the vacuum tubes on which its operation depended were too great a handicap. Two years later, researchers at the University of Pennsylvania completed an electronic computer called ENIAC. About the same time, IBM produced the first practical commercial electronic calculator, which came to be known as the IBM 604, and deliveries of this unit to customers were started in 1948.

Many people in many places were working independently on EDP hardware development. In the decade from 1950 to 1960, although IBM continued as the major producer of equipment, competition among equipment producers resulted in an extraordinarily rapid advancement in the production and capability of EDP equipment.

Question 2: There are two words that keep cropping up in articles on computers that are seldom made clear—what do the terms "hardware" and "software" mean?

Answer: Hardware refers to the physical equipment of the computer. A number of key units are linked together to form the system. These units constitute the following:

The central processing unit. This serves the arithmetic and internal-storage functions. It is used to house the program and the material the program is acting upon. (The capacity of the internal-storage unit is a primary factor in determining the power of the computer.) It also directs the other units toward the steps to be performed.

Input units. Data can be entered into the computer through terminals located thousands of miles away or through nearby units. Wherever they are located, the input units also serve as external storage.

Output units. These serve the function of getting the processed information out of the computer. They include the printer, magnetic-tape units and equipment for graphic display. (The latter two also can be used in connection with input.)

Software is the trade's term for programming and programming systems. For example, a program for a desired type of inventory control is software. So is a computer language system such as FORTRAN (Formula Translation) or COBOL (Common Business-Oriented Language), which permits computer users to use the terminology they're most familiar with in helping to prepare programs. FORTRAN is designed mainly for engineers and scientific people, COBOL for general business use.

Some observers feel that the future of computer usage lies at least as much with the software as with the hardware. According to the editors of *Fortune:*

"To an appreciable extent, the computer revolution

has become a revolution in software. Given a good machine, a system of suitably assembled electronic parts, everything depends on how it is used and what is put into it. In a sense, a computer represents an unrealized potential, something to be shaped by man's ideas. Roughly speaking, software is for a computer what education is for a child." [1]

One element of software that has become a viable product on its own is the computer program. Many companies have learned that both time and money can be saved by acquiring computer programs that have been developed by other firms, institutions, the government, and so on. Similarly, companies can market their own programs as one means of maximizing their return on computer investment.

Traditionally, most programs have been available from manufacturers of computer hardware, others from a nationwide computer-program rental service. Now a publication has been started which acts as a clearinghouse for programs—the *ICP Quarterly*.

The lists of programs available in the publication include this pertinent information: title of the program, hardware configuration, programming language, number of programs, terms, price and whom to contact. Under "Programs Wanted," an example of a listing reads as follows: "Accounts Receivable and Sales Analysis. IBM 360 Mod 30—Tape and Disk."

The catalog consists mainly of three kinds of programs: scientific, commercial and utility (the latter being those that are related to the operation of data-processing equipment, such as for sorting functions). Most of the programs can be obtained by leasing, making royalty payments or by outright purchase.

Question 3: Have managers' early fears of the computer subsided?

Answer: For the younger manager without a vested interest in the status quo, the computer represents no

---

[1] Gilbert Burck and the editors of *Fortune, The Computer Age and Its Potential for Management* (New York: Harper & Row, 1965).

threat of change. The reaction is different with the older men. Many of these still resist and resent the computer.

Frank H. Hawthorne, a systems specialist for General Electric, asserts, "The trouble with a good many managers is that they cannot appreciate something new. They just will not adapt to the new sciences." [2]

Hawthorne then goes on to describe his attempt to help a top marketing executive become aware of the computer's potential: "You might think that he would have been prepared with enough simple math to at least recognize some of the computer's potential for solving marketing programs. But he was not. Unfortunately, his ostrich attitude is all too typical of today's middle manager."

The *Dun's* article then goes on to say, *"Hawthorne's is one of a growing chorus of voices that are expressing disenchantment these days over industry's largely unimaginative, and surprisingly negative, response to the challenge of the tireless robot brain. The fact is that behind the closed doors of the business world, a silent but nonetheless bitter battle is being waged. It is not too much to say that today's middle manager is often tense, worried and trying by almost any means at his disposal— in a few cases, actual sabotage—to short-circuit the electronic newcomer. In trying to preserve at all costs a comfortable status quo, he is foolishly creating internal problems so knotty for many a company that top executives think they may take years to solve."*

Question 4: Exactly why do managers, even those with supposedly strong job security, view the computer as a monster?

Answer: With or without justification, the computer is viewed by some people and in some quarters as a primal threat. Complains one systems analyst, "I find many executives who feel the same way about the computer as primitive man felt about lightning. They don't understand it; they're afraid of it and endow it with supernatural powers."

Setting aside this free-floating fear of computers, there are other complications that prevent some managers from treating the computer as what it really is, a managerial tool with a vast potential for helpfulness:

Resistance of the comfortable. "I'm only going to be around for a few more years," explains one production manager quite candidly. "There's no point in my getting all involved in new methods and equipment." In short, some managers, justifiably or otherwise, "cannot be bothered" to adjust to the changes that computerization involves.

Resistance to dependency. "I know what I'm talking about," insists one manager. "Once we get a computer in here, we've got to change everything to suit that damned machine. I don't want to be dependent on a piece of hardware. I want to feel that I have some job latitude. Frankly, I enjoy playing my hunches. When you bring a computer into the business, you change the game."

Another executive with a somewhat similar feeling points to another aspect of computerization with alarm:

"Victimized by programmers." One businessman whose knowledge of computers is based on his observations of a friend's business operations said, "I visited Pete the other day and he was having a session with a group of his computer people. It was the most ridiculous and disheartening sight I have ever seen. Literally, they didn't understand one another. He was talking *business* and they were talking *computerese.* I'm afraid the others one-upped old Pete. They very quickly made him feel like a dunce who didn't know what he was talking about, a kindergarten kid who had stumbled into a seminar on astrophysics."

Question 5: How rapidly is the technology of the computer developing?

Answer: With extreme rapidity. One authority has indicated that if airplane technology had developed at the same rate of speed as the computer, we would have gone from Kitty Hawk to jet planes in eight years.

One particular reason for the rapid development of

the computer is that it's the very opposite of a one-purpose tool. It can be used for purposes ranging from producing mail-order lists to solving abstract scientific problems. And each area of application is a front on which further advances are being made.

As varied as the applications of the computer are today, as great as are the changes that computerization brings about in a company, these are merely the beginnings of more profound developments. Every indication promises further change—new hardware coming out in a continuous stream, new applications, and software also constantly proliferating.

The chart on pages 194–195 lists four generations of machines. And these, it must be remembered, have appeared within a scant two decades.

Question 6: One way of taking some of the mystery out of the computer is to spell out the backgrounds of some typical "computer experts," that is, executives who work directly with computers. Can you supply a thumbnail description of a few of these?

Answer: Consultations with executive recruiters who have placed executives of this type have turned up the following four case histories:

Manager A. Man aged 38 with two degrees in business, bachelor's and master's. Started out as systems analyst with a large industrial company, continued in that same function with another company for two years, and spent two years with one of the large management-consulting firms. Then spent the following three years with two different large publishing companies as corporate manager of systems and EDP. For the last four years he has had a similar job, with the title "Corporate Manager, Systems Procedures and Programming," with a very large textile firm.

Manager B. Man aged 45 who has two degrees in business. Spent four years with two different public-accounting firms. For the last 15 years has been with a large steel company working as staff accountant, supervisor of analysis and statistics, assistant manager, accounting systems and procedure services. Last six years of that period he has been corporate manager, data-processing services.

Manager C. Man aged 39 with two business degrees. Spent first three years as a systems analyst with a large chemical company. Spent following six years with one of the large consulting firms in systems and EDP work. For the last four years has been manager of corporate systems and programming with a large consumer manufacturing company.

Manager D. Man aged 38, undergraduate degree in mechanical engineering, MIT; MBA from Harvard Business College. Spent eight years with a large consumer products company, first in mechanical-engineering work and then was shifted to their computer operations in the controller's department, where he spent the majority of the eight-year period. Moved ten years ago to one of the very largest of the oil companies and has remained in the computer field. Is now in charge of the total computer and systems operations for one of the large area operations of EDP. Carries the title of "Assistant Controller."

One of the executive recruiters supplying the above information made two additional comments: "A man of forty-five is unusual in such a group. Most of them are in their thirties." And, "Most of the universities that have business colleges have added management sciences, that is, computers and operations research, to the curriculum."

Question 7: How does a company know whether it needs a computer or computer service?

Answer: First, remember that the main function of a digital-computer system is to process data. It does this for two reasons: *(a)* to handle paper work faster, more economically, more effectively than before; *(b)* to provide faster, more extensive, more accurate information on which management decisions can be based.

However, knowing what the computer can do is only half the story. The other factor has to do with how im-

Four Computer Generations and How They Differ

Computer Generation	Some Distinguishing Technical Features	Systems Approach	Level of Systems	Benefits	Environment Required
1st Generation	Vacuum tubes Punched cards Limited magnetic core Machine language coding	Conversion of existing applications	Accounting Clerical	Savings in personnel displacement Absorption of future work load due to expansion Increased accuracy Procedurization	Pioneering attitude Procedurization Knowledge of existing methods Investment in new tools
2nd Generation	Transistors Magnetic tape Expanded magnetic core Symbolic languages including COBOL	Segments of new management information system Management science applications	Technical Middle management support Operating management control	Use of techniques not previously practical Restructuring of information systems Supplement to management's analytical capacity	Willingness to use existing systems in new ways People who can analyze abstract problems Higher order techniques

3rd Generation	Micro-monolithic circuitry Disk storage Real-time and time-sharing capability Operating systems	Large-scale systems Logistics applications Company-wide systems Total systems approaches	Management planning and analysis Corporate headquarters coordination	Interlocking of sub-systems Vertical and horizontal extension of computer use Speed	High level competency in systems design and computer programming Willingness to change local ways for company good Long term, heavy investment
4th Generation	Significant simplification of systems and programming analysis Increased reliability Increased flexibility Confidentiality	Extension of vital decision-making process	Top management planning and decision-making	Sharpening of most vital element of organization	Rigorous analysis of top management functions Business research Availability of high level management systems analysts Willingness to make vital changes

As computers evolve towards increasing sophistication, systems levels and environments become more demanding and the need for qualified personnel becomes urgent. Projection shows this trend will continue.

Source: Chart appears in *Administrative Management,* March 1967, in "Personnel and Software: Third Generation EDP Dilemmas," by Edward A. Tomeski, president, Systems and Management Innovation., New York.

portant the processing of data is to company operations. It would probably pay to use a computer if the data to be processed meets these specifications:

1. The work is repetitive. That is, however varied in content or complex it is, the same procedure is followed time after time in processing it.

2. It is of sufficient volume. But suggesting how much is "sufficient" is a little like answering the question "How high is up?" This is a judgment that must be made.

3. It involves calculation. The computer is particularly adept at solving problems involving addition, subtraction, division and multiplication, and it does these at fantastic speeds.

4. It demands high accuracy. If there is little room for error in the work of a department (that is, an error could cost considerable money), then a computer, with its extremely high rate of accuracy, is an obvious and natural possibility.

5. The work is not subject to frequent change. To do the work desired, a computer must be told what to do. That is, the work must be programmed. This can be both expensive and time-consuming and, therefore, short-run jobs are usually out of the question.

Question 8: Judging from the help-wanted ads, there seems to be a problem in finding people to operate computers. Is there any special reason for this?

Answer: The major reason simply reflects the fact that the computer is a fairly new piece of equipment, so that new people must be trained with the specific skills needed to carry out appropriate job functions.

For example, here are some of the "new jobs" that computer operations have created:

computer operator	project director
computer programmer	supervisor of computer
tape librarian	operations
systems engineer	systems analyst

However, there's one aspect of working with computers that has recently come to public attention. An official of the Australian Council of Salary and Professions Association stated that white-collar employees need to be protected against the strain of working long hours with computers.[3]

The Australian official reported that computers seem to impose a new kind of strain on office employees. Instead of the worker being in charge of the speed at which work is performed, the computer dictates the pace—and this factor seems to create nervous tension in some people. Another forced-pace factor is that the work is tied to deadlines that result from the centralization of processing and the need to stick to a strict schedule in processing incoming and outgoing data.

From another part of the world comes another caution signal. The Japanese Ministry of Labor has set protective standards for that nation's key punchers. A six-and-a-half-hour day with three rest periods, one in the morning and two in the afternoon, was recently decreed to protect them from an alleged "key-punch neurosis."

Question 9: What are the dollars-and-cents aspects of computer installation?

Answer: The question as asked may sound a little like asking how much does an automobile cost, but actually it's an incisive question, because its answer can reveal a good deal about computer operation. Here's the way one expert puts it:

"The way for a manager to learn about computers is to ignore the equipment. Forget about the blinking lights, the spinning tapes, the clicking relays. Just learn the costs involved."

What the expert is suggesting is that one approach EDP not as a collection of hardware but rather from the point of view of "What must the manager understand about the practical aspects of computer service to use it intelligently?"

One way to get this information is to explore the experience of managers who have done work with EDP-

---

[3] Reported in *Industrial Relations News*, September 9, 1967.

service companies. What are the costs of using such a service? The following paragraphs describe in simple terms what is involved in working with an outside EDP organization.

Charges for processing data under a tailor-made EDP program can run from a few hundred dollars to several thousands, depending on the complexity of the job, type of equipment used, and so on. In any case, the service bureau will provide a proposal showing each step required to prepare and process the material, and the cost. (The costs indicated, of course, are subject to change and merely indicate the range in which they tend to fall.)

Generally, there are three main categories of costs that a prospective buyer of EDP service needs to know about:

Systems time. The service center may recommend that one of its systems analysts study and streamline the clerical procedures preparatory to programming its data for machine processing. This, of course, is a one-time cost. Rates are generally $7 to $10 per man-hour for systems work relating to punched-card operations, $10 to $15 for work on systems to be set up for computer processing.

Wiring time. If the job will be run on a computer, a charge will be made for preparing the computer panels, etc. It usually runs from $7 to $25 an hour, depending on the type of machine used. Generally, the more complex the machine, the higher the hourly rate.

An important step in the preparation is "debugging." This is a procedure by which a program once set up on a computer is verified by running test cards, spotting errors and making changes to eliminate them.

Machine time. This is the charge for processing data through the center's equipment—key punch, card sorters, computers, and so on. Rates vary with the type of machine. Some typical charges:

Key punch: One center quotes $4.50 per hour; other quotations range from $4 to $6.

Computer: Rates vary with the type of machine. A typical charge is $100 per hour, with a range from $40 to $400, the latter charge for the largest type of machine.

Aside from hourly rates, charges may also be made on a per-transaction basis. For example, one center does a considerable amount of processing for brokerage houses and bills them according to the number of items processed. In such cases, the center estimates on a certain volume and comes up with a cost per hundred or per thousand items.

Another factor in machine rates involves what the centers call "prime time." Prime time is day operation; nonprime time, night operation. Nightwork may run as low as 50 percent of prime rates because of its lesser desirability. This is an obvious bargain for management to consider if deadlines and work schedules permit.

Question 10: What are some representative types of computer services available to the businessman?

Answer: This question can be answered both generally and specifically. The chart below provides the general answer. In the paragraphs following the chart are a series of specific services a variety of companies have had performed with the help of an EDP service center.

Types of EDP Service

Service	Business Uses	Benefits
Machine accounting	Payroll Accounts receivable Sales records and reports Cost accounting	Machine processing of operations previously done by hand. Results faster and usually cheaper. This type of EDP application helps cut costs.
Research Technical and engineering analyses	Market surveys, opinion polls, tabulation and analysis of research figures, stress-strain problems, and so on.	Usually one-shot jobs; business applications generally confined to R&D function.
Management guidance	Production control Inventory control Operations planning	This type of application helps supply answers to questions like, "Which is the best location for my new warehouse?" "How much of Product A should be produced next month, compared to Product B?" Experts say this is the growth area for EDP.

In addition to the general services indicated in the chart, here are some examples of how companies, even small ones, are using EDP in their operations:

Speed collections: A New Jersey paint manufacturer sends his invoices, cash receipts and other credits to an EDP service center every ten days. Within 24 hours, he gets back a list of all transactions on each account with the starting and ending balances.

At the end of the month, the service center prepares an aged statement for each account and an aged trial balance showing amounts due: current to 30 days, 30–60 days and over 90 days.

Major benefit has been the improvement in collections, particularly from smaller accounts. Statements are in the mail by the second working day of the month, as compared to the tenth working day under the old manual procedure. But equally valuable are quarterly sales analyses that the manufacturer now gets as a by-product. These reports provide information he was unable to get previously: sales by town, by individual salesmen (current and previous year) and by customer.

An average of 2000 invoices per month are processed. Between 700 and 1000 statements are sent out monthly. *The average monthly cost to the paint manufacturer for these services is $350.* (Here again, costs indicated merely represent charges being made at one point in time.)

Pinpoint advertising and promotion efforts. An advertising agency with a soft-drink account sends data on consumption patterns, plus the audience makeup of a variety of newspapers, magazines and TV and radio stations, to its EDP center. Within a few hours, the agency gets back a report showing the most efficient combination of media for promoting the beverage. *Cost of the machine time is $125.* The complete programming—that is, the design of special procedures for the equipment to handle the job—has been done previously.

Tighten inventory control. A St. Louis automobile dealer has been able to increase his parts sales and reduce his inventory investment by use of a computerized inventory-control system. The dealer supplies his EDP service center with a punched paper-tape record of weekly sales and receipts of spare parts. The tape is created in the regular course of daily work on a billing machine. The EDP center calculates a minimum in-stock guide level for each part, based on current demand, and furnishes the dealer with a weekly parts order showing items needed to replenish his inventory.

Before using EDP, the dealer reports he had a $32,000 inventory of 6888 different types of parts. With EDP, his investment dropped to $20,000 and he trimmed his inventory to 6103 parts numbers. At the same time, monthly sales jumped from $6100 to $8200. *The average monthly cost to the dealer for this service is $290.*

Obtain current information on sales trends. A bakery headquartered in a small Georgia town has 80 route salesmen. At five o'clock in the afternoon, the men return with their record sheets showing sales, returns, stock on hand and collections. This information is put on punched tape, which is then fed into an automatic data transmitter connected by direct wire to Atlanta. By 2:00 A.M., the EDP center in Atlanta has processed, analyzed and printed out the sales reports of the day's sales. The report is then sent back to the bakery by bus or train carrier, arriving at 6:00 A.M.

The enormous advantage of EDP to this company lies in the greatly improved control management has over the sales effort. With a detailed profile of each route, the sales manager can tell exactly how each man is doing. For example: Are "stales" (returns) too high in a particular item? The reports help decide if the routeman is ordering too many or if sales have slacked off. No "stales" on a particular item? The salesman may be underordering and losing sales.

"Under the old system," says a company official, "it took several man-hours to analyze a route manually— and with eighty routes, this was too costly to do every month. Using EDP, we now have the information available monthly, and it is produced along with the rest of the report."

On the matter of costs, he states, "Dollar for dollar, we're spending about the same, but we're getting a great deal of additional information a lot faster."

Question 11:   What is the actual experience of working with the computer?

Answer: The fact is, nine managers out of ten, unless they're directly concerned with the operation of the computer itself, may have *little or nothing to do* with computer operation.

The machinery of the computer may be invisible, since the average manager does not get within touching distance or even sight of a machine. And firms that "use" computers often do so through an EDP-service firm. Others may share time on a computer and have only terminals on their own premises.

And possibly most important, the interface or relationship between the manager and the computer is often limited to the computer operators. In other words, the average manager will be working not with the computer but *with technicians who run the computer.* His problem—and it can be a very real one—is to learn how to communicate with the computer technician. He must be able both to understand and to make himself understood. It appears, then, that for the manager to learn how to "live with" the computer, he must learn how to live with the technicians that operate the computer.

Question 12:   Let's assume a manager is about to change jobs and is going from a noncomputerized to a computerized type of operation. What are the key changes that might take place in his business way of life?

Answer: This question was posed to Joseph B. Vandergrift, president of a management-consulting firm that bears his name specializing in operations research and computer applications. The following is based on his response:

Speed of information. The executive must prepare himself to receive information much more quickly than before. Between the transaction and the report of it, time will be telescoped. Specifically, he will be getting reports one day after a transaction that before may have taken two or three weeks. If an EDP department is on its toes, a statement of monthly operation can reach him within two days. Previously it may have taken 30 days, even more.

Amount of information. Take the example of a sales manager's reporting situation. In precomputer days, after several weeks had gone by, the manager could count on getting some kind of analysis of sales results from Accounting—broken down by sales area and individual salesman. With a computer, he will not only get the same report in two or three days, if the input has come in on time, but he can have breakdowns on sales figures in almost any way he wants them—for example, by size, by customer, by price lines, by color, style, and so on.

Necessity for preplanning. Once the manager, whether he's in production or sales, is assured of getting performance feedback quickly, he has the time to develop and adjust his planning. For example, consider the company with multiple sources of supply, multiple manufacturing locations and multiple distribution centers. The executive can plan now well in advance in order to make the right "mix" of buying, manufacturing and warehousing. He can turn over his forecast requirements, which can now be much closer to actual needs, so that goods are produced at the right location, shipped from the lowest-cost source and arrive in time to meet customer demand.

Changes in operational control. Somewhat the same elements that make it possible for the "computerized manager" to plan also give him greater operational control. If anything goes wrong, adjustments can be made quickly. The manager can know on a day-to-day basis where his supplies are, what his machine capacities are. He can transship in an emergency without risking the loss of customer satisfaction.

Becoming computer-minded. As a result of the previous steps—the speed of information, amount of information, opportunity for planning and improved operational control—the manager's job tends to change in several basic ways. For one thing, his whole sense of pace must be speeded up considerably. His ability to make swift changes must give him a new sense of flexibility. While he may not think like a machine, he can be concerned with such matters as sources of supply, production capacity and sales demand as quantified factors to be manipulated and balanced off for optimum profitability. Adding up all these factors, one could say the executive who masters them has become computer-minded.

Outlook

What can one say about the further development of the computer as a management tool and its continuing impact on the executive?

It's difficult to assess a phenomenon that, as Winston Churchill might have said, "tumbles the future about like a plaything." Capabilities of the computer, now just appearing, are awesome:

1. Optical scanning, already commonplace in computer operations—now used by banks for "reading" identification numbers printed in magnetic ink—will progress toward wider reading potential.
2. Translation from spoken to the written word—now limited to a set vocabulary stored in the computer—is sure to break through to even wider and more flexible application.
3. The "talking computer" now being developed doesn't simply repeat stored words but "speaks" by combining basic lip, throat and glottal sounds, much the same as the human being does. It will be heard from increasingly in the future.
4. The amazing capability of graphic display—the cathode-ray tube terminal, only a few years old but now almost taken for granted and used routinely by draftsmen, design engineers and for visual recall of stored data—will find additional breathtaking applications.

As far-reaching as these advances will be, one can surmise that they eventually will be incorporated into the workings of business and society and that managers will learn what they must to live with and use the computer tool and its auxiliary capabilities.

However, for one aspect of the question of the computer and its continuing development, there is no present answer. In his book, *Privacy and Freedom,* Alan F. Westin[4] states the problem:

"The setting—the marvels of microminiaturization and circuitry, chemical synthesis and projective psychiatry—is new. But the choices are as old as man's history on the planet. Will the tools be used for man's liberation or subjugation?"

Which way the computer goes depends *not* on the hardware of the future but on its software—attitudes, values and mankind's regard for itself.

POINTS FOR EXECUTIVE THOUGHT AND ACTION

"What should the executive know and do about computers?"

In one form or another, this question has haunted career-minded managers, specialists in management development and observers of the management scene. Obviously, a question of this large, amorphous dimension can trigger all the latent insecurities of any of us.

One sure answer is, "Don't fight the computer." And the reason for this reply is *not* that the computer can do no wrong—for there are countless documented cases of unsuccessful applications and installations. The reason is that the computer is an inextricable part of the future of management. The managers who accept this fact and capitalize on it will unquestionably reinforce their career prospects. Those who "reject" the computer—not for specific applications, but as a business and management tool—will eventually stand out and be at the same disadvantage as the horse-and-buggy driver on a modern superhighway.

Without intending it to be so, the above paragraphs tend to echo an ominous, threatening note too common in any discussion about computers and their impact on the business scene. To quickly establish a more constructive color to these Action Points, consider the following suggestions for positive thought and action in winning your way in a computerized world:

[4] Alan F. Westin, *Privacy and Freedom* (New York: Atheneum, 1967).

1. *Prepare yourself emotionally.* Examine your thinking and feelings closely, spot and eliminate the last shred of any "It can't happen here" psychology. Don't kid yourself that it can't happen. Eventually it must happen —*everywhere*.

Reject defeatist thinking and doubts about your ability to master computer know-how, to the extent that it will keep you updated within the context of your particular job.

Remind yourself, if necessary, of your relevant assets —experience, skills, general know-how—that will make it possible, eventually, for you to view the computer as just one more management tool.

2. *Find out the computer's relevance for your company's operations.* The computer is penetrating various industries with different rates of speed and in irregular patterns. Here are two sources for clues as to what's coming:

a. *Other industries:* Banking, insurance companies, types of business that require massive record keeping and rapid access of stored information have computerized broadly. In other industries, check to see whether the raw-materials operations, the manufacturing or the distribution ends have had computer experience that can reveal the shape of things to come for your area of interest.

b. *Your own industry:* Check computer applications, as well as you can, in companies that lead the parade in your industry. While many pacesetters don't publicize their changes, the information about experience, particularly where it's been successful, is often reported in trade or association journals, even the daily press.

3. *Prepare yourself practically.* Go back to school? Yes. More and more training and educational opportunities for computer know-how are being offered business people and the public at large. A conference with the institution offering the courses can help you select those appropriate to your needs.

TWELVE/OUTSIDE SERVICES ON EXECUTIVE CALL

"When I first started in business," says J. P. Beem of Hadlyme, Connecticut, "the only outside service available to us was linen service. When I retired, there wasn't a single business need for which we couldn't call in an expert, from decorating a reception room to designing a new product."

The time span to which Beem refers is 1916 to 1961. Following World War One, the American business community witnessed an unprecedented proliferation of services. Some individuals set up shop on their own as psychologists, engineers, statisticians, accountants. Others organized companies which eventually employed hundreds of people and billed millions of dollars annually.

There are many different types of business-service firms. One large group provides "physical services" such as the maintenance of buildings and grounds, repair of equipment, and so on. Usually a company calls on these if it has no facilities to do the work itself or figures an outsider can do it more expertly or economically. For example, employee cafeterias are often run by an outside concessionaire because the company doesn't want to be bothered getting into the restaurant business.

Another type of service firm—and the kind to be dealt with in this chapter—is the one that offers consultation and guidance in various areas of business operations. Companies hire such firms to supplement or extend the capability of their own staffs. For example, a president wants to investigate the feasibility of electronic data processing, but no one within the company is sufficiently knowledgeable to make the study. He calls in a consultant who specializes in EDP. Or a chemical company, pressed by competition, may decide that it should pursue research and development in an entirely new area. An outside laboratory, familiar with the particular kind of research, can supplement the firm's own R&D department.

Management services in perspective

Let's look, for a moment, at management services in the broader context of the growth of service industries in general.

While the economy as a whole has been flourishing over the past decades, two segments—manufacturing and services—have been growing at very different rates. Manufacturing establishments have increased slowly, service firms have literally exploded. The figures below show the recent trend:

	Number of Establishments		
	1963	1954	Increase
Manufacturing (20 or more employees) ..	100,500	90,478 +	11%
Services	1,961,673	785,589 +	148%

The growth of management-consulting services, in particular, was given impetus by the rapid expansion of business after World War Two, as problems of organization and personnel bombshelled many organizations. These problems were so basic in nature that companies often called in experts simply to diagnose the particular malady or combination of maladies from which they were suffering.

The promotional brochure of one company, Fry Consultants of Chicago, New York and Zurich, indicates the broad nature of services these experts offered:

"We provide a general business-counseling service equipped to work with a client on most business problems with the ultimate aim of helping the company increase efficiency and earnings. Our assignments generally fall into these categories:

general-management services,
marketing services,
merger sales and acquisitions,

industrial-engineering & production services,
institutional services,
management-information and data-processing
  systems,
operations research,
personnel-evaluation services,
international services,
executive search."

The so-called general management-consulting firm, such as Fry, offers the same total services to business as the medical internist or general practitioner offers a patient. Since the general consultants are the backbone of the outside-service fraternity, it's important to understand how they work.

The general-management consultant

By 1929, the number of firms in the general-management field had grown to the point where the practitioners themselves felt the need for an organization that would set up standards and methods to protect legitimate firms from fly-by-nights. The Association of Consulting Management Engineers, known as ACME, was incorporated in 1932. The membership has multiplied many times since its inception, although many excellent individuals and firms still operate outside the association. (The following information is largely derived from ACME.)

As of 1967, there were approximately 2600 management-consulting firms in North America. While many of these are small firms offering specialized services, approximately 125 of the largest firms offer a broad range of management services to clients.

Methods of operation differ from consultant to consultant. Some firms confine their work to a single *industry* —such as textiles or transportation. Others specialize in one or more *operating areas*—production, marketing, finance or personnel. In 1966, billings for individual consultants and consulting firms in North America were approximately $725 million. More than three-quarters of the nation's larger businesses and countless smaller ones utilize the services of management consultants.

Management consultants see themselves as professionals offering skilled help in diagnosing and treating management problems. They both *recommend* optimum solutions to problems and help *implement* the recommendations when necessary.

As the consultants see it, the basic value offered a client is objectivity. "There's no substitute," says a proponent of the consulting firm, "for the impartial, fresh viewpoint, free from personal interest, internal loyalties, company tradition or preconception."

Here is ACME's own description of the help its members render:

"While each client's situation is in most respects unique, none is completely without precedent to the experienced consultant. A consultant who serves many clients deals frequently with situations that may confront the individual concern only once in a decade. From this broad experience, the consultant has learned what problems to anticipate, what action to take when unexpected obstacles arise, what reactions to expect from the people involved and what ingredients are necessary for a successful project. Analytical skill is a third advantage. Although he does not have a monopoly on this skill, it is the consultant's business to know how to find the real problem and its underlying causes, determine the conditions for its solution, and the end results which should be achieved by the solution. Finally, consultants can devote their full-time attention to the problem at hand and carry it through to completion thoroughly and expeditiously, free from distracting day-to-day operating responsibilities.

"In their work with clients, consultants also play vital roles in transmitting an improved understanding of modern managerial knowledge, skills, tools and techniques and in helping their clients to anticipate and cope with technical and other kinds of change."

As noted previously, rapid advances in technology have created new problems for business managers. Specialized knowledge is required to install, apply, control and use new systems such as EDP, PERT, operations research, etc. Not surprisingly, management consultants have responded to this need by offering highly specialized services. A large consultant may have experts in many different areas, each heading a group of specialists. A smaller firm may limit its services to one or two specialists. In the following sections, brief descriptions of the more important special areas will be given.

What do to until EDP comes

Consultants that provide help and guidance on the installation of EDP equipment have enjoyed particularly rapid growth in the last decade. Manufacturers of EDP hardware will also advise the potential customer, but many companies considering a transition to EDP feel that they will get more objective guidance by using a service not committed to a single line of equipment.

An advertisement of one such firm[1] spells out the problems to which the firm addresses itself. Below is the essence of the advertisement:

ELEVEN QUESTIONS FOR PRESIDENTS CONSIDERING A COMPUTER INSTALLATION

If you are contemplating a major data-processing center, here are eleven questions you should be asking your staff:

Will the choice of location for the center best serve your interests—immediately as well as in the future?

Will the layout of the center incorporate the most efficient flow of traffic among those departments that support or depend on it?

Will the plan permit maximum internal flexibility for adding and rearranging peripheral equipment?

Will it have adequate provisions for physical expansion to accommodate additional "hardware" and staff?

Will the center have built-in operational reliability?

Will it have safety features to help protect your investment as well as service commitments?

Will it have provisions for maintaining information security?

Will the working environment attract and hold the skilled personnel you require to get the maximum benefit from your investment?

Will the capital cost of the new installation bear a realistic relationship to the anticipated benefits?

Will the planning, design and construction of the computer center be handled so as to assure on-schedule and within-budget completion?

Do you have the internal resources to plan the new installation to assure satisfactory answers to all these questions?

An Austin FACILITY ANALYSIS is one of seven Austin Engineering-Economic consulting services designed to assist clients in analyzing facilities that will reduce operating costs, increase efficiency, and enhance the company's public image.

---

[1] The Austin Co., Cleveland, Ohio.

One multiplant laundry organization considers objectivity so important that it hired *four* consulting firms to conduct studies that would assist in computerizing the cost factors of individual plant operation. Not until the fourth consulting firm turned in its report did the laundry executives feel they had a practical basis on which to proceed.

In most cases, firms considering the use of electronic data processing *must* call on outside help to make the transition. The laundry experience suggests the advisability of more than one study to have the benefit of comparison. Other procedures that can maximize the benefits of outside consultation will be found in a series of general recommendations toward the end of this chapter.

Market-research companies

After World War Two, business became increasingly market-oriented. One sign: The post of vice-president, marketing, became one of the newer, more glamorous and most influential ones in the corporation. Another was the outpouring of articles and books on "the marketing concept."

In simplest terms, the marketing concept means that a company orients all its functions toward the problems and opportunities that exist in the marketplace for its products or services. For example, before a new-product idea is started through the development stage, the marketing potential for such a product is established so that *all* the stages of development—design, packaging and distribution—are influenced by the marketing situation.

With the growth of the marketing concept, there developed a need to investigate specific market situations. To fill this need, the marketing-research firm appeared on the scene. Operating with three main types of personnel—statisticians, marketing people and a field force of trained interviewers—marketing-research firms develop a project study based on a client's needs, survey the market and tabulate and interpret the figures.

For example, Audits & Surveys, now among the largest market-research firms in the business, was founded in

1953. Numbered among the firm's clients are automobile manufacturers, radio-TV firms, metal fabricators and chemical plants. In 1966, Audits & Surveys had a reported annual volume of ten million dollars and operated in Latin America, Europe and Canada, as well as the U.S. A brief description of several recent studies conducted by Audits & Surveys indicates the scope of service firms of this type:

Audience Rating Measurement Study. This study of techniques for measuring radio audiences was sponsored jointly by the Radio Advertising Bureau and the National Association of Broadcasters. Its objective was to compare audience data developed by a variety of diary and recall techniques and to validate these against measurement standards set up particularly for this purpose.

Yellow Pages National Usage Study. The Bell System telephone companies sponsored a detailed examination of how many, how often and why people use the Yellow Pages. In this study 19,737 adults, 20 years and older, were interviewed by 909 interviewers during the month of June 1963. More than 160,000 IBM cards containing the data from these interviews were fed into computers. Before narrowing down to those actually interviewed, the interviewers contacted 18,644 households and listed 75,470 adults, 20 and older. The questioning techniques were first pretested with hundreds of consumers in individual small-scale projects. Subsequently, a major pilot study in eight key cities was used to further refine the questioning techniques.

Automotive Study. This research program was the largest continuous effort on the part of any American manufacturer to evaluate his advertising specifically and the role of advertising generally.

Scheduling of the automotive study was controlled through critical-path techniques. For example, the questionnaires of an automotive wave are checked in, quality-graded, edited, coded, transferred to over 40,000 IBM cards and computer-processed. The complete report was delivered to the client 23 working days after the last questionnaire was received in New York.

Retail Distribution. This service reported to clients annually the *effective retail distribution* of their product(s) and those of each principal competitor. The words *effective retail distribution* meant "distribution in retail outlets which carry the client's type or category of product(s)."

This distinction is important because it meant that the product's distribution (let's say the product is sponges) is measured—not against *all* grocery stores but against all grocery stores *which carry sponges,* all drugstores *which carry sponges,* all variety stores *which carry sponges,* etc. This concept of "effective distribution" is very different from one which measures against all grocery stores, drugstores, variety stores, etc., whether or not they carry the product category, points out Solomon Dutka, founder and president of Audits & Surveys.

To the manager whose responsibility includes one or another aspect of marketing, obviously an outside research firm can be of considerable assistance. Some standard problems, however, have from time to time revealed an Achilles heel. For example, product tests run in localized areas have produced results not duplicated by a broader marketing effort.

One example of a marketing-test failure, not representative but still discussed in marketing circles, had to do with a test of a dog food. A competing firm, hearing of the test, staged a sale of its own competing product in the test area during the test period. Obviously, the test results were not representative.

Another source for error lies in the interpretation of the market situation. A classic example of one such error is the Ford Motor Company's marketing of the Edsel. Ford spent thousands of man-hours and millions of dollars to find out the kind of car consumers wanted. The results were incorporated in the now-famous Edsel. Instead of a bonanza, the company found it had a dud on its hands. The features the public had told the researchers they wanted failed to lure them when actually embodied in the car.

Psychological services

"Engineer Barnes is blocking on that new project. Says he hasn't had a new idea or insight in the last two days."

"Have him see the staff psychologist at once."

That's an exchange we may find to be routine in the 21st Century. Certainly it's not too farfetched to expect that in the next decades, psychological obstacles to creativity may be exorcised by a professional psychologist. Nor is it too extreme to foresee the day when the average company includes on its staff one or more psychologists. As a matter of fact, many of our larger companies—Du Pont, IBM, GE—already have psychological or psychiatric advisors on their staffs.

Today, a sizable number of consulting firms offer psychological services to the businessman. The field has grown in size and in variety; the expansion reflects to a large extent the increased emphasis on the human factor in business. Companies now recognize the difference in productivity between the right man in the right job and one who gropes along in a job for which he is basically unsuited. The psychologist, by helping in the selection of keymen for given jobs, can prevent such errors.

In the typical case, the psychological-services firm starts with one specialty and gradually enlarges its line of activity. For example, when The Personnel Laboratory of Stamford, Connecticut, opened up for business in 1944, it offered only psychological testing. Over the years, partly as a result of client requests, it added recruiting, supervisory training, job evaluation, personnel audits and a variety of consulting services offering management guidance in matters of selecting, hiring, promoting and retiring personnel.

King Whitney, president of The Personnel Laboratory, suggests the underlying rationale of the psychological service:

"The psychologist's objectivity and expertness in understanding human behavior are useful in dealing with the problems of managing, motivating and developing subordinates. Sophisticated and perceptive executives, in particular, often undergo considerable anguish in

making decisions about subordinates, because they are aware of the effects of their own personal involvement with them. The psychologist is frequently able to help the executive recognize his own hostilities, fantasies and guilt and to put them in proper perspective so that decisions can be made which are realistic. By the same token, subordinates themselves will acknowledge facts about their attitudes and limitations from outside counsel that they would never accept from their working superiors. Thus, executives employ psychologists to help subordinates cope with their own deficiencies."

The service line offered by BFS Psychological Associates of New York, another source of psychological services, is fairly representative of the help available from a large firm. Here is a brief summary:

Employee-attitude audit. A large metals-fabricating company started to get an extremely high turnover among production employees. Work was seriously impeded. Management's impression was that the turnover was the result of low wage rates.

Interviewers were sent into the company to talk with personnel at four levels—top management, middle management, supervisors and rank-and-file employees. The interviews were conducted in depth to build a realistic picture of feelings about the company and company relationships. The multilevel approach was used to offset individually distorted perceptions.

The BFS staff concluded that low wages were not the basic source of the problem. The real villains were inadequate training and orientation of new employees and poor screening of job applicants by inexperienced supervisors.

To remedy the situation, the psychologists recommended training of supervisors in effective personnel management and an employee-selection procedure that strengthened the supervisor's hand in initial screening.

Performance review. A menswear firm felt it was handicapped by the inadequate management skills of its field sales manager. Also, it was felt that younger salesmen, especially those with management potential, weren't being brought along fast enough.

The service firm conducted a behaviorally oriented review of salesmen's and managers' job performance. Observations of actual performance were made, along with a study of performance records. All information was analyzed and compared with management's analyses and performance ratings.

BFS staff members were sent into the field with the company's salesmen to identify those behavioral characteristics that seemed to lead to success or failure. A rating program was then developed to be used by managers.

It was felt that the formalized program gave managers more objective and specific standards for rating their subordinates' performance. This program helped identify and reward the more promising men and made it easier to pinpoint and correct weak performance areas. The company, after one year of trial, reports satisfactory positive results.

Testing. Of all the psychological services used by the manager, testing is most controversial. Yet there is no doubt about the widespread use of tests. *The Harvard Business Review* conducted a survey on practices in the field, asking, among other questions, "Who tests?" The answer:

"Every sort of company, from small businesses to the industrial giants. Tests are used by publishing houses, advertising agencies and management consultants, electronics firms, insurance companies, steel companies, airlines and banks; in short, the butchers, bakers and candlestick makers of modern business."

Over half of the executives who responded to the survey questions reported that their companies were at the time using tests for selecting or promoting, transferring and developing salaried personnel.

King Whitney, president of The Personnel Laboratory, describes the contemporary executive's approach to the psychologist's evaluation of personnel:

"To reinforce his own opinions and conclusions about people—or to revise them, as the case may be—today's executive uses the clinical and industrial psychologist in

a variety of ways. In the selection of new employees, for example, he calls upon the psychologist to provide him with insights into the intellectual and emotional makeup of candidates that he himself cannot always obtain from his own interviewing or reference checking. Testing is usually a key tool for the psychologist's appraisal."

The subject of psychological tests and the uses to which managers may put them is too complex to be treated adequately in the present limited context.

Suffice it to say, however, that testing in business has been and will continue to be a controversial activity because the state of the art is undecided. There are groups both for and against. *Opponents* raise objections like these:

Testing derives from the field of psychology (still regarded by some businessmen as "that sex-and-bathroom nonsense").

Job candidates, particularly those in upper echelons, often resent being asked to submit to tests.

Alternatives to testing—interviewing, past performance, etc.—are less "technical" as evaluation tools, and they don't require a specialist to interpret the results.

Tests add just one more factor to the many involved in a hiring decision—and often they confuse rather than help, because they may seem to conflict with past job performance.

Tests represent an additional cost in the recruiting process.

The *proponents* of psychological testing—and there are many—have ample evidence to support their claim that the experience is often favorable. Many companies have indeed discovered that by judicious use of tests they can reduce turnover, improve the performance of personnel and maintain a high level of executive competence. As for the psychologists themselves, the consensus is that although tests are fallible, they are far more valid and reliable than personal judgments or subjective assessments. With this statement, it is difficult not to agree.

King Whitney adds a final caveat: *"Psychological services are no different from any other advisory services.*

The secret of making the best use of them is to recognize that while their contribution is significant, it is still limited. Decisions in business today must be based on considerations that take into account all aspects of the operation of an enterprise—finance, organization, products and markets—and it would be a mistake to let a psychologist's viewpoint prevail in matters that require well-rounded business judgment."

Brainpower on call

Ordinarily, the last assist one might think a manager would look for is someone to do his thinking. Yet, in recent years, a number of organizations have appeared that will, for a fee, take on the job of wrestling with a company's larger strategic problems. These are the so-called think tanks that have grown up since World War Two.

The Rand Corporation, one of the earliest in the field, was organized in 1946 by scientists who had participated in World War Two planning. Some 20 years later, several hundred organizations had come into being, forming a multimillion-dollar industry.

The government is one of the best customers of these service firms. But top business managers, impressed by the array of brainpower these organizations represent, have come to see in them high-powered consultants who can be tossed company problems that required the "big think"—in other words, consideration of a basic policy or operational strategy.

The nature of the problems which business has brought to these service organizations ranges all the way from basic marketing questions to problems of company operations 20 or 30 years in the future.

Some examples of the information business has sought from the think-tank organizations to assist in future planning: the implications of the hippie movement, the shape of the world in the year 2000, and the problems of a "postindustrial society" in which more time may be spent at leisure than at work.

A brief description that gives some idea of the approach and scope of one think-tank operation, the Hudson Institute, Croton-on-Hudson, New York, was recently offered by the *Wall Street Journal:*

"Hudson charges cost plus a fixed fee for its work, which comes to about $46,000 per man-year. As a tax-free, nonprofit institution, it turns back extra funds into pet projects. Such an undertaking is its 'futures' program, which has resulted in a book to be published by Mr. [Herman] Kahn next month. The book is entitled The Next Thirty-Three Years: A Framework for Speculation.

"It is a fantastic collection of extrapolations and insights. Among 100 'very probable' technical innovations envisaged by Mr. Kahn are the capability to choose the sex of unborn children, artificial 'moons' to light huge areas, automated housework, inhabited undersea colonies and programmed dreams.

"The book also outlines 'ten far-out possibilities,' including major modification of the human species, interstellar travel, laboratory creation of artificial live plants and animals, and 'antigravity.' "

Of course, to the casual reader, Herman Kahn offers some of the excitement of reading science fiction. To the businessman, it provides a context—perhaps fantastic, but better than none at all—for thinking about his company, its directions and growth in the decades ahead.

Management services—boon or bane to the manager?

Outside management services represent both a promise and a threat to the user:

The *promise* lies in the possibility that the consultant may help a firm capitalize on situations or solve problems beyond the capabilities of its own personnel.

The *threat* is that key individuals may feel that their prestige is at stake and refuse to cooperate. An inside personnel executive, for example, may not be pleased to have his company president bring in an outsider to help analyze and prescribe for a manpower difficulty that presumably lies within his area of responsibility.

In short, the use of outside consulting services is not an unmixed blessing. If a consultant's services always justified the fee, theoretically a company could skyrocket its profits simply by using an array of consulting talent.

While many companies beset by policy or operating difficulties use outside help most successfully, disillusionment with the consulting process can also occur.

Reports the top executive of a textile firm, "We were experiencing severe growing pains; so we called in a consulting organization to help us reorganize. The consultants created an unholy mess that took two years for us to straighten out. We almost went bankrupt in the process."

A bank followed the recommendations of another consultant that it let one-third of the staff in a particular department go. The consultant had "guaranteed" this labor saving when he took on the job. Result: The bank found itself badly understaffed and unable to build up the department until many months of costly overtime work had passed.

The better consulting firms make no secret of the possible pitfalls. They frankly admit getting complaints from dissatisfied clients. Some typical samples:

"All we got was a lot of blue-sky suggestions for improvements. No one could figure out how to implement the consultant's recommendations in any practical way."

"They picked the brains of our own people, rehashed what they learned and tied it all up in a fancy report. They didn't tell us anything we didn't already know."

"The consultant had a formula that involved a prepackaged solution. They never bothered to analyze our particular needs."

"The consultant picks up all the experience. When he leaves, the experience goes with him. It would be better to have our own people learn whatever there is to learn."

The emotional component

While some criticism of consultants may be justified, there's no question that many managers react adversely to the idea of outside help out of a fear that their own jobs or reputations will be questioned. Managers who feel this way often put serious obstructions in the consultant's path. (One management consultant refers to them as "dragons"—they refuse to let an outsider into their baili-wick.)

Such executives are actually shortsighted, because they bar improvements in their companies that might well open up new opportunities for themselves. From a purely practical standpoint, today's and tomorrow's manager should regard consulting firms as one more source of assistance in helping him perform his job or run his company more efficiently. At the very least, he should understand how outside consultants work, the situations in which it may be advisable to call on an outside expert, and how to work effectively with an outside consultant. The section immediately following gives some helpful recommendations.

POINTS FOR EXECUTIVE THOUGHT AND ACTION

You and your company can benefit from the wise use of outside services, particularly those services that come under the heading of management consultants. However, a word of caution. Experienced executives will tell you that there are many instances of great sums spent in vain and tremendous amounts of time lost, to say nothing of major troubles stirred up, by the unwise use of consulting services. Who is to blame in such instances of managerial chaos and catastrophe? Of course, it could be the consulting firm or even the individual consultant. But, as the client, you and your company can develop an almost failproof procedure that can help you get the benefits of management consultation without suffering the possible failures and losses. When you supply accurate answers and data to the following key questions, you are well on your way to gaining the benefits and avoiding the pitfalls:

1. When should you consult a consultant?

Management consulting probably is desirable when any one of the following situations exists:

When you or your company needs "know-how" in a management area. The need may come about because there's no one qualified to cope with the problems in question on your staff. Or you may have people on the staff assigned to this function, but they need help because of the magnitude of the problem or because it is a highly specialized one, specialized beyond the experience of present staff members. For example, you may want to locate a new plant site, purify water, modify a pollution-causing plant condition, install a pension plan, conduct market research in connection with a new product, get an objective evaluation of employee attitudes or develop a battery of tests to improve your selection procedures.

When a big job must be done quickly, an outside firm can provide qualified personnel who can devote their full, uninterrupted time to the urgent work. For example, you may want to do a test-selling job of a particular product in a given area. An outside firm can hire the salesmen, train them, deploy them as needed and evaluate the results. And you may accomplish all this without interference or disorganization of your regular sales operation. Many other crash programs, ranging from maintenance to research and development, similarly may be handled by an outside firm.

When your company is heading into unfamiliar fields, a new product or a new type of operation may require expertness not available to you. The guidance, particularly in the early planning and implementation stages, of experienced specialists and executives can help you avoid major errors. This consideration is common in this day of acquisitions, mergers and product diversification.

When your organization or operation is suffering from major unidentifiable trouble, the consultant can save critical weeks and months in analyzing and assisting in prescribing for the organizational ailments at the bottom of the difficulties. His objectivity and fresh view can help offset the myopia that is both common and understandable because regular staff members are too close to, or have become bogged down by, the harassing problems.

2. Evaluating a consulting service

It's an all too frequent practice to choose outside service firms haphazardly. A personal recommendation by a business colleague, a reference to the firm in a business journal, may be the single basis on which a selection is made. True enough, personal recommendation is a fairly reliable point of judgment. But it's only one of several guidelines that should be used. Similarly, a firm's reputation as it exists in your industry or in the business community at large cannot be discounted. But here again, it constitutes only a single reference point.

A seven-point checklist can help you to evaluate the desirability of a given service firm. It is a multipronged tool, taking many points of judgment into consideration, and it is weighted in such a manner as to actually help you come up with a numerical score. Accordingly, you can use it to compare two or more competitive services.

To use the chart below as an evaluation tool, mark the appropriate box next to each factor. Then add up the numbers next to the boxes and compare the totals for two or more firms. (The numbers weight the seven factors according to their relative importance.) Other things being equal, the firm with the highest rating "wins."

Factors	OK	So-so	Poor
1. Physical facilities:			
a. Appearance of offices	4 ☐	2 ☐	0 ☐
b. Type and size of staff	4 ☐	2 ☐	0 ☐
c. Atmosphere—calm, dignified, professional	4 ☐	2 ☐	0 ☐
2. Length of time in business	10 ☐	5 ☐	0 ☐
3. General reputation of firm (or recommendations)	12 ☐	6 ☐	0 ☐
4. Intelligence and maturity of the contact man you deal with. (Does he seem to know his business and understand yours?)	8 ☐	4 ☐	0 ☐
5. Intelligence and maturity of the man who will do the actual work. (How favorably does he impress you?)	8 ☐	4 ☐	0 ☐
6. Fees—discussed in advance and equitable	12 ☐	6 ☐	0 ☐
7. Familiarity with your line of business	12 ☐	6 ☐	0 ☐

3. How to develop an effective working relationship

This is really the crux of the matter. How well you and other company personnel work with the outside service firm is the most important factor in determining the benefits gained. Face up to the fact that this relationship poses many potential difficulties. The mere presence of an "outsider" itself can create uneasiness. It's a situation in which "letting well enough alone" *won't* do. The individuals from the service firm will require help in winning the goodwill and cooperation of company personnel. Here, based on a staff recommendation, "Working with a Management Consultant," by the Research Institute of America, is a recommended procedure:

Introduce the representatives of the outside service firm as though they were new employees joining your staff. You may do this in person, by a memo announcing the project and the service firm's participation in it, or both.

"Level" with the consultant and let him know that you expect him to do the same with you. It is important that he be told—either by you or other company personnel—the realities of a situation. This means both good and bad, both the superficially observable aspects of a problem and the hidden (and often more relevant) factors. Get down to cases. Help the outside experts to get a clear picture of the procedures, conditions, personal obstacles, hopes or fears that are relevant to the project.

Establish a single point of liaison. You want to minimize distortions and overlapping efforts. By having a major point of contact—typically this would be a single highly placed executive in the client company—you provide a communication point for feedback on all parts of the project. This also constitutes control and provides some measure of progress, as well as an opportunity for danger signals should trouble develop.

Simplify procedures. It's important to minimize distortions and to get continuity in the project. Accordingly, see that the consulting experts and other personnel have mutually agreed upon the following:

    a. Specific information, services and preparation needed for the project.

   b. A flexible pattern for meeting together to keep projects moving toward completion goals.

   c. Minimum disruption of regular company operations.

   Controlling the project. Periodic progress reviews are desirable to help you keep tabs on how the project is going and to take decisive action as needed. A weekly or monthly review, even if brief and informal, can keep the consultant on his toes and the company informed. These meetings also create the opportunity for forward planning. Keeping track of costs will undoubtedly be important at all stages. You might ask the outside experts to submit, along with progress reports, comparison of actual versus estimated costs of the project following each review meeting. If you yourself are not the financial executive, you will undoubtedly make him happy by requesting monthly billings from the consulting service that are itemized for the different charges incurred.

4. Applying the consultant's recommendations

   It's amazing how often an outside service firm's recommendations end up in the wastebasket. In some cases, this may be a highly costly but desirable outcome. For example, circumstances may have changed so radically that the recommendations no longer apply. However, the following steps can insure effective implementation:

   Explore all suggested alternatives. Most service firms, unless the service is called on to do a specific job rather than to investigate a problem, will come up with alternative courses of action. A group of the company's most qualified people should be in on the evaluation of these alternatives so that the one selected—if any—will have the greatest general backing.

   Be prepared for argument and resistance. As a manager, you must not be surprised by the possibility of a negative reaction to the outside expert's findings. You and your company will have to decide whether the position is valid and will have to deal with it accordingly.

   Request a plan of action. The final report you get from the outside service should state not only "what to do" but "how to do it." Also, make certain that this final report is fully discussed before the consultant leaves the job. This move makes it possible to clear up any misunderstandings, as well as to resolve any new questions created by the report: What can be done about the things that may hamper or prevent follow-through? Which other parts of your company's business will be directly affected by the recommendations? What sort of instructions and policy statements will be needed?

Finally, remember that a good outside service firm can be an invaluable tool in helping you and your company resolve critical problems. But the best test of a consultant's worth is *your* ability to implement his recommendations and pursue them to successful ends.

PART FOUR/THE FUTURE

The future of the executive lies in the increased degree of his professionalization and the continuing importance of his social role.

Along with his place in the social scheme of things will be a shortened time span in which his education and experience remain pertinent. Obsolescence, already a threat, will become a constant prod. Education, a more and more perishable commodity, will have to become continuous in order to keep the wolf of obsolescence from the office door. At the same time, development and training facilities will become more widely available within business itself. One striking example was provided by the following sentence from a recent news release:

"A permanent center is being created to offer courses in plant management, accounting, finance and internal controls, sales marketing and distribution." Perhaps this sounds like the curriculum for an up-to-date business college. Not so. It's the program announced by the Pepsi-Cola Company for its management institute in Phoenix, Arizona.

THIRTEEN/THE 21ST CENTURY EXECUTIVE

Executive Luke Long kissed his wife good-bye at the door of the corporation's apartment house and walked across the green lawn toward the administration building. It had been a great party, he reflected; he and Jane along with several managers and their wives had decided to wind up the celebration in the company's sumptuous quarters rather than fly the 500 miles home.

Crossing the threshold, the clean, colorful expanse of his office gave him quiet pleasure. "It's a great relaxing room," he usually said to visitors who noted the decor.

The morning was special. He touched a button on his desk, and the panel on the wall lit up, showing the time, date, temperature and weather forecast for the next 24-hour period. He was fully aware of the historic nature of the occasion. From his desk he took his camera, attached the tripod, and aimed it at the wall, allowing a blank expanse beside the lighted panel. Then he set the self-timer and posed himself so that his head and shoulders filled the open space next to the lighted square.

It was a good picture for his album, he decided, as he removed the finished color print from the camera. It showed him smiling, next to the frame which showed the time to be 8:15 A.M. EST; the weather prediction, fair with light clouds. The date was January 1, 2000.

• • •

" . . . our lives and freedom depend largely upon the skill and imagination and courage of our managers and engineers, and I hope that God will help them to help us all stay alive and free."

So says Kurt Vonnegut, Jr., in the introduction to his

novel of the future, *Player Piano*.[1] Implicit in the statement is not only the hope we now place in the managerial group for our future well-being, but also the uncertainty we feel when we contemplate tomorrow's world, which, to our present-bound eyes, embodies many political, cultural, economic and technological unknowns.

One thing we do know: If our society continues to develop along present lines, the manager of the next millennium will become a supremely crucial figure, for he will hold in his hands the welfare of the state and of the people. It will be the manager's ability to produce goods and services at an unparalleled rate that will keep our civilization viable and enable it to meet the continuing challenges that arise with each new generation: penetration of frontiers, be they of outer space or the ocean depths; increasing the physical comfort of more people; and providing the context in which the most gifted among us can continue to probe for the answers to the twin mysteries, the meaning of man and the riddle of the physical universe.

In Kurt Vonnegut's world of the future, the manager becomes a member of an elite, responsible for the physical part of national life. The author describes, tongue in cheek, but nevertheless making the point, "Dr. George Proteus was at the time of his death the nation's first National Industrial, Commercial, Communications, Foodstuffs and Resources Director, a position approached in importance only by the presidency of the United States."

It's quite likely that tomorrow the head of the giant corporation will equal the top politician in personal power. An idea greeted with derision some years ago, that the well-being of the state depends on the health of business corporations ("What's good for General Motors is good for the country"[2]), will seem like the most commonplace common sense.

The belittlers

Not everyone joins the chorus that predicts a bright,

---

[1] (New York: Scribner's, 1952).
[2] Attributed to Charles Wilson, ex-president of General Motors, while serving as secretary of defense.

power-wielding future for the manager. There are many antimaterialists, for example, who would like to see the importance of the business world diminish in favor of "human values." They refuse to show deference to the managerial high priests—certainly not in preference to moral, spiritual or humanitarian leaders.

Many intellectuals, too, espouse a kind of "occupational" democracy. Perhaps appropriately, the point is made in an editorial in *Punch*, the English humor magazine:[3]

The case for ludicrously high managerial salaries goes like this: "We work hard," say the Beechings [Ed. note: refers to Lord Beeching, head of the nationalized railways], "harder than other people, and we face frightful responsibilities; our decisions affect the lives and livelihood of millions and determine the profitability or otherwise of great businesses; so we should be paid accordingly." Lord Beeching obviously considers himself to be worth much more than ten times an ordinary man because he happens to deal in large figures. But is Lord Beeching really more important to the state than a doctor charged with the duty of diagnosing disease, a signalman who controls the fate of thousands of railway passengers, a chancellor of the exchequer, a prime minister, a schoolmaster, a nurse, a refuse collector . . . ? The Beechings of this world, it seems to me, have never latched onto the fact that in our complex society we are all necessary to the programme of living. Some, it may be, are more equal than others, but only the most stupid of men would suggest that some are more necessary than others.

We can be sure that the *Punch* editor, having delivered himself of his democratic message, felt good about it all day. A conceit embedded deep in our Christian heritage equates beggars and kings. But, as a practical matter, the *Punch* editor knows very well that he doesn't pay a boy the same for cutting the lawn as he does the repairman who fixes his telly. Just as the laborer is worthy of his hire, so is the manager—although the latter may be first to argue that money is not his major incentive.

3 *Punch*, August 23, 1967, p. 1.

Targets for tomorrow

Of course, no one wants to see supercorporations turn men into automatons. What the antibusiness people often fail to admit is that as yet, there's no proof that the two concepts are mutually exclusive: that it is possible to have a business-oriented state *and* good, creative, happy citizens. Forward-looking executives see this dual goal as their target for the future.

To develop a picture of the executive tomorrow, say in the 21st Century, it is necessary to examine executives from six angles. They are:

1. the professionalism of the executive
2. the manager's social consciousness
3. the manager's political rapprochement
4. the new technologies
5. generalism and specialism
6. the ultimate executive

It is on these points that we depend to answer the question, "How will today's manager become tomorrow's?"

1. The executive as professional

To say that tomorrow the executive will be a professional is not new. A variety of experts and observers of the business scene have been saying the same thing of today's managers, even yesterday's. But there is a difference both in meaning and import in the professionalism of tomorrow's managers. First, let's look at what "professional" means:

"One of the ways in which a 'profession' emerges is through development of an underlying fundamental or theoretical understanding of its common activities. As the knowledge and skills developed become more describable, each generation may teach the next. A body of literature develops, centers of education spring up to prepare novitiates, and standards of performance, conduct and ethics appear. The profession becomes more 'professional.'" [4]

Now let's see how close the executive of today has

---

[4] J. P. Barger, president, Dynatech Corp., in H. B. Maynard (ed.), *Handbook of Business Administration* (New York: McGraw-Hill, 1967).

come to answering this description.

When, back in the 1940s, people wrote of the business executive as a "professional," what they meant was that a *nonentrepreneurial executive* had emerged, a new kind of top man who did not found, own or claim kinship to the owners of the company he ran. This individual operated by entirely different rules, both by background and motivation, than his entrepreneur predecessor.

They assumed that this nonowning manager necessarily did his job "like a professional," that is, according to a fairly clear, if abstract, standard of performance, while observing a certain amount of objectivity in his acts of diagnosis and decision making. (As we shall see, this was not quite true.)

The repeated assertion that managers were professionals, however, was viewed with suspicion by some skeptics. This suspicion was reinforced when, as the years passed, the same accolade was thrust on frontline managers—supervisors, foremen, department heads. It was felt that the statement "The manager (foreman, supervisor, etc.) is a professional" was calculated and manipulative, the objective being not only to boost the individual's self-esteem but also to push him along in what the "establishment" felt to be a desirable direction.

Analysis of the professionalism of the manager is helpful because it not only evaluates where the manager stands in the scheme of things but also the ways in which he is not a professional and may never be.

Philip W. Shay, executive director, Association of Consulting Management Engineers, writes of the "emerging discipline of management":

"... we can clearly see that we do not have an organized, systematic body of knowledge or discipline of management that is formal yet practical and applicable. Since the first decade of the 20th Century, there has been an unprecedented increase in our knowledge of selected aspects of management. But there is, as yet, no fully developed discipline which helps make the tasks of the manager effective and rational, understandable and understood."

Well-known sociologist William J. Goode, in a much-reprinted article addressed to librarians,[5] set forth criteria by which people in a particular kind of work can judge their professionalism. Let's see how Goode's standards for the professional apply to managers in business. (The "ratings" used should be taken as entirely subjective approximations.)

In general, Goode notes that a profession is autonomous, is organized in professional associations, and its members receive higher incomes than most workers. In addition, he sets forth these specific characteristics:

A body of knowledge. A profession must have at its core an organized system of abstract principles. It cannot of mere details, however vast in quantity. Applying this measure to management, one must say that there are few generalized principles of management which have universal acceptance. Consider the area of production, for example. One might say a management principle is, "Work must be planned in order to proceed smoothly." In one sense that's an unassailable piece of common sense. But in another sense the word *planning* becomes ambiguous. In the bustle and rush of the ordinary production department, a minimum amount of "planning" may take place. Even on the higher echelons, work planning may be limited only to trying to make sure that there will be enough raw materials and facilities available to approximate the demand at any given time.

Further, in the sense that a medical student can study medicine out of textbooks and learn a body of information that will fit him to diagnose and treat hundreds of different human ills, management is clearly not a profession. For one thing, the "diseases" as well as the "treatments" tend to be affected by temporary or local factors that make each problem and each solution unique.

A noteworthy example is the incentive system used by the Lincoln Electric Company. Lincoln's incentive-management plan was started in 1934 to create worker-management identification by various means, including open-

---

5 William J. Goode, "The Librarian: From Occupation to Profession?" *Library Quarterly*, October 1961.

communications bonuses for suggestions on methods and cost improvement, etc. The results at Lincoln were highly successful, and other companies tried to duplicate Lincoln's approach. With two exceptions, they failed.

The failures were due to the presence of local situations —attitudes, methods of management, employee values— that negated or unbalanced the Lincoln system. Accordingly, where principles cannot be applied in seemingly similar situations, the very foundations of professionalism are lacking.

On this point, then, one must say that management rates low—let's say 10 or 20 percent on the factor of a "system of abstract principles."

The employers or clients of the professional believe that principles of the profession exist and that they can be used to solve problems. What Goode means here is that the user of the professional's services must feel that the "professional" isn't merely a master of common sense or logic, but that he has at his command a set of guides that will lead him safely from diagnosis to treatment.

The business world is of two minds on this point. On the one hand, many "traditionalist" top executives, possibly aware of their own lack of professionalism, consider the whole subject so much bunk. Others feel the whole professionalism bit is just so much window dressing.

There is another group of executives, making up in numbers what they lack in traditional power, who believe almost naïvely that the trained manager is indeed the possessor of special skills and principles. Such companies would hire an executive recruiter to find a top executive to come into their troubled company and "clean up the mess." They have an almost childish faith that if only they pay enough, the master professional will perform up to expectations.

Accordingly, we'll rate the manager 50 percent on this measuring point, because in this case professionalism does get some support. Goode's next criterion:

The profession must not only possess knowledge but must also help to create it. Management measures up here, because it has helped and is helping create management theory. The proliferation of books and publications, conferences and seminars on both the practical and theoretical content of management is the visible evidence. Moreover, behavioral scientists are producing an ever-growing series of theoretical propositions that apply to contemporary management. Consider Lewin's contributions to leadership, McGregor's to motivation, etc.

On this point, rate the professional proclivities of management and its experts at 80 percent.

The profession must be the final arbiter of any dispute about what is and is not valid knowledge. Here, management doesn't meet the test, and there's not much room for argument. Almost *anyone* can second-guess a manager's decisions, including his wife. And certainly, when it comes to top-executive performance, stockholders have no hesitation in setting themselves up as a judgmental group. One must, forthwith, rate management professionalism a zero here.

The profession largely controls access to its knowledge through control over school admission, school curricula and examinations. In a limited and subtle sense, management does control access to itself. For example, management has directly or indirectly helped establish the curricula of business schools. And, in the hiring process, certain centers of learning are given preference over others. And, of course, in the internal-development program, companies control the flow of individuals into the development courses. This rating would be about 60 percent.

A profession is "service-oriented." (By this statement, sociologist Goode means that a decision of the true professional is not properly based on self-interest of the professional but on the need of the client. The professional practitioner defines what the client "needs," even though it may not always be what the client wants.) The manager's "client" is, of course, his employer and, in the average case, he's expected to deliver what the company asks for. True, on the upper echelons, executives may have greater latitudes in defining their own areas of responsibility or the procedures by which they will do their jobs. But the question may be asked, "Are

they performing in the role of employer or professional?"
A 50-percent rating would seem to be called for.

The professional must at certain points make sacrifices.
For example, the practitioner may be asked to contribute
services to those who cannot pay; members of a profession may be asked to risk their lives or reputations—the
scientist is expected to publish the truth possibly at the
risk of losing his job, the lawyer to defend an unpopular
case, or the clergyman to oppose even the initial sin.

Occasionally, in management, one does find the manager who insists on "doing what he thinks is right" even
though it may be against the policy or mores of his employer. But this is very much the exception rather than
the rule. A low rating on this point—say, 5 percent.

*The profession spends both time and money in seeking
superior candidates and giving them better training, even
though this increases competition in the field.* By this criterion, management certainly does qualify as a profession.
Possibly more than most other professions, it has devoted
a tremendous percentage of its total energy both to improving the art/science of management itself and in developing superior candidates and practitioners. A 100-
percent rating seems justified.

Finally, Goode makes a statement that is particularly
enlightening:

*"No obvious steps can be seen through which an occu-
pation must pass on its way to professionalization. All
those which have been noted in literature take place
more or less salubriously, or, phrased differently, the elite
members of all high-ranking occupational groups seem to
know what to do and try all the moves they can to accomplish it, formulating a code of ethics, founding a
professional association, promulgating favorite legislation,
establishing curricula for professional training (preferably in a university), making appeals to foundations for
funds with which to develop a new professional knowledge, writing articles to explain the unique contribution
of the occupation, making protests against inaccurate
stereotypes of the occupation, and so on."*

Although the present score is low, management seems

to be moving—perhaps groping is the better word—in the *direction* of professionalization, even if actual achievement is problematical.

In sum, we see the manager as continuing to progress toward the goals of professionalism, meeting some, falling far short in others. He will become skilled in regularized and recognizable techniques that, increasingly, will be teachable, so that the new manager entering his assigned office on his first job will feel as capable as the young doctor who has served his internship and residency and hangs out his shingle.

2. The manager and society

The social values of business, tiny seedlings in our own day, will become flourishing sprouts on the business scene by the year 2000. One prophet has already sounded the keynote:

"The objective of just 'making money' is not sufficient. In our world, perhaps because in America our affluence is so great, this has become a slightly tarnished idea, no longer appealing, especially to the new generation of college youths." [6]

The growing social consciousness of the business executive, already touched on in chapter 4, will not only affect the operation of companies but will also be revealed in a much greater participation of business executives in the social and political world outside.

A recent front page of the *New York Times*[7] featured two items that indicate the executive's growing preoccupation with civic and national affairs. One item described how business leaders had joined civic, labor and church leaders in a move to persuade the government to "reorder national priorities" and concentrate more heavily on the "urban crisis." They called for action on everything from creating more jobs to the problems of housing, crime and air pollution. On the same page, the headline, "113 Business Leaders Back a Temporary Rise in Taxes,"

---

[6] Harold Bramen, ex-director of public relations, Du Pont, *Corporate Management in the World of Politics* (New York: McGraw-Hill, 1965).
[7] August 25, 1967.

capped a story describing business leaders' support of a tax to ease the government's budgetary burdens.

The business executive has been devoting more of his time and energy as an activist in the social sphere. One revealing case history was provided in a publication of the Research Institute of America recently: [8]

"At a time when businessmen and top executives are beginning to talk seriously about social responsibilities to their communities, several companies have actually taken the initiative in becoming 'good corporate citizens.' As a result, there are increasing examples of cities that are getting new infusions of executive time and talent—not to mention corporate money—in their attacks on social problems.

"One of the most striking examples of social leadership is that of Pitney-Bowes, Inc., the mailing-machine and office-equipment manufacturer. This company has a long history of pioneering progress in community and minority-group relations. With a payroll of some 3000 employees at its headquarters in Stamford, Connecticut, Pitney-Bowes management is extremely cognizant of the company's economic impact there and has attempted in many ways to use its influence for the common welfare. Several years ago, for example, the company began employing large numbers of marginally qualified personnel, including school dropouts, and developing special training and education programs for them. As a result, the company now has an unusually high proportion of Negro employment and has been singled out for laurels by minority groups and the Office of Economic Opportunity.

"The latest Pitney-Bowes move will no doubt enhance that reputation. That company has created a new position, manager of community relations, and appointed an articulate young Negro to fill it. The appointee, Charles A. Ukkerd, is a former Pitney-Bowes salesman who, as an avocation and with the aid of a one-year leave of absence, recently acquired some practical experience in social-service work.

"Broadly speaking, Ukkerd's total responsibility will

[8] Research Institute of America, *Alert*, August 1967.

be to (1) throw the company's considerable influence solidly behind any municipal or federal program that will benefit Stamford's citizenry, but especially its Negro population, and (2) to open and keep busy new channels of communication between the company and city officials, local politicians, religious groups and other community organizations. There are several long-range objectives, only a few of which will be of direct benefit to the company. The major gain will probably be in winning public favor and goodwill.

". . . Pitney-Bowes is not alone in its social concern. Reports from across the country tell of stepped-up company-community-relations efforts by dozens of firms. For example, the pharmaceutical maker Smith Kline & French has stationed employees in a run-down section of Philadelphia to give residents information on everything from job opportunities to medical care and welfare problems. As a result of the Detroit riots, Ford has set up a staff to correlate government, community and private efforts to repair social damage and 'build new bridges.'

"Small firms, too, are becoming active. In Cleveland, six small manufacturing companies have donated $25,000 each to a fund that will guarantee interest-free loans for renovating slum properties. Five small banks, also in Cleveland, are behind a move to rehabilitate and finance $250,000 worth of slum housing. The banks' senior officers will direct the projects and, after completion, turn the mortgages and properties over to nonprofit church and civic groups for management."

3. The manager as a political creature

In the 1950s, a strong trend developed in some business circles for executives to become active in politics.

Business interest in government participation stemmed from three factors:

Me-tooing labor. The labor movement had organized to back political figures in elections. Franklin D. Roosevelt, for example, had pivotal backing by unions in his presidential campaigns. Business chafed at the political edge labor had gained and felt that it, too, might profit from the same game.

Local-politics enlightenment. Many corporations, especially those in smaller towns where the community centered on the company economically, felt that "company" men should run for office or otherwise participate in local affairs. Advantages could be gained in everything from fending off complaints about nuisance elements—noise, smoke, odors, water pollution—to tax advantages.

National-politics enlightenment. Similarly, on the national scene, it was felt that the business viewpoint could be given new luster and be made more acceptable if emissaries of the business community participated in government activities either as consultants and specialists or as elected officials. This tactic, it was felt, would help business in the delicate area of government regulation of business activity—everything from control of interstate commerce to utilization of natural resources.

But in the world of the future, the rapprochement between business and government will be much more intimate. In some cases, it may even be impossible to say where business ends and government starts. The main reason behind this development is the increasing identification of government power with economic growth.

Whether it's to wage war or to wage peace in today's world of planetwide technological advance, governments have come to realize that their real power base is the health and potency of their economies. It is in this atmosphere that tomorrow's manager may have to be half businessman, half politician.

One observer of the business scene states his view of the situation like this:

"The interests of business and government have become closely meshed on several fronts. The business executive discovers many times that his major problems are becoming distinctly less 'business' and more 'societal' in one or another of their aspects. Increasingly, he is discovering that the societal problems appear governmental in nature. Through regulatory agencies, as a purchaser of vast quantities of goods and services, by the use of subsidies, taxes, spending and other techniques to

promote certain goals, as a 'partner' in solving social problems and as a competitor, government manifests its relationship with business in numerous and complex forms." [9]

Held, whose affiliation with the Brookings Institution gives him the opportunity to survey the political and business fronts, states the implications for the manager: *"The disciplines of political science and political economy must be made more meaningful and relevant to effective business management in a modern, changing world."*

4. New technologies, new managers

When we seek to project our thinking into the future, it's usually by extrapolation. We take present situations and trends and develop them in some fairly logical manner to produce "the world of tomorrow." What often happens, however, is the major oversight, the failure to take into account new developments that create new situations. Certainly, among the X factors in the development of tomorrow's world are the new technologies that will create new products, new industries and, in some cases, new modes of life. Once the list is started, it can doubtless be added to almost endlessly by anyone who reads in either of two sources—science fiction or engineering and scientific journals.

However, one need only name a few new products and services to suggest the new opportunities and new jobs that will be created for tomorrow's managers.

William G. Ryan[10] in a stimulating article recently listed half a dozen developments that managers will be concerning themselves with tomorrow:

The electric automobile. Although development work on electric automobiles has never completely stopped, the vehicle that traveled the streets of the 1920s seemed to represent the height of the development. However, on October 3, 1966, Ford Motor Company announced the

---

[9] Walter G. Held, "Executive Skills: The Repertoire Needs Enlarging," *Columbia Journal of World Business,* March/April 1967.

[10] William G. Ryan, "Six Technologies in Search of a Manager," *Business Horizons,* Indiana University, Winter 1966.

development of a "breakthrough battery" which may make the electric auto once again a practical vehicle. Clean air and quietness are two of the obvious benefits.

Jumbo jet transports. The carrying power and speed of the supersonic transport, or SST, as it is known, are tremendous. Equally tremendous are the problems to be expected. But the management of a fleet of SSTs will be challenging indeed. As Ryan says, "If one makes the most reasonable assumption about tripling usage of planes, and so on, even assuming that the average flight will be only 60 percent filled, half of the U.S. fleet will be able to deliver from 45 to 50 million passenger-miles each year."

High-speed surface travel. The monorail and pneumatic-gravity tube are just some of the new ways of speeding up surface vehicles. The Hovercraft type of vehicle promises rapid transit over difficult terrain—such as desert and swamplands—as well as over water.

Ryan concludes his list with *waste management* (the answer to the "garbage explosion"), *the integrated circuit* (miniaturizing complex electronic components and minimizing error-prone connecting operations such as soldering), *the information industry* (efficient production, storing and retrieval of information materials).

Other authorities have forecast the creation of entire new industries and companies that will spring up from research in these fields:

Oceanography. Millions of dollars have been committed to exploring the floors of the oceans—not to find the lost continent of Atlantis—but to find new solutions to a number of the world's problems. To name a few:

Food for the growing population. In the deep, dark depths grow nutritious seaweeds and plants which, properly processed, could be a new source of food.

Fuel. Mining oil from the ocean is already a reality; in future it could be a major industry.

Minerals. Iron, gold, copper and a host of minerals lie undiscovered under the rolling waves. New tools and techniques will make it possible to bring them to the surface and into commercial use.

Ultrasonics. Sound waves are the invisible servants of

man in many fields: washing machines (cleaning without liquid), detection of flaws in metals and machinery, high-speed dentists' drills—the list is endless.

Lasers. These concentrated beams of light cut, weld, bore and otherwise work materials ranging from paper to metal. Lasers are also aiding surgeons in such jobs as mending a damaged retina in the human eye.

Electronics. This already growing field has even further extensions in the future. One of the most promising is fluidics. Based on the principle that gases (air for liquids) can direct jet streams of fluids and move heavy parts, fluidic devices are operating computers, replacing valves, substituting for moving parts in mechanisms, etc.

Space research. Space exploration has already given rise to a number of new industries, ranging from miniaturized parts like transistors to new metals that can withstand extremes of heat and cold.

5. Generalist and specialist

In tracing the parameters of the future manager's job, an old controversy takes on realistic significance: What will be the worth of the generalist's skills compared to those of the specialist?

The question tends to arise in two situations: when a key job is being filled and when a young man is deciding on his college education. For example: Company A needs a manager for a research-and-development department. Should the recruiters look for a man with broad management skills and experience, who could be taught the technical background of the R&D activity? Or should a scientist or engineer be sought, who could be taught the management skills required to lead the work group and tend the administrative chores?

The second focus of the problem has to do with college education. From the point of view of the young man interested in a business career the question becomes, "Should I take a liberal-arts degree and expect to get my technical training on the job? Or should I take a business course and leave the cultural broadening to informal pursuit later on?"

The answers to the first question, recruiting for a job requiring both managerial and technical skill, go something like this:

"Employers say they want a generalist," says one executive-search consultant, "but when the chips are down, they hire the specialist and take their chances that they'll be able to teach him how to be a manager."

A top executive who has faced this hiring problem often in the operation of his electronics firm says, "It's an individual matter. I look for either a specialist or a generalist, but try to ascertain, by psychological testing and checking on his personal and career interests, whether he has a *capability* to learn the half of the job with which he's unfamiliar."

The plain fact is that in industry today, both courses are followed, and both turn up successes and failures. The executive who says he looks for the *capacity to learn* is probably on the right track, because flexibility and willingness to acquire a new set of skills seem to be the keys to successful accomplishment. The specialist who admits, "I don't really like to tell people what to do," or who says, "I hate paper work," isn't likely to break through these obstacles rooted in personal rigidity. And the same is true of the skilled manager who has a strong reluctance to "get into all that technical stuff."

As for the college undergraduate who must decide between liberal arts or business training, it's likely that the future will make his dilemma obsolete. In the present period, coming to an end in the 1960s, it is still possible to enter the world of business with a liberal-arts degree and to progress on the basis of skills acquired en route.

But tomorrow, the job of management itself will be increasingly technical. While the old-fashioned administrative and human-relations skills could be picked up by a bright youngster through exposure to a good boss or even a good book, tomorrow's skills—for example, the mastery of PERT techniques and ability to stimulate the creativity of groups and individuals—are not so readily grasped. Accordingly, formal training in management is becoming increasingly necessary for the person who is interested in a management career.

Some of the people who argue the generalist-specialist question seem to harbor the mistaken idea that the generalist and specialist are at opposite ends of a single continuum. In one sense, they may be. That is, there seem to be certain aspects of the personality that dispose an individual either for or against generalism or specialization. The extroverted person seems to have a predisposition toward management, particularly the interpersonal aspects. The introverted person seems to fare better as a specialist, particularly one who works on his own.

But in the functional sense, being a generalist refers to management-oriented duties, and being a specialist refers to technical duties, such as those of the scientist or engineer. These two types of responsibility are *not* extensions of one another. Whether or not they touch or overlap depends on the capability of the individual.

At any rate, what is suggested here is that specialists *and* generalists will be required to run tomorrow's business enterprise. And these trends may be expected:

Continuing specialization. Splintering of areas of expertness will follow in present directions. We have seen it significantly in science and engineering. For example, the science of physics continues to add specialties: atomic physics, astrophysics. The electronics engineer of yesterday now has second-generation successors who specialize in solid state, fluidics, and so on.

And specialization in management will also proliferate. For example, yesterday the executive in charge of a company's finances had a clearly defined job: All money matters were his domain. Today the finance function is divided among an investment specialist, loan specialist, tax expert, and so on.

Continuing generalism. The generalist will continue to be needed—perhaps even more than before. As specialization proceeds, the need grows to coordinate and integrate diverse activities, to give them overall direction. Interdisciplinary unity, the teaming together of a variety of specialists, will require a generalist's skills.

And, just as in the sciences one sees considerable interdisciplinary mating—the social psychologist, the bio-chemist—look for the engineer–finance officer, the ma-terials-handling purchasing agent, the salesman–product designer, and, of course, the overall manager to direct them toward company-decided goals.

In the world of tomorrow, it may well be difficult to tell the engineer from the manager, the scientist from the engineer, and the engineer from the rank-and-file employee. The educational preparedness of many mana-gers will be highly technical. The scientist or engineer who aims to function in the business world will get his training in the university well before he sets foot in the arena of enterprise.

6. The manager as artist

In this text, we have talked repeatedly of what today's and tomorrow's executive will be doing. In this chapter, we are talking not only of the executive tomorrow, that is, of the immediate future, but especially of his succes-sor—let's say, the executive at the beginning of the 21st Century. This executive, working in a science-fiction world as far as equipment facilities and techniques are concerned, will still carry with him the problems of leadership and capability that exist now and that also be-set the leaders of the Stone Age.

To extrapolate from today's world, tomorrow will be one of extreme flexibility. To extend the period of self-usefulness on the business scene, the manager will be in a continuing fight against obsolescence. Education, al-ready a highly perishable product in our day, will be-come increasingly so tomorrow. For example, it has been said that what a man learns to earn an engineering de-gree today is good for about five years. Repeated re-treading will be required to maintain viability in almost any field, be it medicine, engineering or management.

In the years ahead, it can be assumed that the manager will walk farther down the road toward being a profes-sional. His training will bring him closer to the accepted standards of professionalism, academically speaking. And, as far as his job is concerned, his behavior will even more closely resemble the professional, for standard diagnostic techniques will be applied to problem situations and standardized remedies will be prescribed, assuredly with a higher degree of predictability than is possible today.

In addition to the problems and procedures that will preoccupy him, a considerable part of his activity will depend on his individual propensities. The fact that these capabilities will continue to have a place in the world of business suggests that management is an art as well as a science.

It can be properly argued that every profession embodies an artistic element. Surgeons, for example, are complimented for their "artistry." It's the potential and latitude for creativity that will give a manager the opportunity to practice his profession as a technician *and* as an artist.

Making the transition

How will today's manager become tomorrow's? How will the contemporary manager—in the transitional stages of professionalism and yet still the creature of his seat-of-the-pants past—develop into the sophisticated, self-assured manager of tomorrow?

In all probability, the metamorphosis will occur through the manager's growth in social participation and more stringent self-imposed standards of his job performance. His skills will develop toward two extremes: the "hard" sciences on the one hand, such as physics, chemistry, biology and mathematics; and the social sciences on the other: psychology, sociology, political science, and so on.

That such a paragon will run tomorrow's corporations may seem doubtful. But this is the projection that must be made to adequately extrapolate from today's trends.

We must avoid what English scientist-writer Arthur C. Clarke calls "the failure of nerve." In anticipating the future, Clarke suggests that the two handicaps to our crystal-ball gazing lie in the failure of nerve and the failure of imagination. The former results from our balking at weighing facts available today and drawing logical conclusions, because these conclusions seem unbelievable. It was this failure of nerve, for example, that prevented many scientists of the preflight era from accepting the imminence of the airplane.

It seems obvious, even from today's scant evidence, that the positions of top management in tomorrow's world will require individuals who have the utmost in education and mental ability. And in the lower-management echelons, specialists will be expected not only to know the answers within their immediate areas of responsibility but to be able to function effectively in interdisciplinary groups.

While management will continue to be the most practical profession, managers will rise to new heights in understanding and applying abstract ideas and theories. The challenges facing tomorrow's executive will not be limited to what we now think of as the "business world."

Social and political considerations, as well as cash profits, will preoccupy the manager of tomorrow. It may well be that reality will outdistance Kurt Vonnegut's prediction that the importance of the top business leader will match that of the president of the United States. One day both responsibilities may fall on the same man.

FOR FURTHER EXECUTIVE THOUGHT

Bell, Daniel (ed.). *Toward the Year 2000: Work in Progress* (1968). Houghton Mifflin Co., 2 Park St., Boston, Mass. 02107.

Brown, Harrison, et al. *The Next Hundred Years* (1958). The Viking Press, 625 Madison Ave., New York, N.Y. 10022.

Foreign Policy Association (eds.). *Toward the Year 2018* (1968). Cowles Education Corp., 488 Madison Ave., New York, N.Y. 10022.

Kahn, Herman, and Weiner, A. J. *The Year 2000* (1967). Macmillan Co., 866 Third Ave., New York, N.Y. 10022.

Uris, Auren. *Keeping Young in Business* (1967). McGraw-Hill Book Co., 330 W. 42nd St., New York, N.Y. 10036.

INDEX